Advanced Praise for

The Washashore

"Take a trip through time and tides with young sleuth Emily Cartwright as she arrives on the island of Martha's Vineyard just in time to set about solving the island's biggest mystery—the disappearance of island matriarch Ann Simpson. This suspenseful historical mystery, set during the Prohibition era and rich in period detail, will keep readers up and burning the midnight whale oil. A thoroughly engaging and delightful read!"

—Margaret Meacham, author of
Secret of Heron Creek and *Oyster Moon*

"Fast-paced with a gripping storyline, *The Washashore* delivers an insider's peak into Prohibition-era Martha's Vineyard, where high tea happens during the day and rum-running happens during the night, and newly transplanted Emily finds herself caught right in the middle. A must-read that'll leave you on the edge of your seat."

—Lorraine Besser, PhD, author of
The Art of the Interesting

"Marshall Highet and Bird Jones have crafted more than a mystery—the precise, poetic details transport readers, like a time machine, to the rum-running, gambling, tipsy world of Prohibition-era Martha's Vineyard through the eyes of washashore Em, a naive but plucky transplant from Nebraska's dust bowl."

—Traci O'Dea, author of *Waving* and
Restricted Movement

"The characters of *The Washashore* are wonderful creations—all of them, even the minor ones—so they are great company, and their dark-tinged adventure keeps the reader (this one anyway) engrossed and guessing. All in all, an excellent read."

—Bruce Bennett, author of
Navigating The Distances and
Just Another Day in Just Our Town

"Excellent storytelling is the backbone of this thrilling, Agatha Christie–like page-turner. Wonderfully paced with terrific details laced throughout, boasting a fabulous setting, insightful research, and timely vernacular. I so loved the world of this book that I didn't want to leave it. *The Washashore* truly made me feel like I was seeing Martha's Vineyard through Emily's eyes, and feeling the change, overwhelm, and excitement of her transition."

—Lisa Davis Mitchell,
Middlebury Town Hall Theater

"*The Washashore* transports the reader in place and time. In the middle of an intensely suspenseful moment, I found myself rereading a line of comic relief. And the food! You can practically taste what's on the page. I've never had tomato aspic and now I don't need to!"

—Cintra Horn,
Ashley Hall School

"*The Washashore* vividly captures Martha's Vineyard as it was a century ago: an island caught between its rural past and its growing popularity as a summer resort. Marshall Highet and Bird Jones embroider an exciting story with details that make the place and the era come alive. Along with Emily, their intrepid Midwest-born heroine, we probe the deeply buried secrets of small-town life, feel the boom of the surf on deserted ocean beaches, smell the tang of salt and seaweed at low tide, and hear the rumbling engines of rumrunners' powerful launches on moonless nights."

—A. Bowdoin Van Riper, research librarian,
Martha's Vineyard Museum

"Should Amelia Earhart, Bessie Coleman, and Zelda Fitzgerald ever recruit a fourth comrade, they'd choose Emily Cartwright—prairie born, flapper tested, and fearless enough to conquer the roaring tides of 1929."

—Richard J. Mihans, author of
My Guiding Star

"F. Scott Fitzgerald typified the Prohibition era as a Presbyterian nymph, but this is not a novel about Prohibition where it is set. It's a story about an orphaned teenage girl, Emily, who leaves the hard plains of Nebraska in 1929 to find a home. She washes ashore on the glacial island called Martha's Vineyard, where her maternal aunt has a not-too-welcoming mansion. With her story set against the beautiful scenery of 'The Island,' the sailing on its coastal and offshore waters, and a murder mystery, Emily has to dig into her Midwestern values to try to understand, cope, and find a home. I have no doubt that her older contemporaries, the worldly Gatsby, His Honor Frank Skeffington up in Boston, and Don Corleone down in New York, would have cheered her on. I certainly did. A great summer read!"

—Bob Crimmins, JD, master of theology

The Washashore
by Marshall Highet and Bird Jones

© Copyright 2025 Marshall Highet and Bird Jones

979-8-88824-712-9

All rights reserved. No part of this publication may be reproduced, stored in a retrieval system, or transmitted in any form or by any means—electronic, mechanical, photocopy, recording, or any other—except for brief quotations in printed reviews, without the prior written permission of the author.

This is a work of fiction. All the characters in this book are fictitious, and any resemblance to actual persons, living or dead, is purely coincidental. The names, incidents, dialogue, and opinions expressed are products of the author's imagination and are not to be construed as real.

Designed by Suzanne Bradshaw

Published by

3705 Shore Drive
Virginia Beach, VA 23455
800-435-4811
www.koehlerbooks.com

THE WASHASHORE

—

Marshall Highet
and Bird Jones

VIRGINIA BEACH
CAPE CHARLES

For my mother, Bushnell Pearce Henry (1920-2022),
a woman for the century.
With love, Bird

For my mom, Nancy Bryan Blair,
who always knows the way home.
Love MM

Preface

The "rumrunner" occupies a peculiar and romantic spot in the American imagination. Rumrunners, at least at their start in the Elizabeth Islands, were the good guys. They were not highwaymen or gangsters but fishermen, extraordinary boat handlers, and superb navigators. Their exploits demonstrated nerves of steel and enough daring and righteous indignation to satisfy the likes of Han Solo.

Rumrunners' boats, like the Millennium Falcon, were not expensive yachts but tough, working fishing boats. Sometimes they were painted black and refitted with airplane engines for speed and mufflers to diminish the engine's roar and avoid detection. The modifications were done in small shipyards in out-of-the-way creeks and tiny harbors, mostly by local mechanics or the captain himself. As a group, they were totally opportunistic, and, really, in the face of their stark reality, who wouldn't be?

Life as a fisherman in the 1920s was not easy or lucrative. An oral history from the archives on Martha's Vineyard retells the story of one woman whose husband was a fisherman. She had several kids and could not afford the grocery store even for the most basic supplies. After school, her son hunted rabbits and squirrels to add to the larder. Her existence consisted of bone-crushing poverty and a life of endless work. Food came from the sea, the forest, and the garden. As romantic as this sounds to our twenty-first century sensibilities, it was nothing more than backbreaking work to preserve a measure of pride and family stability. The word *grit* comes to mind.

Then, one day, her husband came home with ten brand-new ten-dollar bills, and she went to the grocery store. From then on, the husband would disappear, usually in the dark of the moon. She would wait up for him, knitting. When he got home, she never asked questions; she simply accepted the change in their fortunes. Their life was better—not sumptuous, not perfect, but better. He was a rumrunner.

Rumrunning was the unintended consequence of the Eighteenth Amendment, which itself was a response to women getting really tired of their husbands spending their paychecks in bars and taverns rather than supporting their families. The Woman's Christian Temperance Union arose out of the real need to protect families from the "scourge of drunkenness." Unlike the family farm, work in factories took individuals away from home and hearth. The hours were long, the money not terrific, and the experience mind-numbing.

Payday also meant pub day, and often wages were left at the bar rather than brought home. Because of this, women were, in large measure, supportive of Prohibition, as were factory owners and progressives. These three groups, unlikely bedfellows for sure, felt that more government control was necessary to promote prosperity and reestablish the moral order in people's lives.

The movement became entangled in evangelical fervor and class divisions, and was ultimately politicized in the form of the amendment. Simply put, it became illegal to buy and sell liquor, which opened the door to rumrunning, or the illegal booze trade.

In the early years of Prohibition, accomplished mariners marveled at how easy it was to make serious money. There were men like Bill McCoy, who inspired the term *the real McCoy*. Bill was impossibly handsome and charismatic. He was also an extraordinary mariner and businessman. He specialized in premium whiskey and managed to buy it from offshore ships and resell it. His territory extended from Miami to Martha's Vineyard. He made a fortune, and he became known as the genuine article; if you bought booze from Bill, it was always *the real McCoy*.

Frank Butler and his high-speed boat, the *Nola*, became famous for outrunning every coast guard cutter between the Vineyard and New York City. He was a brash, daring individual with a personality that was larger-than-life. He enjoyed respect and admiration among his fellow rumrunners at home on the island. And these are but two of many that captivated the American imagination during the roaring twenties.

In 1923, the territorial waters limit went from three miles to twelve. What that meant was that the rumrunners had to go twelve miles offshore to meet cargo vessels (mostly Canadian and British) loaded with alcohol; spirits, wine, and beer were the most common.

Rumrunners typically operated on moonless nights and always without running lights to avoid detection. They often hid their cargo by building false compartments in the bilge to house the crates or barrels. Fishermen would often disguise their cargo under their catch. They would go out at night, pick up contraband, and then go fishing, putting their catch on ice so it concealed their *other* cargo, thus maximizing profits. Eventually, rumrunning became a Mob activity. In fact, the Mob's toehold in New York City was a direct result of the early success of rumrunners. Eventually, the whole enterprise took on a violent and lethal cast. Gatling guns were mounted on boats and full-on shoot-outs were the order of the day.

On December 5, 1933, the Eighteenth Amendment was repealed; with it came the end of rumrunning, closing a colorful but deadly chapter in our past.

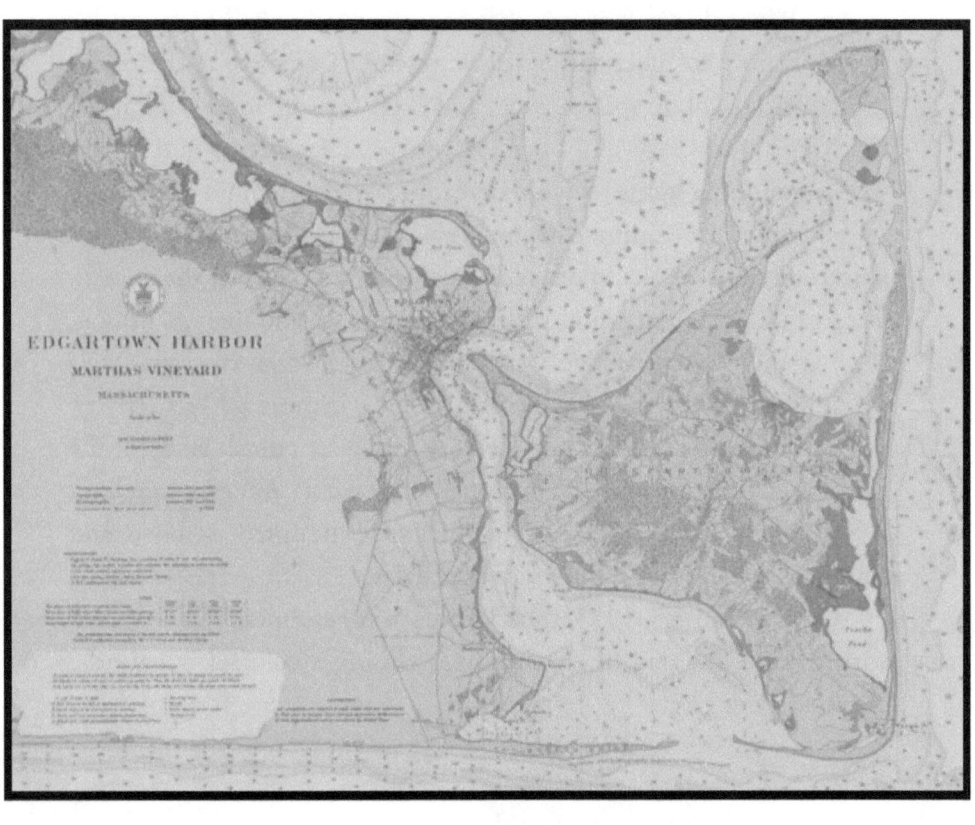

Chapter 1

Edgartown, Massachusetts
1929

The first step Emily took on the island was an unsteady one, to be sure. Her booted foot threatened to slip on the gangway from ship to pier, slimy with sea spray from the rough water on either side. When she stepped off, Emily couldn't help but let a prayer to St. Nicholas escape her lips, thanking him for safe passage. Since it was a very high tide, the decline of the gangway was steep, making the ladies gasp and clutch the railing and the men stop talking to one another to watch their feet.

Another wave of nausea washed over her, so much so that she had to let the others pass as she rested her head against a piling—the vertical beam jutting from the water; the cold wet wood made her overheated face feel better. When she could, she continued after the crowd of passengers bustling to the packed-dirt clearing beyond where a line of Model T cars stood waiting, belching out clouds of smoke. Standing on land proper made her feel a smidge better, but only because Emily knew mentally that there was solid ground under her, rather than the bucking ocean. It was more a psychological shift than anything else, but it helped her start to get her bearings in her new home.

She couldn't blame herself. Only a month ago she'd been a sixteen-year-old Nebraska farm girl. Yesterday morning was her first ever glimpse of the ocean, and it was certainly a violent jolt.

Although her trains had been on time across the high plains and into the more densely populated East, her steamboat—the *Nantucket*—was delayed in New Bedford due to foul weather, making her trip from Blue Hill, Nebraska, to Martha's Vineyard, Massachusetts, eight days instead of seven. She'd had to sleep in the ferry terminal in New Bedford the night before. The seats had been narrow and hard, and the pervasive smell of fish and fuel was still stuck to the back of her throat. Her head hurt, her back hurt, and she was miserable because of it.

The porter plunked her steamer trunk down as Emily scanned the line of cars. How was she to know who was to pick her up? She had wired Aunt Isabel from the ferry terminal in New Bedford as soon as she'd heard the boats had been canceled due to the weather, but maybe the message hadn't made it through the churning seas. How would they know to come get her? Who was coming? Was anyone?

Anxiety curdled her stomach for the seven hundredth time during her forced journey to the East Coast. She would have to wait for as long as she could, then abandon her trunk to see about a telegraph office or police station where she could ask the whereabouts of Isabel Hewett, her aunt and now, sadly, legal guardian.

It had not been an easy trip, but Emily, thus far, had not had an easy life. With no siblings and missionary parents, she had helped her family build up their small place and did what needed to be done. She was a farm girl, and she could handle herself around foaling mares and dust storms. Crossing a storm-wracked Buzzards Bay on a ferry alone was another matter altogether.

And now she was finally here, in the place where her mother Constance had grown up with her much older sister Isabel and a crowd of servants. Her mother had woven countless stories redolent of luxury but stiff with rules and expectations. When Constance had died of tuberculosis four months ago, Emily had the unenviable job of reducing their entire existence to cash money and a few choice belongings, and she'd bought her tickets to the enigmatic East to live with family she'd never met, after the exchange of a flurry of letters.

Emily didn't know what to make of her new surroundings. Taking a seat on the steamer trunk as the first few tendrils of cold crept through her coat, she pulled it more closely around her and wondered what an acceptable amount of time to wait would be. She decided on half an hour to an hour, if she could take the cold. The aftermath of the rain and winds still held the sky captive in a prison of iron clouds, and the dark came down early for April. The damp air clung to her skin and crept in at her cuffs and collar. She shivered and crossed her arms.

While she waited for someone who might or might not come for her, Emily took stock of her surroundings. The *Nantucket* had dropped off its passengers and their luggage on a wooden pier jutting out into a sickle-shaped harbor filled with stout fishing rigs and a few sleek sailboats. Across the water, a slice of land was visible through the fog, but Emily couldn't figure out whether it was another island or part of Edgartown. Up until this afternoon, she'd never set foot on the island of Martha's Vineyard, the homeland of her mother's people, or any island for that matter, as her entire life had been spent on the flat, wide expanse of the high plains amidst a lot of sky and not a whole lot else.

The pier behind her was made of wood, topped by a clapboard structure that offered protection from the rain, with a viewing deck for those brave enough to clamber up. It loomed over her in the gathering darkness like a protective giant.

Across the clearing ringed with tire tracks, a dirt road made its way over a narrow causeway and disappeared into the tattered fringe of town, spreading up a gentle slope in front of her. Buildings, mostly of gray shingles and white trim, with a few brick ones thrown in, dotted the landscape as far as she could see, with the elegant white spires of a church rising over it all.

Of course, Emily came from the land of squat single-story buildings, one notch above sod houses. The first Europeans in Nebraska built homes of dirt and dried grass. When it rained, the old-timers said, mud dripped from the roof onto the people inside for as long as the rain came down. For Emily and her parents, a wooden cabin with a sturdy roof to hold out the ever-present wind and protect them from the cold and heat had suited them just fine, in its simple way.

But these stalwart and practical island buildings were also beautiful to look at, with weathered, overlapping shingles forming a buttress against the wet sea wind, and white trim peeking cheekily through the fog. On the prairie, in her other life, she'd gotten used to the monotony of the flat landscape. Here she was repelled by the angles and alleys, the denseness of the architecture disappearing into the sea mist and coming night. It was all just too strange and close together.

In the distance, a foghorn hooted, and the beam from the lighthouse periodically strafed the clouds above and around her. The minutes slowly passed, each one slightly colder and darker than the one before. And was that a raindrop? More rain? A big boat chugged by in the harbor, its hull slapping water, motor churning, metal and wood creaking. Blending in was a growl that she at first supposed to be a smaller boat, but turned out to be an approaching vehicle.

Reaching down for the straw farm hat that had always shaded her face from the hot prairie sun, she found that it had rolled off her trunk and sat in a puddle. With an inward groan, she shook it, spraying mud droplets from the ruined straw. Well, there was nothing to be done about it at the moment, as her mother would've surely said.

From the mist, a Model A truck came bumping into the dirt clearing, making a large semicircle and pulling up alongside Emily and her steamer trunk. The balsam-green vehicle jerked to a stop, and a man in a tweed cap and vest with a red woolen scarf leaped out. He made a clumsy bow in front of Emily, doffing his hat and running a hand through the black hair underneath.

"I assume you are Miss Emily Cartwright?" the stranger asked.

Emily nodded, relief flooding through her to finally be found, to be named, to not be abandoned on this rock in the middle of a strange ocean. "Yes, are you from Aunt Isabel?"

"Mrs. Hewett sure isn't going to like the sound of that," he commented in a thick Irish accent, eyes twinkling. "I'm John Patrick. My pals call me Pat. Hop in."

Emily's relief was palpable as she made her way around the front of the truck. That was certainly an odd welcome. A fine rain had started to fall, like needles against her cheeks. John Patrick huffed as he heaved her trunk in the back. Emily slid into the passenger seat, grateful to be out of the weather.

John Patrick poked his head in the driver's side. "Just in time."

Emily glanced through the windshield at what she could see of the harbor and the darkening sky: a bank of even denser clouds was bearing down on the wharf, so close it seemed she could reach up and tear off a piece of the murky material. "Looks like a terrible blow." John Patrick's accent made *blow* sound like *blew*. "This all you got?"

Emily nodded.

"You sure? No other worldly belongings?"

Emily looked at him blankly and held up the carpet bag she carried.

"Righty-o." John Patrick jumped in, the cab settling under his formidable bulk. "Off we go."

"She isn't going to like what?"

"Pardon, Miss Emily?"

"Aunt Isabel isn't going to like the sound of what?"

"Oh, she isn't going to like you calling her Aunt Isabel, I'll warrant," John Patrick said, grinning a handsome, devilish smile. "But my niece will certainly enjoy having a new little friend around. Better get underway before the squall is really upon us." The truck sputtered to life as John Patrick slammed the gearshift forward.

At that very moment, the rain picked up, like sheets of water thrown from a laundry bucket onto the windshield. This wasn't like any rain Emily had ever known. It was a strange, horizontal rain. And, with John Patrick's comment, it felt like it had been dumped all over her heart, drenching it in icy cold. This whole place was unfamiliar and damp and misty when all Emily had ever known was a dry constant wind with nothing to stop it but open sky for miles and miles. She had never felt so alone in all her life.

John Patrick, oblivious, rattled on as they rumbled across first the dirt causeway and then the road to town, telling her about the streets, buildings, and shops they were passing. He appeared to be in his early thirties or so. "There's Manny the boat builder's place, and here's the Edgartown Market."

Through the slowly fogging window, Emily saw snatches of plate windows, clapboard buildings jostling for purchase on narrow streets. She couldn't shake the feeling of extreme claustrophobia. After the miles of trains, with the dirty cars and children wailing and steel clanking and rails shrieking, this small truck hurtling through the dusk-drenched trees and unfamiliar structures, with Pat hurling out his helpful geographical interest points in a broad Irish brogue—"there's Dr. Slate's, you'll be wanting him if anything goes amiss"—seemed to be the center of the whole universe. Nothing else existed except this very moment.

As darkness fell and the already-steady deluge somehow continued to increase, all of it—buildings, boats, docks, trees—disappeared into a wall of mist and rain. Emily leaned her overheated cheek against the cool window and thought about the wide-open expanse she called home. She missed her mother, their friends, and especially her horse. Even though she wanted to pepper Pat with a million questions about Aunt Isabel, the house, and her mother's childhood, not to mention that strange offhand comment he'd made, her eyelids soon fluttered down and, exhausted by her seasickness and the long grind of travel in the aftermath of her mother's death, she suddenly fell asleep, as if she'd dropped off a cliff.

Emily was awakened by a stiff jab to her shoulder. She woke up as quickly as she had fallen asleep, sitting straight up and trying to remember where she was. Was she on a train? A station? A boat?

"Miss!" a dark shadow hissed at her. "Miss Emily?"

It all came rushing back, where she was, *who* she was, and who the hissing shadow was. John Patrick. Pat to his pals.

Emily clutched her carpet bag. "Are we there?" she asked, her eyes peering through the windshield, past the gloom of rain and fog, at the hulking behemoth of the house before them. The rain was coming down so hard on the roof of the truck that it almost drowned out all conversation.

"Yes, Miss, we're here at Hydrangea House," Pat practically yelled from the driver's seat. "And a hearty welcome to you." He straightened and, satisfied that she was not going back to sleep, jumped out of the truck, turning to the task of lifting her steamer trunk from the back.

Emily gingerly grasped the handle on the inside of the car door and pulled, recoiling as the door sprang open into the rainy night. She was more used to jumping off wagons than clambering in and out of cars. She hadn't seen many automobiles, and had only ridden in them occasionally, most recently at her mother's funeral.

Dragging herself, her wrecked hat, and her carpet bag out with her into the cold, piercing rain, Emily felt the weight of all that had happened push down on her shoulders. She couldn't take another step on this soul-wearying journey until she knew where to go, and she didn't know where to go until someone told her, so she just stood there, cold rivulets running down the collar of her too-thin coat.

She probably would've stayed there forever if a shadow holding a light in one hand and a giant umbrella in the other hadn't darted out of the monstrous building into the squall. The shape ran straight to Emily's side and, transferring the light to Pat, gripped her elbow in a firm hand.

"Oh, ye poor wee wet thing!" The woman held the umbrella up as high as she could to help keep the rain off. "Come into the kitchen. We'll find you a spot of something." She threaded her arm around Emily's waist with companionable certainty and urged her forward, toward the doorway. "John Patrick, you great galumphing ogre, you!" the woman hollered though the rain.

Poor Pat was following them with Emily's steamer trunk hoisted onto one shoulder and the light in the other. It was a strange contraption—not a lantern, more like a candlestick, but Pat was holding it wrong, and the light was coming out one end; Emily was too cold and wet to make heads or tails of it. Pat looked up, eyes wide.

"Could you have not gotten the girl inside to my fire first and then set about the luggage?" The woman bustled Emily through the door, stepping her over the stone stoop and leading her into a warm room. Then she let go of Emily's waist and disappeared to help Pat.

Emily had been deposited next to a squat black stove that sat in the middle of the kitchen like a smug toad. She could feel the heat roll off it as if the sun itself was trapped inside. Emily shivered all over for a full minute, a puddle forming at her boots. When she didn't feel as if she was going to dissolve, she looked around at the rest of the room.

It was a large and well-appointed kitchen, but simple. The wide counter behind the stove was wooden with divots, scratches, and dents up and down its length. Open shelving ringed the room and two enamel sinks sat side by side on the far wall. The floor was tile and the walls a mint color, an odd contrast that gave the room a modern feel. This room alone was almost the size of half of her house back home. It was the biggest kitchen she'd ever been in, except for the church kitchen, and that didn't count.

She could hear Pat and the woman, whom she assumed to be her aunt, arguing softly behind her in the small foyer as Pat dragged the steamer trunk across the floor.

"I'm telling you, this is all the lass had. There are no other bags or trunks down at the landing, and I asked her meself if it was all. She said 'twas this and the bag she's holding now, the carpeted one. It was one of the only things she said before she tuckered right out, the poor little mouse. Look at her now—she's dead on her feet."

Emily pulled herself together and turned to greet her hostess. She didn't know how much more she had in her, but she hoped it was enough to properly greet her Aunt Isabel, just as her mother had trained her to do. She hadn't known about any uncle named John Patrick. Maybe her aunt had remarried an Irishman?

"Aunt Isabel?" Emily tried as best she could to pop a curtsy, but her boot leather was extra stiff from the cold wet and she had a hard time.

"Oh, Maiden Mary, would you look at her?" The woman crossed her arms across her wide belly and laughed. "Your poor mouse is so tuckered out she thinks I'm the lady of the house." When she straightened, Emily realized she was about the same height as the woman, who had reddish-tawny hair in a braid to her waist, a smattering of freckles across the bridge of her nose, wide-set gray eyes, and an easy smile.

"No, Miss Emily," the woman said, enunciating each word. "I'm Bridget, the cook and all-round housekeeper. This is John Patrick, me brother."

Pat lifted his cap and nodded at Emily, giving her a smile. "Or just Pat, if you fancy." Even the swath of black hair falling into his eyes didn't hide how blue they were.

The woman's firm hand found its way under Emily's armpit. Deftly, Bridget sat Emily on a tall stool near the stove and turned, plucking a cloth-wrapped loaf of bread from the open shelf behind her and plunking it on the counter. She grabbed a serrated knife from a knife block and, as she sliced bread, kept up her chatter in an accent as thick as her brother's. Pat busied himself by pouring out two cups of tea.

"It's Mrs. Hewett, me, and Pat. We're all she's got now, but we're enough. If we're having visitors then I send for my daughter, Fiona, to help us out. She's at the Howsons' down by the boatyard. You'll be in her room. But first, a cup of tea?"

Emily nodded, so happy to be anywhere other than a train, station, terminal, or car that she couldn't say a word. She was discovering the East was somewhat like where she came from, there was just a lot more of everything here—people, cars, dishes, bread. It made sense, her tired mind reasoned. People couldn't bring that much stuff all the way out there to the high plains of Nebraska. She suddenly felt a pang of sorrow for giving her mother so much grief about not bringing more out with her, about not having more. Her poor, sweet mother, buried out there and left behind, along with her father and everything else Emily knew.

Tears threatened while Bridget bustled about like an attentive hen. As Emily's eyes began to burn, Bridget plunked a mug of tea in front of her, along with a crock of marmalade. The housekeeper scooped a piece of bread off the cutting board with her dishcloth-covered hand and, with a broad butter knife, spread marmalade on it, slapping it in front of Emily before starting on another piece.

"You've been well tested on your journey, I'm sure," Bridget said, handing her brother his piece of bread, the orange swath of marmalade glistening. "Pat, take this and get the girl's trunk up to Fiona's room. I've put fresh sheets on the far bed by the wardrobe, that'll be Miss Emily's—" When Bridget said her name, Emily noticed, her face got kind of funny. It crumpled at the edges, revealing a deep well of sadness. Pat didn't react; he merely glanced at Emily and then folded the bread in half, popping all of it into his mouth and swallowing it down with a generous gulp of tea.

Her exhausted brain couldn't quite put it all together yet, so she gave up trying and simply concentrated on lifting the bread and tea to her lips, sipping, chewing, swallowing. It was excellent bread, rivaling what they used to get from Ingrid Gustafssen at home. As Bridget tended to the final chores in the kitchen, Emily kept her eyes trained on the marmalade crock like it was a beacon of home. And it was, in a way.

The glazed crock had a wide round mouth that made it easy to reach inside with a spoon or butter knife. Emily knew it was easy to reach in with a spoon because she had done it many, many times, as had her mother with the crock's twin back home. But that crock, their old crock, was gone, parceled off in some other family's things.

Tears threatened again and Emily squashed them down with more bread, its smooth, warm, mellow taste tempered by the bite of marmalade. Just like her mom used to make. If she closed her eyes, she was almost back in her mother's kitchen, instead of this strange one. She finally stopped trying to quell her tears and let them come, her head in her hands. When she finally pulled herself together, she wiped her eyes and looked around.

Pat was nowhere to be found, but Bridget was busy with the innards of the stove and a black iron poker. When she noticed that Emily had recovered herself, she straightened and held out a washcloth, newly damp.

Emily took the washcloth, pressing the hot wet material gratefully to her eyes. She stayed that way for a few moments and then looked at Bridget, who was back to stirring the coals around in the belly of the stove.

"That's good," she said quietly.

"I know how you feel. I myself was just a wee one when me and Mam and Pat came over for the first time, from the old country. It wasn't easy. But it does get easier, I can tell you that." She shut the door of the stove with a clang and straightened, brushing her red hands on her apron. "Let me show you where you'll be bedding so you can get out of those wet clothes and get some rest."

Emily nodded. "Thank you, Bridget. You've been so kind."

Bridget smiled and grabbed her hand. "I've been wantin' you to arrive, Miss, to bring some sunshine to the place." Just as quickly, she let go and bustled toward the doorway they'd come through.

To the right in the cramped foyer was the large wooden door to the outside, rain still hammering on its other side, and a small set of wooden stairs curling up and away to the left, into the darkness. The staircase was so narrow, it must've been quite a treat for Pat to get her trunk upstairs.

Bridget was halfway up, her skirts filling the small space as she ascended. Emily followed until the stairs opened onto a wooden hallway with four closed doors. As they walked, Bridget pointed to each room in turn.

"This one is mine," she said, indicating the first door, "and the one all the way down on the left is the bathroom. The first on the right's for storage as Pat sleeps at the back of the garage. The last one on the right is yours, Miss. My Fiona will take the other bed when she's about."

Bridget opened the door and pushed it wide, stepping aside for Emily. The room was small but cozy, two twin beds stretching out from the far wall with a circular window between them. Close to her was a reading lamp and a chair, with a table next to the pairing. Her trunk sat at the foot of one of the beds.

Bridget pulled a nightgown out of the small dresser that sat next to an equally small wardrobe on the wall opposite. "Here, use this one of Fiona's so you don't have to get all of your clothes out of your trunk to find the one thing tonight."

Emily took the nightgown from Bridget's outstretched hand and nodded her thanks. With a last smile, Bridget withdrew from the room, and the door latched with a *snick*. Emily undressed quickly and donned the other girl's nightgown, which was pretty short in the legs but a good fit through the shoulders.

The room cozied up against the big chimney leading from the kitchen stove, so it was as warm as a fox den. Emily slipped under her covers, the first proper bed she'd felt in a week, and closed her eyes. Her body was so chilled from the rain that the unfamiliar bed felt toasty and heavenly in comparison. She didn't think she'd be able to sleep with what she'd been through, but, just like with Pat in the car, she fell asleep so fast she couldn't remember pulling up the counterpane.

When she awoke, she had to take a few moments, staring at the unfamiliar ceiling with the familiar disorientation of a constant traveler, to put all the pieces back together. Where was she? How did she get here? Whose nightgown was she wearing?

She acclimated herself to the room and the knowledge that she was at Hydrangea House, or home, whatever that meant for now. The weight of her travels and travails, and the high ledge she was about to vault in meeting her Aunt Isabel, *the* Aunt Isabel, at breakfast made Emily want to curl up into a ball in the center of the bed and close her eyes against the world. But of course she couldn't do that.

The urgent need to rise and visit the bathroom soon made itself too pressing to ignore, and Emily decided to get up and have a look around. She got up out of her warm bed and stretched, then pulled the counterpane up to neaten it. Bridget must've visited again because there were a pair of old slippers and a thick, oft-washed bathrobe hanging by the door. Fiona's, Em supposed as she shuffled into it.

After she'd donned the leather slippers, she poked her head outside and scanned the hallway. No one was about, so Emily took her chance and made her way toward the last door on the left. She twisted the knob too hard and banged open the door, feeling a bit like a sheep in a stall, and fell into the bathroom, which featured all-white tile and a clawed bathtub taking up most of the left side. A sink-and-mirror combo was located next to the tub, and a toilet with a pull chain sat opposite the door.

This toilet was a new contraption for Emily, who had used an outhouse for most of her life and had only used indoor plumbing in the many transit stations and terminals she'd recently visited. She stood staring at the toilet for a thoughtful moment before making use of it. It was mostly self-explanatory but, she thought as she pulled the chain afterward and the water *whooshed* away, an absolute modern marvel.

As her mother undoubtedly would've advised, Emily smiled at herself in the mirror, a fake smile which, after a moment, turned into a real one. At the thought of her mother, she realized she'd need a bit of a scrub before she was presented at the Court of Aunt Isabel, something else her mother would've insisted upon.

It took Em a minute to get the water temperature in the tub right as she didn't trust the showerhead, and she didn't use much water, as she was water-conscious to say the least—only an inch in the large basin. Bridget had once again thought of her and left out a towel, face towel, and washcloth. She felt exceedingly better after squatting down and giving herself a once-over with hot water and the bumpy lump of soap she found next to the tub, with a good rinse at the end.

In the bathrobe again, she trotted down the hallway to her—or Fiona's—room. Now she had to dress, and it presented a bit of a conundrum for her. Mama had told her plenty of stories about Aunt Isabel, so Emily knew that she was headed for a high-stakes breakfast. She only had three dresses to her name, two plain and one fancy, and none of them would really do. Emily flung open the top of her steamer trunk, which exploded in balls and folds of cotton and clothing, her quilt, two books, one framed family picture, her mother's silver candlesticks, and anything else she'd been able to think of saving from her previous existence in the whirlwind of sickness and death and funeral and packing.

Emily pulled out the wine-colored wool dress that she'd worn to her mother's funeral and held it up to her bathrobe-clad body. *What's the weather like?* she wondered. That would make a difference.

When Emily pulled aside the gabardine curtains and peered through the round window under the eaves, she was treated to a wonderful vignette, like a picture-postcard. A wide avenue purled away, lined with houses and white picket fences, and then, further on, boxy stores and red-brick sidewalks. The road unrolled down to the harbor, concluding in a dark-blue splash. A mixture of farm wagons, people pushing carts, and cars bumped down the main street, and, out on the indigo harbor, two sailboats scudded by, and a fishing boat chugged to sea. In the far left-hand corner, she could just see the white lighthouse, standing sentinel at the harbor's mouth.

Unlike the night before, today was going to be beautiful. Emily didn't know much about the ocean, but she knew wind, and the way these trees were tossing their crowns and the clouds were quickly moving across the periwinkle-blue sky told her it was blowing hard out there. Maybe she'd be glad of her woolen dress after all.

Dressing rapidly, Emily tried to do something with her hair, flattened from sleeping so deeply, and decided that a braid would be both quick and passable to her aunt's scrutiny. A smoothing of her strong dark eyebrows and she felt ready to meet the dragon. Or was she? Perhaps she'd never be ready, but at least now she was presentable.

Chapter 2

The kitchen was much brighter and warmer in the morning, daylight illuminating all its nooks and crannies. Bridget stood at the counter, putting plates and cups on a tray. She was filling a silver pitcher with steaming milk when Emily entered, waiting quietly in the doorway.

"Oh!" Bridget said when she finally looked up. "Good morning! There you are, Miss! I'm afraid we can't be as chatty as we were last night. Mrs. Hewett has asked to see you as soon as I set eyes upon you."

Isabel Hewett always had breakfast in the parlor so she could get the best light with which to read her letters and newspapers—or at least, that's what Bridget said as she finished the tray and gave Emily a once-over with a sharp glance, smiling encouragingly. "This'll just have to do until we can find better. Follow me." Bridget untied her apron and threw it down, taking up the silver tray and sweeping toward the set of double doors, clinking softly as she went.

Emily steeled herself and followed in Bridget's wake as she backed through the double doors, which opened onto a long hallway opulently done in maroons with gold accents. A staircase unfurled grandly to Emily's right, its thick wooden balustrade carved with grapes, leaves, and vines. Emily goggled at everything, the ornate cuckoo clock they passed, clicking and chiming to itself, and the thickness of the rug under her feet. The hallway opened into a foyer with a black-and-white floor, an unlit chandelier glistening high above the stairs. There were rooms to either side, and before veering left after Bridget, Emily got an eyeful of the front door. A stout wooden affair, it was painted a cornflower blue. There was a slot for mail and an ornate doorknob, which was, hands down, the fanciest doorknob attached to the fanciest door Emily had ever seen.

Across the parquet floor to the right was an open doorway leading into a gleaming dining room, and then, as Emily looked down the hallway beyond, she saw a cubby tucked into the wall where a black telephone lay inside, sitting on a table, a lamp with a green shade spotlighting the curvature of graceful metal. She'd seen telephones before and used one, once, but she didn't know anyone with a telephone in their home. Em tore her eyes away from these wonders to enter the parlor.

Trailing into the room after Bridget, Emily finally snapped her eyes ahead of her, and into the steel-trap gaze of Mrs. Isabel Hewett. Emily closed her slightly gaping mouth and brought her shoulders back. Aunt Isabel appraised her unflinchingly, immobile as a statue in a museum, a small woman with upswept silver hair, astonishing violet eyes under stern brows, and a high-collared, filigreed blue dress. Emily could almost feel her mother's light pinch and dutifully popped a curtsy.

"Aunt Isabel," she started from her bowed position. "I'm very glad—"

"Oh, stop that." Aunt Isabel's voice was deeper than her diminutive status belied.

Em lifted her head and looked at the older woman quizzically.

"Come seat yourself at the table like a normal guest. No need for formalities this early in the morning."

The woman was sitting at a round wooden table in a bay window of the cheerful parlor; on a small chintz pillow behind her perched an alert-looking dog, white and brown, eyes trained on Emily but otherwise not moving a muscle. The organdy curtains framed the picturesque view outside, barely competing with the art that lined the walls, jammed together like pipes in an organ.

"Sit down, please," Isabel said and arched an eyebrow in Em's direction.

Emily pulled out a chair to sit in, feeling very out of place. Bridget was there in a moment, bless her, with a teacup and a welcome squeeze of her shoulder. "Coffee or tea, m'dear?"

Emily thought for a moment. She was usually a tea drinker, as her mother had been, as well as her father, but coffee sounded good. Maybe she was a coffee drinker after all and had just never given it a chance. "Coffee, please."

Everyone was silent as Bridget poured out a cup of hot black coffee and then held the silver pitcher of milk up with a questioning raise of her eyebrows.

"Yes, please, and a little sugar."

Bridget added milk and sugar, then placed the coffee and saucer at the top of Emily's plate. The place setting itself was stunning, and looked to Emily like something royalty would dine on at the highest of state affairs. And here they were about to have breakfast on it. She could hardly believe it. The white china was ringed with flowers of bright coral, and the rims of the two plates in front of her, as well as the matching teacup and saucer, all looked like they'd been dipped into melted gold, but only the rims. These foreign accoutrements were placed on a white place mat with a silver fork and a linen napkin expertly folded in a triangle atop it all. This at least she recognized. Her mother always made sure there were napkins at the table. Emily took it, unfolding the cloth in her lap.

"Glad to know we have *some* manners for rough stock," Isabel murmured from the head of the table. "Now, why don't we try and get to know one another?"

Bridget appeared anew, this time with a serving tray of eggs and sausages balanced on one forearm and a silver spoon held in the opposite hand. Emily was helping herself to eggs when she felt the hot weight of her aunt's gaze on her again. She gave the serving spoon back to Bridget with a murmured "thank you" and turned toward her aunt.

Isabel was poised, a cup held aloft in her beringed hand, still staring, and obviously waiting.

"Aunt Isabel," Emily began. "I'd like to take this opportunity—"

"Let's dispense with *that* forthwith," Isabel said curtly, clattering the cup back in its saucer. Emily cringed; the china was apparently stronger than it appeared. "I am not Aunt Isabel, I have never *been* an Aunt Isabel, and I shan't be starting now."

Emily stared at her napkin, twisting it in her lap. *You certainly are an aunt, as you are my mother's sister*, but her good training stopped her from speaking the words aloud. She didn't know why this woman was so angry with her or for what. She took a shaky sip of coffee to fortify her nerves and realized it was excellent—dark, strong, and sweet. She felt a little better upon the warm sugary concoction hitting her stomach.

"Well," she returned evenly, "what would you like me to call you?"

"Mrs. Hewett to start with, I suppose," Isabel rejoined, picking up her cup again and taking a dainty sip. Her long patrician nose almost dipped into the liquid. Her violet eyes flicked back to Emily's. "And then there's the matter of *your* name."

My name? Em scrunched up her nose before she could stop herself.

"Do you have a middle name, niece?" Isabel sat there, regarding her, teacup once again paused in mid-arc to her mouth. Emily was speechless. What was this line of questioning? In the meantime, Bridget reappeared at Mrs. Hewett's side with another small silver tray (*Is everything made of silver in this house?* Emily wondered), this one stacked with the morning's mail.

"My middle name is Frances," Emily finally offered, "but I'm not particularly fond of that one."

"And I'm not particularly invested in which name you are fond of." Mrs. Hewett worked one of the letters open with a knife, slitting the seam at the top and letting the handwritten letter slide out into her waiting palm. "I am not fond of your first christened name, so Frances it shall be while you are in my care."

Emily felt a spurt of distaste in the back of her throat. She took a sip of the strong coffee to wash away the bile. She could hardly believe that this woman shared blood with her sweet mama.

"If you say so, Mrs. Hewett," Emily said, replacing the cup as gently as she could.

Isabel fixed her with another long stare until, apparently satisfied, she nodded and placed a small pair of spectacles at the end of her nose to read her correspondence.

Bridget met Emily's gaze and gave her a sympathetic half smile. Well, at least Bridget was kind. That was something.

In the hallway, the telephone rang, a noise so unknown to Emily that she jumped in her seat at its clanging. It sounded like a bell trapped under a metal bucket. Bridget put down the tray and bustled out.

"Hello, Hydrangea House," Bridget answered in a moment from the hallway. The nearby placement of the phone cabinet made it easy to hear the conversation. "Oh, hello, Thankie."

A pause.

"She's at breakfast at the moment, could it wait?"

Another pause. A clock chimed the quarter hour in the hall.

"I will see if Mrs. Hewett is available, Thankful."

When Bridget came back in, she had a confused look on her face. "Ma'am, Thankful Downs, the telephone operator, is on the telephone with some news for you. She wouldn't say what it was."

Mrs. Hewett looked at Bridget thoughtfully, then pushed up from her place at the table, her elegant silk robe brushing the tops of her golden slippers. The dog was off his cushion in a moment and stayed glued to his mistress's left side as she glided across the parlor floor, her passage silent. She didn't seem that much older than Emily's mother, Constance, who had died at the too-young age of forty-six, but Emily knew that Isabel was older by quite a bit, and had partially raised Constance after *their* mother had died. Em wondered how many years were between them, or if they were once close; her mother rarely spoke of her life before Blue Hill unless pressed, and then only with reluctance. She would have to ask Bridget for more details in a spare moment.

After Mrs. Hewett had left, Emily ate sausage and moved the eggs around her plate as she listened to the conversation in the hallway.

"Hello, Thankful . . . Yes, thank you. Please be expedient; I am meeting with my niece."

There was a pause while Mrs. Hewett listened.

"It *can't* be!"

A long pause.

"Are you absolutely certain, Thankie?"

Another long pause.

"I appreciate the forewarning, Thankful." Her aunt's voice had changed, dropped, gotten more gravelly. "I won't forget it. Please call back at the house if you hear anything. Anything at all."

There was a clang as Mrs. Hewett ended the phone call. When she reentered the parlor to stand in the doorway, she looked pale and diminished. Bridget hovered just out of view behind her shoulder. The dog was behaving in a manner that Em had never seen a dog behave—he did not move from her side and didn't even glance at the sausage Emily was holding in her hand.

"I'm sorry, Frances, you must excuse me. I've . . . I've had a nasty shock, I'm afraid."

"What is it, Mrs. Hewett?"

Her aunt clutched the doorframe, her knuckles white beneath her rings. "I'm afraid my dear old friend Ann Simpson's boat has been lost at sea, and she on it, which seems . . . somewhat impossible." The older woman shook her head from side to side. "Frances, I . . . I'm afraid I must leave you and return to my chambers. I apologize for the abrupt welcome. Please finish your breakfast at your leisure. Bridget?"

"Here, madam," Bridget said from behind her.

"Come, Connor," Mrs. Hewett said to her dog, who didn't need the reminder, and then she was gone, the dog at her heels.

Emily soon heard their footsteps on the stairs and then, in some unknown room overhead, the squeak of a bed. Abrupt welcome? She could laugh; there had been absolutely nothing welcoming about her first hours at Hydrangea House.

Despite her anger at being newly named Frances—her least favorite moniker, worse even than Emmy—Emily, who referred to herself as Em, wondered who Thankful Downs was. She tried to finish the eggs on her plate as she was not a girl who left anything at the table, but this whole interaction had gone so wrong so fast that Emily felt thoroughly seasick again. She poked at the congealing egg globs, such a contrast to the intricate coral roses traced around the edges. Then she abandoned them and set about studying the many paintings hung across the walls.

The parlor, Emily supposed, was not as elegant an affair as the formal dining room, which, if her mother's stories held any water, was the fanciest room of all. In any case, this parlor looked plenty elaborate to Emily, with azure wallpaper forming a wonderful backdrop to the framed artwork packing the small room's walls.

That wasn't altogether correct; art didn't just pack the walls, it was practically all the walls were made of. It was as if Aunt Isabel had taken all the art in a museum and hung it in one room. Emily's eyes devoured the wondrous glimpses into other lives. There were charcoal sketches in gold frames, small oils and watercolors of faraway streets and bazaars, and stern-looking portraits. The wallpaper with its intricate golden designs peeked out from behind all the sketches, oil portraits, etchings, and landscapes. Emily was not experienced in the ways of manners and high society, but she knew a fair deal about art due to her mother's tutelage. Emily perused the walls as her mother's lessons—perspective, shadowing, depth—came to life in front of her.

She was leaning in for a closer look at a tiny watercolor of what could only be Italian hillsides at sunset or dawn when Bridget swept through the doorway with yet another tray and started to pile plates and breakfast detritus onto it. She seemed preoccupied, muttering to herself as she haphazardly stacked the plates. Watching her work gave Emily the itch to help or do something with her hands, so she collected the silverware in front of Mrs. Hewett's place close by, handing them over to Bridget, who looked at her in a funny way as she took them. Emily then followed her out and down the hall into the kitchen, where she instantly felt more at ease. Pat was sitting at the wooden table in one corner, eating another slice of bread and washing it down with a mug of tea.

Bridget thumped the tray down. Emily stood near the double doors empty-handed and looked around.

"Good morning, John Patrick," she said sociably. "Pat."

Pat looked as large as she remembered him and almost seemed out of place indoors, like he belonged in the wild. He nodded at her and swallowed. "Good morning, Miss."

Emily wondered if *Miss* was Pat's tactful way of getting around her name and silently applauded him for it.

"Miss Bridget?" she said to Bridget's broad back where she was already getting started on the morning's dishes at the sink.

"Ach, Miss Frances. Bridget is fine enough for me."

"Bridget, then. Tell me what I can do. I'm not very good at having idle hands."

Bridget gave her an incredulous look over her shoulder, her wet hands glistening in the suds in front of her.

"I can churn, grind corn, or do any kind of kitchen work you've got," Em continued. "I especially like working outdoors, like in a garden, or with animals. Do you have any animals out back?"

There was a pause in Bridget's hand motions in the sink, and Pat also froze in his corner, Emily noticed.

"Do you mean pets, Miss?" Pat asked from across the room.

"Not pets, farm animals. Cows, goats, chickens?" Emily asked hopefully. "I can kill a chicken, pluck it, and get it roasting in no time at all."

"No, Miss Em—Frances, we don't have anything like that here." Bridget pulled her hands out of the sink and dried them on her apron.

She faced Emily and gave her a smile, which somewhat loosened up the taut tug of loneliness in Em's chest. They didn't even have any animals? What was she going to do with her days?

"Why don't you head up to your room and unpack. It always feels better to have your things all in order, doesn't it?" Bridget wiped her hands and steered her toward the back of the kitchen. "Fiona will be about midday. You'll see the Mrs. again at dinner, I'm sure, as she never misses it. Maybe you can take a walk around the town with Fiona, get your bearings? You mentioned a ruined hat to Pat last night."

"Did I?" Emily couldn't remember that.

"That you did. I asked Mrs. Hewett about it and she said you and Fiona could go on down to the Edgartown Market and pick out a new one."

"But Bridget, I can't get a new hat." Emily's cheeks burned as she thought of her dwindling purse and careful corner-cutting at every Woolworth lunch counter at all the stations she had been through over the last week. "I'm afraid I don't have the money."

"Don't mind that, my dear. I'm sure you can put it on Mrs. Hewett's account, and it won't be any trouble at all." With that Bridget turned back to the sink, and Emily left the kitchen to climb the stairs to her room.

On the stairs, she heard Bridget snort. "Did you hear that, Pat? Could you imagine the first Miss Emily—the daughter of the house—asking if she could kill a chicken or pluck it? I hardly think so."

Pat guffawed from his corner.

Emily stopped on the narrow stairs. So, this was interesting. There was *another* Emily, it seemed. A "first" one. A daughter.

My word, another Emily? This would explain the hubbub about her name, she thought as she started up the stairs again. They both named their girls Emily? She was under the impression that they never spoke after Mama's inglorious escape to the West. Where was this Emily now? Not here, that was for certain.

As she entered her room, which was even more cramped with the introduction (and explosion) of her trunk, Emily got down to the task of unpacking.

Bridget was right, it was nice to straighten up her things, but it also made her intensely sad. She missed her mother more than anything. Her father had been a wonderful man, quiet and kind, with a helpful hand and positive words anytime she fell or took a scrape. But it was her mother that Emily had been closest to out on the prairie, especially after her father had died in a farm accident when she was twelve. The last four years had been especially hard on them both. And then Mama's illness. And now this.

Her jam-packed steamer trunk brought back an onslaught of memories as she unearthed her mother's most treasured worldly possessions, the ones that Emily couldn't bear to sell or give away. The silver candlesticks, a family portrait in front of the house they'd built together, and Constance's jeweled comb, a remnant of her debutante days, Em remembered, fingering the inlaid pearls. Along with these treasures, her steamer trunk contained everything else Em had thought, back in Nebraska, she would need for her new life.

She put the two books on the shelf and hung her other two dresses in the wardrobe next to Fiona's shorter ones. Her wardrobe consisted of the aforementioned dresses, a coat still damp from last night's rain, one pair of boots, a muff, and a winter hat, along with her ruined straw one. She also had a scarf and mittens her mother had knit her, and an assorted collection of underthings and socks.

The more she lightened the load in her trunk, the heavier and sadder she felt. Her spare possessions, some of them passed down, seemed to carry the weight of her family's history. Her *real* family, not this one. Why did her mother send her here? What could Mama have been thinking? Why couldn't she have just stayed in Nebraska, with the Lawtons who lived on the next farm over?

Em used a shelf below the mirror to store the few items of her *toilette*—brush, soap, a small scrap of ribbon. The one picture went next to her bed; it showed the three of them, her mama, her dad, and her, standing in front of the wooden beam house they'd built in Nebraska, all with proud smiles. Emily snorted as she looked at their beaming faces; they wouldn't have been so proud of their accomplishment if they'd ever been in a house like the one in which she was currently standing. Which, she realized, her mother had. But her mother looked just as proud as the others in the photo, even more so—she was ecstatic.

Emily didn't know much about her mother's circumstances directly before she'd left for Nebraska with Em's missionary father, only that the disaffection had been utter and complete and Mama's face had gotten a pinched look whenever Em had asked her to reminisce.

In the picture, just peeking around the side of the house where she definitely wasn't supposed to be, was Juniper, Emily's horse. She remembered how upset her mother had been that Juniper had ruined the picture, a formal family portrait. Emily had tried to convince her mother that Juniper only wanted to be included in the photograph as a rightful member of the family.

Gosh, she missed that horse most of all sometimes. At least she knew Juniper was taken care of with Ethan Lawton, her fifteen-year-old neighbor back in Blue Hill. He would mind her well, even if he didn't know which exact spot she likes itched behind her ears, she thought, wiping her eyes. Em sighed and replaced the photo on the table next to her bed.

Finally, she spread out the homemade quilt on top of the worn counterpane that was already there, and then she was done. All unpacked.

Her task having taken her all of half an hour or so, she now had loads of time to await whatever Mrs. Hewett had in store for her, if it was anything. Goodness, Emily couldn't think of anything worse than spending the rest of her life up here, itchy from idleness, staying out of her aunt's line of sight.

Her room did feel much more homey, she had to admit, with her things set out, but this was like no other home Emily had ever known, and it was thoroughly unwelcoming. Just as she was starting to feel really sorry for herself, she heard a clattering on the stairs below, steps in the hallway, and a quick knock, then the door to her room was thrown open by a tiny tempest.

A girl, no more than five feet tall, stood in the middle of the doorway with her hands on her hips. "Taking up all the space already, I see?" She grinned hugely at Emily, who, despite her heavy heart, couldn't help but smile back. "You must be Miss Emily, erm, Frances. Aren't you? One of those, at least?" This last part said with an arched eyebrow.

Emily rose from her spot on the bed. "Yes, I am. And you're Fiona? Miss Fiona? Bridget's daughter?"

Fiona nodded enthusiastically, black curls bobbing. "The one and only. And just Fiona, for me."

"Just Emily for me too. So then, this is your room?"

"Right."

"Thank you for letting me stay in it. And for the loan of a nightdress."

"Sure. Not that I had a choice." Fiona stared at Emily. "Well, I'm certainly glad you're here. And you don't look like her, at least your face doesn't, so that's a huge relief."

"Look like whom?"

"Haven't you heard yet?" Fiona paused, a shrewd look coming over her china-doll features. "Of course you wouldn't have. Who would tell you?" She started to revolve around the room, inspecting Emily's few things. "Have you met Mrs. Hewett yet?" she asked as she plucked Emily's comb off the shelf.

"Yes, I . . ." Emily wasn't sure how to relate the disaster of a conversation she'd had with her aunt that morning. "It was . . . eventful."

Fiona snorted and turned a rueful smile Emily's direction. "I'm sure it was." She replaced the comb and sat down on Emily's bed. "Everything's eventful when Mrs. Hewett's around. Did she tell you why you're bunking with me?"

Emily shook her head, watching Fiona finger the tiny stitches of the quilt with admiration.

"No, of course not," Fiona said. "This is the berries, by the way. Such lovely sewing skills you must have."

"My mother helped me."

"I'm sorry to hear about your mother."

"Thank you."

"What about your name, is she having a hard time getting her tongue around it?" Fiona kept her vigilant gaze on Emily's face, watching her reaction.

Emily looked at her through squinted eyes. "Well, yes, in fact. She isn't going to call me Emily, she's going to call me by my middle name. Frances." Emily screwed up her mouth in disgust.

"So I heard," Fiona said.

At first Emily had thought that Fiona was a good deal younger than herself, but after watching her for the last few minutes, Emily was pretty sure they were about the same age, sixteenish.

"This your horse?" Fiona held the framed photo, pointing to the sliver of horse nose just visible. Emily nodded. "Did you tell my mam you wanted to go slaughter chickens or something? She's still talking about it. Can't get over it, apparently."

"I just . . . I asked if there was anything I could do. I'm a little restless." Emily gestured weakly to the confines of her room. "I'm used to working."

Fiona studied her from wise eyes and nodded. "Of course. You're a farm girl."

Emily shrugged and smiled.

"I won't call you Frances, promise, except in front of the Mrs. But how's Em, short for Emily? That way, if we're overheard . . ."

Emily could've hugged her. "That sounds just fine. Fiona."

Fiona reached out and squeezed her hand. "Mam asked me to be kind to you, as you've had a rough time of it. But I don't even have to try! I think we're going to be fast friends."

Warmth surged through Em, starting from Fiona's small palm clasped in hers. "I think so too," she whispered, hardly daring to believe it.

Chapter 3

It was Fiona who finally revealed the mystery of the name, and it turned out to be just as bad as Emily could've imagined. It looked as if she was going to stay Frances for a good long while.

"There *was* another Emily, you're right." Fiona's gray eyes lit up when she was relating an interesting tale like any natural storyteller. "The first Emily was the Mrs.'s daughter, and she died six years back. Didn't you know? Your mam and the Mrs. being sisters?"

"No, they . . . they were estranged," Emily said. "They didn't speak."

"Well, isn't that a shame! We'll have to catch you up. Let me start from the beginning."

Fiona scooted closer to Em on the bed. She was wearing a simple green dress and a handsome tweed coat carelessly thrown over her shoulders and looked like the imp version of her mother—the same gray eyes and turned-up nose and freckles, but with dark curls and paler skin. "See, it was a few years after Major Hewett's death. That was sad, but it wasn't too troublesome for the Mrs. as her husband was a soldier and died bravely in the war.

"The routine here at Hy House"—when Em looked at her, confused, Fiona clarified—"Hydrangea House—was largely back to normal, with most of the first Miss Emily's time taken up with sailing and boating and fishing and social calls and the like."

No wonder Bridget thought it funny when I offered to pluck a chicken, Em thought.

"The girl was made for anything and everything on the sea. Mam called her a little mermaid, that's how much she was in and out of the water."

Even if they did share a name, that was something the two of them did not share; this Emily, the second Emily, was certainly not game for anything and everything on the ocean. She *did* know how to swim, thankfully, as plenty a summer day in Nebraska found her floating around in the Platte, Juniper slurping river water nearby.

"It was fall in 1923," Fiona continued. "I was ten. I remember because the *John Dwight* had just gone down. The *Dwight* was a ship, a rumrunner with a big cargo on board, and, when it sank, everybody went treasure-crazy, taking out any kind of boat and crew to go look for sunken treasure. One autumn day, Miss Emily went out in the afternoon to do some surf casting. And she never came back." Fiona held out both hands, palms up.

There was a heavy pause.

"What do you mean, she never came back? She just disappeared?" Emily was incredulous. "Did she drown? Was she in a boat?"

Fiona shook her head. "She'd gone surf casting, when you fish from the beach, so she wasn't in a boat. She'd been fishing down on South Beach loads of times. Hundreds. And she was always fine. But she didn't come home that afternoon, or that night, and that's when Mrs. Hewett began to get really frantic. They searched and they searched but they couldn't find heads nor tails of her. All they found was her tackle box, washed up at Quansoo. At first they thought what they found was something from the *Dwight*, but they soon figured out that it belonged to the one and only missing island heiress—Miss Emily Bushnell Hewett. It was tragic."

"And Aunt Isabel, I mean Mrs. Hewett? What did she do?"

"Has she done with the auntie stuff too, I imagine?"

Emily nodded. She felt mildly reassured. Maybe she wasn't the only one that rubbed the older woman the wrong way.

"Mrs. Hewett? What did she do? She collapsed. Once they found

Miss Emily's tackle box Mrs. Hewett went to a place that you don't come back the same from."

"Poor woman."

"Yes. She is." Fiona looked around in mock secrecy. "Richest woman I know but also the loneliest. Her crabby behavior over the morning meal is actually the warmest and most talkative we've seen her in years. She might as well have given you a ticker-tape parade."

Emily snorted. "I don't think a ticker-tape welcome parade has a ceremony in which the honoree gets renamed and dismissed."

Fiona chuckled. "I suppose not. A little stern for a welcoming parade then?"

"A little."

A mischievous look came over Fiona's face. "Em, do you want to go see her room?"

Em was aghast. "Who, Mrs. Hewett's?"

"Saints alive, no! I mean Miss Emily's. The *first* Miss Emily's."

Emily almost said no, but a curiosity for her mysterious predecessor had begun to take hold. "She still has a room here?"

"The Mrs. has never changed a thing. All her clothes, everything is still there."

"Will we get caught, do you think?"

"Not by the Mrs. From what Mam says, she's locked up until at least dinner. Asked for a tea tray to be taken up at two. If anyone catches us, it'll be Mam, or maybe Uncle Pat. But I can talk my way past them." Fiona grabbed Emily's cuff, all bravado and gumption. "Come on, where's your sense of adventure?"

"Um, in Nebraska?"

They both burst out laughing. "Left it in Nebraska? I don't believe it. You wouldn't have made it all the way across the country alone without some sense of adventure!"

And then they were up and out the door to visit the first Emily's, the dead Emily's, room, and there wasn't a thing Em could do about it but be borne along like driftwood in a flash flood.

The two crept down the back stairs and into the kitchen, pausing at the threshold while Fiona poked her head in.

"Thought so," she whispered. "Mam's gone off for her spot of tea with Lucinda next door. She is as punctual as the clock in the hall."

Still clutching one another's arms, they set across the broad expanse of the kitchen and through the double doors. The thick hallway rug muffled their footfalls, and they tiptoed so quietly that Emily could hear the precise inner workings of the cuckoo clock as they passed by—wooden clicks, rickety whirls, and muffled chimes.

Instead of going into the parlor, as she had for breakfast, Fiona led Emily across the foyer and up the curved staircase. Unlike the parlor, the tall walls along the stairs were totally bare except for three large paintings and a photograph of a grand house, the whitewashed walls behind making them stand out in sharp relief. Their subjects included a younger, brunette Isabel, an older man in an army outfit, and a young girl of about sixteen, shown in profile, her bright hair piled on her head and one graceful shoulder peeking out of the folds of her dress.

"The first Miss Emily," Fiona breathed from beside her.

As they passed underneath, Emily studied the girl in the portrait and thought she looked capable, clever, and maybe a little funny. A good sort to share a name with.

On the landing, Emily got an eyeful of the beautiful crystal chandelier that hung in the high-ceiling space above the main entrance. Each crystal dangled independently, and Emily could only imagine its sparkling splendor when all the candles were aflame. When they crested the stairs, Emily and Fiona were confronted with a long dark hallway, several doors closed up and down its length. It was longer and darker than the hallway in the servant's quarters, more opulent, and more menacing.

Fiona put her finger to her lips and tugged Emily along behind her. They crept past an austere grandfather clock and a painting of a storm at sea. Doors on both the left and right remained closed and the girls whispered past as the *tickticktick* of the grandfather clock got softer. There were no other noises in the hallway at all, only the wind outside playing with the branches of the trees.

When they reached the third door down, Fiona stopped and looked up and down the length of the hallway with large, luminous eyes. She nodded at Emily, whose heart seemed to have split into two and lodged into each ear, thudding so loudly she was sure even Fiona could hear. Fiona had just put one fingertip on the smooth crystal doorknob when a hand suddenly fell on Emily's shoulder.

Emily gasped and jumped; Fiona gasped too, and they both turned together.

There stood Bridget with a furious expression on her face. Fiona opened her mouth to start talking her way out of their tight spot, but Bridget threw a finger to her lips and pointed down the hall toward Mrs. Hewett's closed door.

Shooing them vigorously with her apron, Bridget urged both girls back down the dark hall to the main staircase. And even though Emily was pretty sure she was already in trouble barely halfway through her first day, she couldn't help feeling like a princess as she descended, fingers trailing on the thick wooden banister, which was as smooth as well-polished leather.

Bridget ushered them down the hall and into the kitchen. As soon as the doors swung shut, she swatted at Fiona with her apron. "Mary Fiona O'Callahan. What could you have been thinking?"

Fiona stammered. "I . . . we . . . Mam, I—"

"Sneaking around upstairs like a pair of common burglars. Is this what you think I meant when I asked you to befriend Miss Frances here?"

"No, ma'am, I . . . I didn't."

Emily didn't know Fiona well yet, but she didn't think she was talking her way past her mother at all successfully. "Bridget, we weren't trying to do any harm, we were just—"

"Please, Miss Frances," Bridget interrupted. "I know you mean well and you want to keep my Fiona out of trouble, but this isn't something you can know about, having just arrived."

This stopped Emily from trying to deflect any more heat coming Fiona's way.

"Fiona O'Callahan. I asked you a question. Is this what you think I meant when I asked you to cheer up Miss Frances?"

Fiona hung her head, barely looking at her mother. "No, Mam, I do not think this is what you meant."

"So what were you up to then?" Bridget's Irish accent got much, much stronger the angrier she became. "You know the Mrs. does not approve of guests millin' about upstairs, especially in *that* room."

"Sorry, Mam."

Bridget sighed and tried to smile at Emily but only half succeeded. "I'm sure this seems all very strange to you, Miss Frances."

"Not as strange as getting a new name the minute I arrived."

Bridget lowered her head in agreement. "It's all connected. Did Fiona relate what happened to the Mrs.'s only child?"

Emily nodded.

"Did she tell you about the state of things?"

Emily crinkled her brow and shook her head.

"Well," Bridget began, leading the girls closer to the stove, which was still putting out heat even on this sunny day. "No one is supposed to go into Miss Emily's, apologies, the *first* Miss Emily's room, except me, once a month, to clean. And the Mrs. whenever she wants. The reason why we're all making the effort to call you Miss Frances is because she doesn't like to hear the name Emily. Not since her own was lost. Mother Mary, I miss that lovely girl." Bridget dabbed at her eyes. "The fact that two sisters so many miles apart named their daughters the same thing is a wonder to me, but the Mrs. won't hear anyone speak of it. So, for now, Miss Frances you shall remain." Bridget smiled and squeezed Em's forearm. She began to herd them toward the back door. "What this all means, however, is that you girls are *not* to be snooping around the first Miss Emily's room, now or any other day. Do you understand me?" She stood them in front of her, glaring at them like they were a pair of two-year-olds with sugar frosting all over their faces and hands. "Answer me, please."

"Yes," both girls said in unison.

"Yes what?"

"Yes, we understand," they mumbled somewhat coherently.

"Good. Now you have an errand to find Miss Frances another hat as hers was ruined last night. Take her down to the Edgartown Market, and no funny business, Fiona. I mean it." Bridget fixed her daughter with another stern stare and then turned a kinder visage to Em. "Here's a loan of my coat." Bridget grabbed a short burgundy coat off a hook on the wall and handed it to Emily to go over her dress as Fiona buttoned up her tweed version. "Yours is still damp, dear. I'm drying it out for you."

"Thank you."

"No trouble." And then Bridget had them out the back door and standing in the drive.

The house looked very different from the way it had appeared in the rain the night before. Instead of a hulking mass of wood, steaming rain, and shadows, the house this morning looked like an absolute dream. It was a white clapboard mansion crowded with windows, adorned with four chimneys, and crowned with a railing-ringed platform. She caught sight of her own window, well, hers and Fiona's, a tiny circle of glass tucked up under the eaves.

While the kitchen door wasn't as fancy as the front door Emily had seen on her way to breakfast that morning, it looked impressive enough to a girl from the prairie. A wide stone lintel framed it, and the girls had to go up and over a slab of granite to get outside. At first Emily couldn't quite understand the blinding whiteness of the drive and why it should be that way, but when she leaned over to inspect it more closely, she found it was made of crushed white shells. Green laurel bushes grew along the side of the house, and stately sycamore trees lined the main road, partially hiding it from view.

Fiona waved goodbye to her mother and wrapped her arm through Emily's as they set off, crunching across the crushed shells to the sidewalk, where they took a left to follow a sloping brick path past an austere white church, four massive Greek columns rising up to the steeples. The village of Edgartown was made up of compact houses of simple clapboard with painted white trim, all save the Methodist church—the enormous columned spectacle neighboring Hydrangea House. Across the street from it were a few tidy-looking houses and then another church. This one, Fiona said, was the Catholic church where she, her uncle Pat, and Bridget attended services. A mix of carriages, carts, and cars filled the one-way street, parked vehicles on one side, and moving traffic on the other, all jostling for space on the narrow thoroughfare.

The girls sallied down Main Street and, en route, Fiona waved to quite a few people. No one asked who Emily was or greeted her, despite some appraising looks, nods, and curious stares. Fiona didn't stop to introduce her either, which Emily was glad for; she was so amazed by the scenery that just looking at everything was a job in itself.

There were a lot more trees in Edgartown than there were in Blue Hill, Nebraska, although Emily's hometown was quite proud of their newly planted windbreaks. White picket fences wrapped with prickly brown rosebushes lined the brick sidewalks here, and the snug cottages pushed up, sometimes half hidden by brush, sometimes so close Emily could've reached out and snapped a twig from the lifeless stems in the window boxes.

This was very different from what Emily was used to, as her house and all her neighbors' houses, even those who lived in town, had yards of dusty space between them. Ranches and farms were miles apart, and in Blue Hill, yards weren't for gardens, except for vegetable gardens. They didn't grow showy flowers like the ones that would be blooming along the picket fences and in the window boxes here in the summer; the only pretty flowers they grew were ones that were useful as well as attractive, like bee balm or catmint. The yards were ruled by the farm animals and were for working, not leisure. Here, the houses were almost decorative, not practical or efficient, a quality that Emily had never witnessed before walking amongst the clusters of well-appointed cottages dressed up by bushes and smart shutters.

Everywhere around them were snatched glimpses and hints of the sea. The air had a salty tang, seagulls called loudly to one another overhead, and the salt spray made Em's cheeks tacky as they walked down the hill. The scene once again reminded her of a postcard, probably a lot like one her mother must've had somewhere at home.

As the sidewalk narrowed and the buildings huddled closer, many of them began to look more like businesses than domestic abodes, with larger, uncurtained windows. The girls approached a four-way crossing where a stout brick bank sat to their right, and to their left boxes of produce lined the sidewalk outside the plate-glass window of a grocer's.

Emily slowed her pace, tugging on Fiona's arm to slow her too. In Nebraska, Em had never seen such abundance before, even though most of the folks she knew who weren't ranchers were farmers. But in all her years, she had never seen a harvest this big thrown together in one place, especially in late spring. Purple cabbages, bursts of green spinach, orange acorn squash, and even the last apples of the season crowded the boxes. It was easily the most splendid thing Emily had seen since she'd arrived, even more splendid than the plush rugs, fancy china plates, or the delicate cuckoo clock quietly churning and grinding its gears in the emptiness of her aunt's vast halls.

Fiona smiled at Emily's look of wonderment and pulled her through the shop's doorway, but not before Em read *Edgartown Market* painted in red script on a white sign overhead.

Inside the building smelled like Kinecki's General Store—perhaps a little more like fish and a little less like horse—and Emily recognized the barrels of grains and rice and oats and the bolts of fabrics against the wall. A long wooden counter paraded down the aisle, bearing a metal cash register and a line of glass jars, each cylinder filled with a different kind of candy in eye-popping colors.

Fiona looked at Em with twinkling eyes and cried, "To the milliner's!" as she spun so her green skirt belled out around her black stockinged legs. She marched off down the aisle and Emily followed with the deep relief of someone who has found a friend in a strange and faraway place.

Chapter 4

In the end, Emily decided (or Fiona decided that Emily should decide) that she would get a cloche hat that was both of the moment and could still provide protection from the elements. The color, a deep blue, looked beautiful against Emily's bright golden hair, Fiona said, cocking her head as she held the hat up against Emily's skin.

After that, the girls wandered through the aisles on creaky wooden floors, taking in all the wares, Emily marveling at the many oddities she saw and Fiona explaining what she could. Em particularly loved a snow globe with a lighthouse in it, imagining what a snowstorm on the island would look like. She thought it looked quite enchanting as she shook it, watching the white particles swirl and dance. Fiona charged the hat to Isabel Hewett's account, and Emily turned down Mrs. Fligor's offer to box it, opting to wear it out instead.

While the girls were leaving the establishment, they were accosted by a white-haired old lady who had a strong resemblance to an owl in that she had the same wide, unblinking gaze, and her overall unkemptness suggested that she'd just woken from a long nap, perhaps in a hollow tree. She practically bumped into them on the threshold just as Emily was putting on her new hat.

"Hello there," the stranger crowed at them, and Fiona's hand tightened on Em's forearm. "Who do we have here? I know Miss Fiona, but who's this?" The lady's tan skin, white hair, and woven shawl made her an ideal New Englander, at least in Emily's regard.

"Mrs. Pritchard, may I introduce you to Emily, I mean Frances . . . Frances, erm—" Fiona looked at Emily for help.

Em stepped up and nearly curtsied, but her experience with her aunt that morning had given her pause about the liberal distribution of her curtsies, as this was 1929. She reconsidered and, instead, nodded at the woman. "How do you do? I'm Frances Cartwright, Mrs. Hewett's niece."

"Oh, that's right. Aren't you newly arrived from Oklahoma?"

"Nebraska, actually."

"My word, how could anyone imagine living all the way out there?" The older woman's voice trailed off. Emily didn't quite know how to answer her enigmatic comment, so she stayed silent. "Do you like it here?"

"Honestly," Emily said, "I haven't been here long enough to get a feel for it. I just arrived yesterday."

"Just washed ashore, then." The older woman kept her ponderous gaze squarely planted on Emily. The three of them were still bunched at the doorway, and a few other customers had to make their way around them to get inside the store. Emily could smell Mrs. Pritchard, a mixture of something musty and floral and a bit rank underneath.

"You're the spitting image of her, you are," Mrs. Pritchard remarked in a high, querulous voice.

"Spitting image of whom?" Emily returned.

"Constance."

When Mrs. Pritchard said her mother's name, Emily felt a surge of joy in her heart, like warm honey. "You knew my mother?"

"Well, of course! For many years, I was the piano teacher for the village's children."

"She played the piano?" Emily said. "I never heard her play. We didn't have a piano in Nebraska. Did she play well?"

"I don't remember if she played well or not. Hundreds of students over the course of my twenty-five-year career, so I don't remember everyone's playing. I remember Constance—" The woman paused as another customer pushed by them with a muffled "excuse me." Fiona politely herded Mrs. Pritchard and Emily out of the doorway and onto the sidewalk.

"I remember Constance Hewett because," Mrs. Pritchard continued, "out of all my pupils, she was the most like a hothouse flower."

"A what?" Fiona asked.

"A greenhouse flower, some sort of specialty bloom that can only thrive under particular circumstances."

Emily had always been taught not to disagree with her elders, but this woman was about as far off as she could be when it came to her mother. Constance had *not* been a hothouse flower, which sounded to Em like someone delicate and finicky. Emily had many memories of her mother doing brave things for the benefit of her child or her family's well-being. One in particular stood out: her mother flushing a prairie rattlesnake out of the vegetable garden and taking its head off with one swipe of her shovel. It was one of Emily's earliest memories. No, Constance was no delicate orchid that wouldn't survive an hour out on the plains.

"Are you sure you have the right person, Mrs. Pritchard?" asked Emily. "Maybe you're thinking of her older sister, Isabel."

The woman clutched her shawl to her throat. "I know my pupils," she said shortly. "Isabel Hewett was a beautiful pianist and a rare talent. Her little sister barely peeked out from behind her skirts, not that I could blame the girl. She was shy, and probably very kind, but seemed fragile somehow. And you are the spitting image of her. Although, the hair . . ." She waved her hand vaguely in Emily's direction.

It was true, her mother's ice-blond locks were different from the thick braid of gold that swung from Emily's nape. But besides that, the mother and daughter had often been told how much they looked alike. They were quite proud of it.

"Yes, my hair is different." Emily felt the old pride surge up.

"Are you a hothouse flower like her, too?"

From beside her, Fiona snorted. "I should say not, Mrs.

Pritchard. Our Emily's a crack hand at almost anything. She's a farm girl, you see."

Emily flushed at her friend's words. Not that Fiona would know if she was skilled at anything, since they'd only known one another for all of two hours. But it spoke to Fiona's loyalty, and Emily was grateful.

"And your mother, she was out there, on the farm with you?" The woman's nasally voice rose.

"That she was," Em said.

"My my," Mrs. Pritchard said, offering another of her vague admonishments.

Fiona propelled Em down the sidewalk. "It's been lovely chatting with you, Mrs. Pritchard, but I must get back to the kitchen at Hydrangea House. Mam will start to wonder."

"Of course, of course, my dears. Give my best to your aunt, Frances. Remember me to her, please."

Emily spoke over her shoulder as Fiona urged her down the sidewalk. "I certainly will, Mrs. Pritchard. Nice to meet you."

"You as well, dear. And don't forget to practice!"

As soon as she turned straight again, Emily caught Fiona's gaze from underneath the brim of her new hat.

"Hothouse flower?" Em whispered.

"Don't forget to practice?" Fiona returned.

They erupted in shared chuckles.

When they'd recovered themselves, Emily noticed that they were not headed up Main Street's hill to Hy House but had cut back down to the harbor. They veered between two cottages, following a footpath shaded by tall trees.

"Where are we going?" Emily asked.

"Let's go take a look at the harbor, so I can give you a lay of the land, or the Vineyard Sound, I suppose." Fiona opened a white picket gate and stepped through, letting Emily pass, then relatching it behind her.

In front of them, a gentle slope led down to the edge of the harbor. Men in oilskins or wool sweaters and caps were working across the various decks of the moored fishing boats. The sea breeze whipped up the street, making Em grab at her new hat so it didn't blow away, filling her lungs with a fresh salty tang. She smiled. This was turning out to be a grand adventure indeed.

Carefully stepping around the muddiest parts of the dirt road, Emily and Fiona made their way down to the water, picking a path between large boxy objects that looked like cages and were called, Em soon found out, lobster pots.

When they walked onto the wooden pier, several of the fishermen working nets and mending lines on their boats called to Fiona and waved, glancing questioningly at Emily, but none asked who she was. The men shouted back and forth to one another in English and in another language that sounded like Spanish, but had more *rsh* sounds.

"It's Portuguese," Fiona explained as they doubled back along the harbor, once again walking toward the intersection of Main and Water Street.

An establishment with a sign out front that read *Papers* had a window peppered with posters—one trumpeting a boxing match in a place called Oak Bluffs. As they walked by the entrance, the smell of coffee came wafting out of the slightly open double doors.

Fiona squealed and stopped. "Let's go grab a frappé."

"A what?"

"A frappé," Fiona clarified. "What, you've never had one? That's baloney! They're the bee's knees, Em! C'mon."

The two stepped over the threshold and threaded their way past a table covered with spread newspapers. An older man with glasses was standing next to the table, screwing up his eyes to read the headlines of *The New York Times* as a tired-looking mum snaked her arm through and snagged the *Boston Herald*. She carried the paper to a bench against the wall near a small stove and scanned the front page, rocking a black baby pram with one foot as she read.

The girls made their way down an aisle to the lunch counter at the back where they both perched on stools and settled themselves, unbuttoning their coats. "Two coffee frappés, please, Mr. Pachico," Fiona said from beside her.

On the other side of the counter, a tan, amiable man with very white teeth smiled at them. "Hello, Miss Fiona, will do. Who's your friend?" He set to work by placing two glasses on the long countertop and a glass-and-metal blender next to them. His black hair and olive skin were a sleek contrast with his white apron and the long white expanse of counter.

"This is Mrs. Hewett's niece, Miss Em—er, Miss Frances Cartwright." Fiona threw an apologetic look Em's way, mouthing *sorry*.

"Hello, Miss Frances," Mr. Pachico said as he measured ice into the blender. "Here for a visit?" It was hard to make out the man's age; he could've been forty or sixty. His skin looked like a well-worked saddle.

"Nice to meet you, Mr. Pachico," Emily said. "Actually, it looks like I'll be here a while. You see, my mother died." Try as she might, Emily couldn't make her voice not waver on the last statement; she wasn't quite used to the idea.

Mr. Pachico paused while pouring milk from a glass pitcher into the blender and gave her a glance from his shark-dark eyes. Emily kept his gaze. She didn't blink; if she did, she was afraid tears might fall. In a moment, he went back to the coffee frappés, whatever they were, by adding spoonfuls of sugar, vanilla extract, a darker syrup, and what looked like cold coffee from a metal pitcher, its surface foggy from the temperature in the fridge. Once all of these ingredients were in the glass blender, he stirred the mixture with a long silver spoon.

"I'm very sorry to hear that, Miss Frances. I also lost my mother at a young age. *Desculpe*." He attached the blender to its base and flipped a switch, filling the air with a metal clattering. The baby in the pram yelped and the mum glared at them from her spot by the stove. Mr.

Pachico looked back at the woman as he calmly finished blending, then flipped the switch off.

He filled tall glasses with the creamy coffee-colored concoction and topped them up with a flurry of whipped cream, sticking a paper straw and long-handled spoon in each before sliding them in front of the girls. "Welcome. And *minhas condolências*, my condolences." He smiled sadly at Emily.

Emily nodded and stared at the cloud of whipped dairy in front of her to keep her vision clear. "Thank you," she said, and meant it.

Fiona watched Emily take her first sip. Emily's eyes widened as the taste hit her mouth. The frappé was sweet, with the smoky bite of coffee and the creaminess of whipped cream and sugar soaking through. In short, it was delicious.

"This is tasty!" she exclaimed, delighted. "In Nebraska, we had ice cream sodas, but nothing quite like this!"

In the corner, the babe was fully awake and hollering its red-faced head off by now, sitting straight up in the pram in an irate froth of lace. Its mum glared at them as she folded the newspaper, dropping it onto the table and hustling the pram out the front door.

The girls settled into their frappés, making short work of the tasty treats, even though it made Emily's teeth ache and head throb to drink it so quickly. After the disruptive squalls of the baby, the long counter was soon enfolded in a lovely warm silence, punctuated by ticks from the stove, the clatter of dishes from Mr. Pachico at the sink, and Fiona's spoon scraping the inside of her glass. Out the glass-paneled door, Emily could see the harbor, the rich blue of the Atlantic peeking through the gray buildings like a wink.

Fiona looked over at her, her eyes bright with caffeine and sugar. "Well?"

"Seriously, Fiona, this is the best. Thanks."

"My pleasure. Let's get home. Mam always gets busy in the late afternoons."

As they were slurping the tail ends of their frappés, a man in a peacoat stomped in, raising a hand to Mr. Pachico as a greeting. He was a large man, not so much in stature, but in presence. He filled up the almost-empty store immediately.

"'Allo, Frank, how's all things?" Pachico asked him from behind the counter.

The man nodded, more interested in the headlines than small talk. In a moment, he commented without looking up, "Bloody shame the coast guard decided to extend their jurisdiction, innit, Pachico?"

Mr. Pachico chuckled as his hands kept busy scooping coffee. "If you say so, Cap'n. Seems to me all it does is make Rum Row a lot longer and harder to get to."

The man guffawed. "That's about the run of it, Alfonse, that's about the run. It also makes the row harder to guard, you know."

Fiona pushed her empty glass across the counter and jumped down off her stool. Emily did the same and was soon resettling her new hat and waving goodbye to Mr. Pachico.

The captain had taken a seat at the end of the counter and was avidly reading the newspaper. As Emily walked by, she read, *Liquor Seized! Mob Blamed!* A picture of two men on a boat with wide smiles on their faces appeared just below, and behind them, boxes and boxes and boxes of what could only be confiscated spirits.

The bell above Papers' door jingled as the girls left. As soon as they were headed back up the sidewalk, hats pulled down against the wind, Emily let loose her whispered questions.

"What was that all about?"

Fiona had the half-lidded, flushed look of someone who has a belly full of coffee and sugary frozen dairy products. "All what?"

"That man? That captain who just came in? What were he and Mr. Pachico talking about? What's Rum Row?"

"Rum Row? It's bootlegger heaven. You know about Prohibition, don't you? Even out there in the Wild West?"

Emily nodded.

"Since 1919, liquor has been illegal everywhere in the US *on land*"—Fiona waggled her pointer finger—"but not by sea, if you catch my meaning. If you stay twelve miles off land, you're safe legally, or at least the coast guard can't arrest you. The rumrunners dash out and pick up the liquor they need. Some stay off shore in the free zone to visit a speakeasy, the *Atlantis*, but most run out, do a pickup, and then run back and sell what they have. So there's one strip of ocean highway—Rum Row—where the floating speakeasies and the boats that bring in liquor heave to and wait for customers. You can see all sorts going out for a spot of their favorite tipple—teachers, preachers, and all the rest.

"That man who just came in, well, he's just about the best rumrunner you've ever put your peepers on. Captain Frank Butler, and he runs the most rum out of anyone."

Chapter 5

Emily and Fiona returned to a quiet Hydrangea House. Although there was evidence of a massive amount of baking and cooking going on in the kitchen, there was no sign of Bridget.

Emily and Fiona were just hanging up their coats on the hooks lining the wall outside the kitchen when Bridget came bursting through the double doors to the hallway, clutching a mass of fabric so bouffant it hid her face.

"Mam?" Fiona asked the moving ball of lace, tulle, and satin. "That you?"

"Oh, hello dears!" Bridget dumped her armload onto the corner table, just inside the door. "Did you find success at the market?"

Emily turned her head this way and that, modeling the hat.

"Oh my. Absolutely fetching, Miss Frances!"

"Thank you, Bridget."

"I picked it out for her, didn't I?" Fiona piped up. "I thought the color was just perfect with her lovely hair."

"It is. Right you are, Fi."

"Oh, and Mam! We saw Mrs. Pritchard, you know, the old piano instructor who lives out on Planting Field Way?"

"You did, did you now?" Bridget was back at the counter, her capable hands mixing up something pink and fishy in a green bowl.

"She went on and on about how Em here is the spitting image of her mum, meaning Constance. On and on. She wouldn't stop, would she?"

"It was mostly a one-note conversation," Emily agreed. "She told us that Aunt Isa—Mrs. Hewett was an excellent pianist whereas Constance, my mother, was more known for being shy. Is that true, Bridget?"

"I wouldn't have called Miss Constance shy, mind you. She simply chose whom to show her true self to, that's all. And she was a bit of a late bloomer."

"What do you mean?"

"Well, she loved to read. And she was quiet, so folks sometimes forgot she was about. My mother, who kept the house before me, was always bumping into her as she swept floors or bustled about. Constance had a special way of going unnoticed."

"Mrs. Pritchard called her 'a hothouse flower,'" Fiona added. "Was she?"

Bridget started to scoop spoonfuls of the pink fish mush onto a wax-papered sheet pan. "Who, Constance?" Bridget paused, looking up at the ceiling before continuing. "No, it wasn't that so much. She was sheltered, sure, but they all are. I've been with this family for decades, since I was only twelve and your mother a few years older, so I knew her better than most. As I said, she was more selective than shy. And Mrs. Hewett was such a grand character, it was hard to come up in her shadow."

She thought for a moment, then went on. "No, Constance always went her own way. How do you think she ended up way out there on those plains?" Bridget asked with a smile for Em before turning and pushing the sheet pan into the oven behind her. Once it was in, she grabbed a long wooden spoon to adjust all the different receptacles baking away in there. "You do look quite a bit like her, Miss Frances. And I think it's wonderful," Bridget added to the inside of the oven. When she turned again, her cheeks were flushed from the heat. "It's like she's come home again. You'd be a lucky woman if you shared both your mother's grace *and* her bravery."

Emily felt simultaneously the proudest she'd ever felt and also like she wanted to break down into tears. She guessed that this was what grieving was about, like Pastor Canton said, rapidly seesawing between emotional extremes without warning. Bridget must've sensed that Emily was close to a raw edge, because she wrapped an arm around Em's waist and led her to the double doors.

"Brace up, m'dear." Emily let herself be led and hoped that *m'dear* was Bridget's new way of not calling her one name or another. "Having you here is warming all of our hearts. A real breath of fresh air. Even if it doesn't always show, we're *all* glad you're here." Bridget pushed open one of the doors to the hallway and urged Emily through. "Go show your aunt the new hat. Fiona will still be here when you get back. She's going to help me with the croquettes."

The door swung shut, cutting off Fiona's groan of protestation. When Emily got to the parlor threshold, the mellow tones of an orchestra playing on the radio reached her, as well as the hiss of a fire. She stood just beyond the doorway, still out of sight, and took a deep breath. Hopefully this interaction would go better than breakfast.

Mrs. Hewett wasn't sitting at the breakfast table when Emily entered but in a tall-backed scarlet armchair, closer to the fire. The afternoon had brought along a late-spring chill, and Mrs. Hewett clutched a beautifully woven shawl around her delicate shoulders. Connor seemed unperturbed by the change of the weather and lay once again on his throne-cushion; he didn't lift his head or open his eyes when Emily entered, but one ear crooked up.

In front of Isabel was a square table, a cut-crystal cordial glass filled with ruby liquid balanced on one corner. As Emily moved toward the fireplace, she could see the table was actually inlaid, like a chessboard, with metal boats strewn across it. The tabletop was made up of two dominant colors—tan and navy—and suddenly the shapes clicked into place in her mind. It represented a coastline, with the polished tiger oak as the land, and the lapis lazuli for the sea. The boats were metal, with tiny wooden masts and booms, and the white cloth sails no bigger than her thumbnail. Emily assumed the coastline was probably close to here.

Isabel was immobile, staring intently at the board. Emily wondered if it was some sort of game and the boats were the pieces. She coughed into her fist as politely as she could, and Isabel glanced up. "Ah, Frances. There you are. Come, sit."

On the other side of the table was a twin armchair, to which Mrs. Hewett gestured.

Emily lowered herself, all the while keeping her head still. She was hoping that her aunt would notice the hat and say something, but Isabel's eyes were trained on the table. The small silver boats had flattened bottoms to make them look as if they were afloat.

"I just can't see, with that prevailing wind direction, why she should be out there at all!"

Emily had no idea what to say to this, having not an inkling of the subject, so she made a mild sound of agreement, something between a "yes" and an "erm."

Isabel looked up, as if noticing her niece for the first time. "What a fetching hat, I must say. Now, please take it off. You are inside after all."

"Thank you for the hat, Mrs. Hewett. I've never had a nicer one."

"Absolutely. We can't have you going about town bareheaded, can we? And we must dispense with this Mrs. Hewett nonsense. We're family."

"But you told me not to call you Aunt Isabel, don't you remember?" Emily asked. This seemed like a trap.

"Ah, so I did. So I did. So much has happened between then and now." Isabel raised a hand to her forehead; a large opal gleamed on her third finger. "I suppose if it can't be Aunt Isabel and it shouldn't be Mrs. Hewett, as you are my sister's daughter, a blood relation, then it should be just Isabel, don't you think?" Her eyes sparkled like amethysts in the firelight.

Emily didn't think Isabel had ever been "just Isabel" in her lifetime, but she was willing to play along. "All right. Thank you for the hat, Isabel."

"That'll do," Isabel said, and turned her attention back to the small silver boats. "Now that the niceties are out of the way, let's ring for tea." Isabel reached out and pulled a bell cord next to the fireplace, undoubtedly setting off a little bell in the kitchen. "I must apologize again, Frances, for my abrupt behavior at breakfast. I had something of a shock, as I'm sure you've noticed."

Emily did notice a difference in her aunt from their conversation this morning. Isabel seemed sharper in a way, like a bird of prey that's just now fully waking up. She was younger than Emily had first suspected, with preternaturally silvered hair. She could easily see how her aunt would be a larger-than-life character, despite being so small-statured. She had, as Emily's mother would say, bearing.

Isabel leaned back to pull a framed photo off the bookcase behind her. It was of a woman standing on the slopes of a snowy mountain, tufts of brown hair sticking out the sides of her woolen hat, a gigantic grin on her face. She had on snowshoes, dark sunglasses, and an intricately knitted sweater to top off the ensemble, and her jaunty stance made her look like just about the spunkiest spitfire Emily had ever seen.

"This is my friend, Ann Simpson, the one I got the call about this morning." Isabel handed the photograph to Emily across the board and picked up a tiny sailboat. "We first met at school, years and years ago."

Emily looked closely at the photo, noting the suspenders and the spray of freckles across the nose. She wished she could see under the sunglasses to the young woman's eyes. "Where is she here?"

"The Alps, the Italian side." Isabel said, with no explanation, as if everyone would immediately know where and what those were. (Fortunately, Emily did, thanks to Constance's stern geography lessons.) "She was absolutely fearless. But not reckless. You know the difference?"

Emily handed the photo back and nodded. "She looks clever. I'm sorry she's in trouble."

"Thank you, Frances. Thank you."

The two waited for tea, listening to the branches tap a rhythm on the windowpane and the percussive pop and hiss of the small cozy fire in the grate.

"There was a story, back in Nebraska," Emily began, breaking the silence, "about a woman in the 1860s. Back then there was a lot of fighting between everyone, native and European, all the time. This woman kept arsenic in a bag of sugar. She understood that the native people had a penchant for sweet things, never having tasted such before, so Mrs. Havisham always kept one particularly obvious bag of sugar thoroughly mixed with arsenic in her pantry. Whenever Pawnee or Fox came raiding, and smashed into her house, she knew they'd go straight to the sugar bag, the one chock-full of poison."

Isabel looked astonished and captivated. "And this relates to me *how?*"

"Mama always admired this lady, Eve Havisham, and called her fearless, not reckless. The point was, she never went out looking for trouble, but if it ever came her way, she was well prepared to meet it."

The fire snapped in agreement.

Bridget had come in during Emily's story with a tray and set it on the round table under the bay windows.

"Well, I suppose she's right, isn't she?" Isabel conceded. "What a lively story, Frances."

Bridget offered Em the plate of cookies—small disks topped with powdered sugar—with a smile tucked into her cheek.

"Miss Frances," Bridget asked after offering round the tea. "Would you like me to take your hat?"

Emily glanced at Isabel and caught the woman's slight nod. "Yes, please, Bridget. Thank you," she said, handing it over. "And thank you for the tea."

Bridget left the room with Em's new hat.

Emily took a sip while scanning the shelves, laden with photos of groups of people on boats, with dogs, at weddings, accepting awards, at parties, and in fast-looking cars. None of them looked as if they had worked a hard day in the field in all their lives.

The fire was the most active thing in the room, creating a warm halo around them both, not unpleasant. Connor sighed appreciatively on his cushion. An ancient oak tree out the bay window kept up its tap-tapping in the gusty wind.

"I'll have to get John Patrick to cut that back, I'm afraid," Isabel commented. "A stately tree nonetheless." She looked lovely, but still distracted. The line between her brows spoke to her underlying anxiety. "As I was saying, my shock this morning stemmed from the news that my dear friend Ann Simpson has gone *missing*, of all things. It just seems so unlikely. I've been gathering information all afternoon. Apparently, Ann was sailing alone on the *Temptation* at about six last night, a little before your boat got into Edgartown. She never came home. This afternoon, the harbor master found the *Temptation*, grounded, out by Cape Poge point. Ann's just . . . disappeared." Isabel's face crumpled as she reached into the sleeve of her dress to pull out a handkerchief with fine needlework on the edges.

"She's disappeared?" Emily couldn't imagine the anguish this might cause her aunt, whose own daughter had gone missing for days and weeks and months.

"Yes, poof." Isabel threw the handkerchief up in a little flourish. "Again."

Emily considered reaching out across the table in a gesture of solidarity, but discarded the idea immediately. "When did they find her boat?" Emily asked instead.

"Early this afternoon. Thankie called again at one. Ann was an excellent sailor, one of the finest skippers in the harbor. It's fairly unfathomable that she would have lost control and drowned. She's been sailing boats since she could walk. Swimming since before that." Isabel spoke these facts with no inflection, perhaps trying to prove to herself that her friend wasn't dead, Em supposed. "But there *was* that line squall that came through last night. Do you remember, Frances? About an hour after you arrived?"

Emily thought of the torrential sheets of rain, like walls of water, coming at them, hitting the windshield with a thump. Sailing in that? No thank you. "I'm . . . I'm so sorry, Isabel. If there's anything I can do . . ."

"Thank you, Frances, that's very kind. Perhaps they'll find her clinging to a buoy any moment now. As you can imagine, I will be on edge until I get news of her. Let's hope it is favorable when it comes." She raised her cordial glass, still half filled with the ruby liquid, and Emily did the same with her teacup. "To good news," Isabel said, barely above a whisper. Emily repeated this, and they clinked rims ever so gently. Isabel took a healthy sip of her cordial and Emily sipped what turned out to be a smoky oolong tea.

After a few moments of sitting by the fire, Isabel put her emptied glass on the table and picked up one of the sailboats again. "The oddest thing is not the fact that the weather would've tipped her over—in that rain there'd be no question. It's the idea that she would go out in that weather at all. Especially alone. It was almost dark as well. She would never have made such a choice like that, never! I cannot understand . . ."

Isabel trailed off, toying with the silver sailboat and staring into the fire. Emily looked out across the dead stark bushes to the austere profile of the Methodist church.

"Bridget tells me that you only have three dresses," Isabel stated. "Is this true, niece?"

Emily flushed when her aunt called her that, momentarily distracted from the thought of her two other dresses hanging in Fiona's wardrobe. "Only?"

"Well, for example, how were you planning to dress for dinner tonight?"

Emily put down her teacup in the saucer with a gentle clink and looked down at herself. She was still wearing the maroon dress she'd donned for her mother's funeral. It was simple, made of wool, and fit her neatly. She and her mother had designed and sewn it together just before she'd died of tuberculosis. It was the last thing they'd done together. "This?"

"That won't do, I'm afraid."

Isabel must've seen the hurt spasm on Emily's face, as she quickly amended her sharp comment. "I just mean we dine with a little more *formality* than you're probably used to in Nebraska, and you may need to augment your wardrobe to befit your new station. As my niece."

Emily took all this in while chewing one of Bridget's cookies, delicately dusted with sugar. She wiped her mouth with the lace napkin before responding. "How do you propose we do that? I could sew myself some dresses, but that will take a while. And I would need a form, and fabric."

"No, no, that will take too long." Isabel shook her head, the large pearls swinging underneath her lobes. "I have a solution, I believe. I have . . . access to some dresses that may work, although they are a few seasons out of date. I am having Bridget air them out and take them to your room. You can alter them as needed. I've asked Bridget to bring you some basic sewing supplies as well."

Emily nodded, a trifle taken aback as she was almost entirely sure these dresses used to belong to Isabel's daughter. "Thank you again, Aunt. I mean, Isabel."

Isabel waved a dismissive hand in Emily's direction. She returned to staring into the fire and to her previous subject. "It's just so out of character for her to be out there alone, at sunset, and to not be aware of the weather. It's all so very *un*Ann!" Isabel's hands twisted the handkerchief in her lap like a writhing bejeweled serpent. "She was always so fastidious about checking the weather. Almost as fastidious as she was about safety. It simply doesn't make sense!"

"Perhaps we'll hear something by dinner," Emily said.

"Yes, perhaps we will." Isabel's sharp gaze went to Emily's dress again. "That one will be fine for tonight, Frances. Please go tell Bridget about my acquiescence."

Emily had no idea what *acquiescence* meant, but she took her aunt's comment to mean she'd been dismissed. With a fair amount of relief, she took a last sip of tea and made her way back to the kitchen.

That went better than expected, she thought.

Chapter 6

Emily didn't find Bridget in the kitchen, although the smell of baking fish, an odor Emily wasn't entirely used to let alone liked, pervaded the room, and the countertop gleamed with waiting silver trays and platters. As she passed through, Emily tried to imagine the effort it took to keep up with these types of standards and expectations in a home. It didn't seem very homey, in Em's experience. In her house, they each had their own bowl, plate, and spoon, which they took care of themselves, cleaning them after every meal to put away. It was a good system.

On the stove, a pot of soup, a dense white paste, bubbled thickly as she went by. Climbing the back stairs, she could hear Bridget singing somewhere above her.

"*There's a rainbow around my shoulder, and it fits me like a glove . . .*"

It was a new song; Emily had heard it in her travels across the country. Bridget was singing it loudly and, Em had to admit, fairly well in a strong alto. When Emily reached the hallway, she realized the singing was coming from her room. Or, the one she sort of shared with Fiona.

"*Let it blow and storm, I'll be warm 'cuz I'm in loooooove. Hallelujah, halla—how the folks'll staaaaaaare, when they see that great big solitaaaaaaire,*" Bridget sang as Emily entered the room, "*that my little sugar, my little sugar baaaaaaby is goin' a-weaaaaaar.*"

Bridget was going through a series of dresses piled on top of Fiona's bed. A hill of underthings heaped on the lone chair in the room, next to the door. Emily silently ogled at the clothing.

The pile on the bed included the most dresses Emily had ever seen in one place, period. Full stop. Not even when she'd helped out at the church bazaar, sorting out all sizes and types of donated clothes. Even the department store they'd visited in Lincoln before a cousin's wedding didn't hold a candle to the first Miss Emily's wardrobe. The pretty dresses modeled on the mannequins in Lincoln looked only a smidge better than the scarecrows out in the fields compared to some of these frocks. And they were all worn by one person, Emily the First, her princess cousin. It was hard to swallow. Honestly, she thought she'd get used to the opulence and wealth at Hy House, but the Hewetts kept on surprising her.

Bridget, oblivious, kept singing. "*There's a rainbow around my shoulder,*" she sang again, hips twitching to her own internal beat, "*and a sky of blue above—*"

Not only was this mountain of clothing the largest Emily had ever seen, it was also the richest. The vermillions, bright sunflower yellows, shiny burnt siennas, and brilliant ceruleans were a mixed miasma of color. The textures knocked her out as well. Fur and lace, shiny satin and matte velvet; it was like looking into a revolving kaleidoscope of clothes.

"*Oh, the sun shines bright, the world's all riiiight, 'cause I'm in looooove—*"

And then, on top was layered the idea that this froth of wealth, this abundance of cleverly patterned fabric and buttons and trimming, was now, all of a sudden, *hers.*

Would wonders never cease? came her mother's voice, echoing through time, until Bridget drowned it out.

"*There's a rainbow around my shoulder, and it fits me like a glove . . .*"

Emily looked down at the lesser pile of clothes on the wood and wicker chair next to her, maybe nightshirts or petticoats, she didn't know. She fingered one light-pink ribbon between finger and thumb. It was slippery and thin.

"*Let it blow and storm, I'll be warm*"—Bridget was giving it her all in what had to be the last verse—"*cuz I'm in loooooo*—" When she finally turned, her mouth the perfect O of an opera singer, she caught sight of Em and stopped singing, flushing bright red in a split second. "Oh! Miss Frances! I'm so sorry! I got carried away. I think of this as Fiona's room, you see, and I often do small jobs in here. I forgot that this was your, that now it was your . . . *is* your room," Bridget stammered.

Em rushed over, grabbing her arm. "Oh please! Bridget! That was wonderful!"

Bridget smiled broadly, all the tension evaporating in a second. "It's the newest one from Al Jolson. I love him," Bridget gushed. She turned and busied herself with the clothes again before looking back at Emily, who was studying the monstrous pile with dismay.

"Miss, are you all right? You look like you've had a turn."

Emily shook her head.

"Is it because they were the first Miss Emily's? Some people get the willies about such things, but I assure you, these were all clean when they were put in her wardrobe. I made sure. And the Mrs. made sure I made sure."

Emily tried to master her expression. "No, no, that isn't it. It's just that I've never seen so many dresses before . . . all in one place . . . at the same time."

Bridget raised her eyebrows, looking at the pile again. "Oh! I hadn't thought of that. Yes, well, you wouldn't have, would you? She was quite different than you are, from one Emily to another. You seem so capable, and she wasn't, at least, not in a practical sense."

Emily's curiosity was instantly kindled, despite her awkwardness about the excess of garments that had taken over her room. "What was she like?" she asked cautiously.

Bridget folded a short-waisted jacket of peach silk over her forearm. "She was beautiful and smart enough to know it. She used it to her advantage." Bridget motioned for her to stand in front of her, the obedient child. With her model in reach, Bridget could then establish which dresses would best suit her. And while she did, Bridget told her about the other Emily, her polished cousin. "Always put together, always in the most stylish clothes, always tickety-boo, as my Nan would say. She and Isabel made quite a pair. Born on the same day, did you know?"

Em shook her head.

"Yes, right around Halloween. Hydrangea House was always the host to some fabulous birthday balls for the two of them, I can assure you. But since Miss Emily's disappearance, we haven't had a one."

Em thought it strange Bridget still referred to it this way, as Emily's *disappearance*, but she didn't say anything as the other woman tucked and pinned and folded around her. Bridget held a blue satin splendor to Em's body, looking at her with inquisitive eyes. Emily took one look at all the buttons and lacy bits and ribbons and shook her head. Bridget nodded firmly in agreement, tossing the ball gown onto the other bed, creating a new pile of castoffs.

"They would often go in paired costumes—themed, you know? Mrs. Hewett would go as a salt cellar and the Miss was the pepper, that sort of thing. It was all very clever and in great good fun."

The process continued, with Bridget twisting her this way and that, sometimes asking her to pull something on, like a coat or jacket, staring hard and murmuring positive affirmations at her willing model. If the process hadn't been so strange and disorienting, it would've been very boring. After a few minutes of this, as Bridget made her one big pile into two smaller piles, Em was restless. She was beginning to feel as if she were being remade into a different person: new place, new name, new clothes. New identity.

"You know, Mrs. Hewett—Isabel—gave me her ac-qui-es-cence"—she said the long word slowly—"whatever that means, for me to wear my own dress for dinner."

Bridget stood in front of her, pinning something tighter on the red riding jacket Emily currently sported. When Bridget heard this, she straightened and smoothed her hair, tucking a wild curl behind her ear.

"She did, did she?"

Em nodded, throat loosening at the thought of getting out of mannequin duty.

When Bridget held up another garment, Emily groaned, slipping out of the riding jacket and holding her arms out for a knee-length pressed blue wool coat which had very fine designs etched into it somehow. Two heavy horn buttons fit the coat snugly around her.

"Just as I thought, perfect fit. It's uncanny. Two sisters, so far apart, naming their daughters the very same thing, and then the girls grow to be the same size and build, too. What about this one, my dear, do you like it?"

Emily looked down at herself, pleased with the weight of the coat and its softness. She rubbed her fingertips up its length.

"It was brand-new when Miss Emily vanished. She never wore it once."

Somehow, Emily felt disappointed. She wanted it to be her cousin's favorite.

"Why don't you take part in one of her pastimes," Bridget suggested, "and head on up to the widow's walk to 'see what you can see' as Miss Emily would've put it."

"What's a widow's walk?" Emily asked, instantly curious.

"Like a balcony, but on the roof. I'll show you how to get up there."

Emily started unbuttoning her coat.

"Keep it on. The wind will be up."

Em nodded and followed Bridget out of the room, gratefully abandoning the shimmering pile of opulent clothing. Perhaps there would be a view.

Bridget took her through the kitchen, which was smelling more like fish with each repeated pass, down the well-padded hallway, and swiftly up the ornate staircase to the second floor. Down the darkened passage, past all the doors (of which there turned out to be three on either side), and finally to a small alcove at the end.

This alcove, which was more like a doorless closet, was unlit and smelled dusty and stale: unused. Both women crowding in left little to no space around the base of a wooden ladder standing sentry in the middle, leading straight up to the ceiling and a trapdoor. Bridget hoisted herself up the first few rungs and put a hand in the middle of the trap, pushing hard. The door flapped into the afternoon, letting in a burst of salty chilled air.

"Ah!" Bridget yanked her hand back, jumping down to Emily's side. "Got me," she said, rubbing her palm, hard. "Like a viper."

"Are you all right?"

"Fine, fine, it's just a sliver." A bead of blood welled from the angry red splinter in her palm. "You find your way up. I've got to get this out and disinfect it." Bridget started away, holding her hurt hand with the other, and then turned back in the doorway, a serious expression on her face. "Careful around the edges up there, Miss Frances, I mean it! Nobody's been up there much, except Pat twice a year and after storms, and the railings could be unsteady—rotting, you know? Don't lean on them too much, and don't lean over. This house can't take any more tragedy."

Emily nodded solemnly at this dark proclamation and watched Bridget retreat down the hall and disappear down the stairs, muttering to her hurt hand. Then she clambered up the rungs into the violet of an early-evening sky, poking her head through the roof of Hydrangea House. Carefully stepping up, Em pulled the trapdoor shut. Then she stepped back and looked around.

A view there was indeed! Not only that, but the widow's walk was the first place Emily felt like she could breathe. Adding to the exhilarating sense of freedom, all around her was the most enchanting panorama she'd seen in her short life.

In disbelief, Emily looked down to check that her feet were still on the ground, and they were, in fact, on a square of flat roof encircled with a railing that looked pretty sound in her view. The widow's walk was about sixteen-by-sixteen feet, with the trapdoor centered in the middle.

Since Hy House was essentially on a hill, its roof was the highest point in all directions. Main Street unraveled past the house and ended, about five hundred yards down the hill, at the wharf backing up to the fishing boats. Small figures in bright colors scurried across the decks, stowing their lines and nets for the night. To the northeast, the lighthouse pulsed in its place at the end of the point, and beyond it lay another strip of land across the dark sea, rising into cliffs that were a defiant red in the last of the day's light at their tallest before they tapered off to a sandy punctuation point. Behind the house, away from the harbor, the sun was setting, dyeing the clouds sorbet shades—peach and orange with violet shadows. The sky behind them was a deep blue, bleeding to indigo. Hydrangea House had some land, it seemed, that Emily promised herself she would explore as soon as she could.

Hy House's trimmed lawns led to beautifully laid-out garden beds and the bony gleam of a dry water fountain. Sunny daffodils winked through gnarled apple trees, and a willow grew by the just-out-of-sight pond, the wind tossing its pale-green spring crown this way and that. As she watched, a carriage jangled by the stone wall that carved the perimeter by a far-off street. The wooden box and shadowy rider were drawn by a dark horse, which seemed ominous, as if the crepuscular carriage was carrying foul messages to an unwilling recipient.

Far off to the west, up the hill and past the Hy House gardens, Main Street grew into a wider road, and Emily thought she could see more stores amongst the smaller homes. Lights were coming on inside the pert little cottages, and cars with headlights jostled for space among the slower-moving cart-and-horse combos making their way home. Somebody was yelling across town; a woman's plaintive cries for "Sam!" reached Emily on the rising wind, along with the rumble and grind of the cars and carts, the distant hoot of boats, and, always, the ambient rush of the ocean behind it all. The ever-present ocean made everything salty, but Emily also detected a whiff of baking bread on the breeze.

No wonder this had been her cousin's favorite thing to do. Stars were popping out of the violet sky and Emily impetuously squeezed her eyes shut after catching sight of the first one, whispering fiercely, "Star light, star bright, first star I see tonight, wish I may, wish I might, that my wish come true tonight." She couldn't think of anything to wish for at first, not really, because everyone knew you couldn't wish for people not to be dead anymore. It didn't work like that. She could only come up with one word to vaguely gesture at the idea of a wish—*home*.

It was getting too dark to be up there without a lantern or flashlight, the new type of light she'd seen on her first night on the Vineyard, so, once the shadows had been swallowed by the dusk and a few more stars had popped out of the firmament, Emily reluctantly made her way back into the house.

She could see better once she arrived on the second floor as electric lights flickered peripatetically down the hallway. As she walked back to Fiona's room to freshen up for dinner, she wondered at the word that had floated up from the pool of her mind when pressed for a wish. *Home*. Here, the balustrade under her fingertips was smooth as she descended, the chandelier glistened and tinkled as the crystal prisms brushed against one another overhead, and the black-and-white parquet floor beneath gleamed as if newly mopped.

Would this place ever feel like home? She glanced at the portrait of the First Emily as she slowly descended the stairs. She doubted it, but as her mother was wont to say—wonders never ceased.

Chapter 7

For Emily, freshening up for dinner mainly consisted of rebraiding her hair and smoothing her wild eyebrows with some spittle and her pinky fingers. A few more ministrations and she was done and on her way to the kitchen, thankful her aunt had acquiesced about her dress. The clang of dropped metal and muttered Irish epithets reached Emily as soon as she arrived in the bright space. Bridget was in the midst of some elaborate dance with the silver serving trays and a pair of tongs. Her cheeks were flushed, and there was a piece of tape stuck to her palm.

"Miss Frances, looking lovely! Go right on through," Bridget told her, nodding in the direction of the double doors. "I'll be in directly." She went back to tonging biscuits into a basket as Em left the kitchen.

This would be her first jaunt to the formal dining room, and she made her way across the checkered floors, past the blue front door, and into the dining room with bated breath. The rectangular room held another fireplace at its far end laid with a small, cheerful fire, but the space was dominated by a long wooden dining table with multiple chairs on either side. On one wall was a gilded mirror, and the ornately carved side table beneath it held a silver tea samovar, which Emily recognized only because she'd gone through an intense reading period that her mother had called her "Russian spell."

A china hutch perched in the corner, done out in deeply polished mahogany and brass fittings. Two candelabras floating above the dining table each held aloft three candles on delicately curved arms, and the silver and mirrors refracted the warmth of the flames back, making the whole room glow.

Aunt Isabel stood by the fire at the mantelpiece in a long formal blue dress with her white hair piled high on her head and held in place with a silver comb encrusted with pearls. Emily was struck by how glamorous she looked. She thought there had never been a creature more at home in her surroundings as Isabel idly fingering her multiple strings of pearls as she studied a clock on the marble mantel.

Emily paused at the threshold, once again momentarily jolted by the fact that this woman was a direct relative of her mama. She could not envision her mother, in her sun-bleached dresses and long swinging braid, at home here. *How could these two be sisters?* she wondered, studying her aunt's profile. But there was something around the jawline, or in the tilt of the head, an echo of Constance, even here.

Isabel turned, a hint of a smile gracing her face. "Ah, there you are, Frances. You should know, I'm quite fastidious about mealtimes, so please be present promptly at seven thirty each evening, dressed, when we can manage it."

Emily smiled blandly, glancing at the clock, which uncooperatively read seven thirty-three, or maybe even seven thirty-two.

"Not that there's anything wrong with that dress," Isabel quickly amended. "Here's Bridget now, with the soup. Let's sit." She held out a jeweled hand toward the immaculately set table.

Bridget carried in a tray as Isabel and Emily took their places at the head and catty-corner seats, respectively. Bridget placed the tray almost soundlessly on a sideboard in the corner as Emily unfolded her napkin onto her lap, Isabel looking on approvingly.

The first course was, as Isabel said, soup, and it happened to be the steaming white paste that Emily had passed multiple times that afternoon.

"New England clam chowder! My favorite," Isabel said, looking at Emily with bright eyes. "Bridget and I have conspired to create this menu as a sample of some of our favorite local meals, as I doubt you've been able to taste many before now."

Emily looked down as Bridget set the bowl on her plate. Two sets of forks, a knife, and multiple spoons framed the bowl, which contained a soup that was the least appetizing shade of beige. The unknown bits and blobs floating around in the liquid didn't help its appearance, nor did the fact that it was being served in a bowl almost the exact same shade as the soup. Em shuddered inwardly; outwardly, she smiled and tried to look eager.

"I've never had chowder before, Isabel. I'm so looking forward to trying it."

Isabel's eyes sparkled in the candlelight as she nodded and picked up her own spoon, dipping it into the chowder. Emily studied all the silverware in front of her, silently berating herself for not paying attention to which spoon her aunt had picked up but deciding it was too gauche to peer over at her place setting.

Many might have been nervous when faced with such a spread of gleaming forks, spoons, and knives, but Emily's mother had prepared her for just such a circumstance. *Work from the outside in* had always been Constance's advice on silverware at fancy functions, and since the only options were a spoon above her place setting or one on the right, beside the knife, on the outside, Em opted for that one. It was closest to the bowl, she reasoned.

As she dipped the spoon into the viscous liquid, she heard a murmur of approval from her aunt's end of the table. She had apparently chosen correctly.

The soup was thicker than she expected and, frankly, better than it looked. The chunks turned out to be potatoes and onion, and the mixture was warm and salty, with satisfying globs of tender clams. Emily ate with delight after a couple of bites, remembering to swipe her mouth with the napkin at appropriate pauses.

"Have you heard anything more about Ann Simpson?" she asked. She didn't know if talking about her aunt's missing friend would ruin the mood, but if the woman was still missing, it was a prudent question. Isabel was probably thinking about her.

Isabel looked up from her bowl to meet Em's gaze, which she hoped was sympathetic. The older woman's eyes gleamed, but this time the sparkle in them wasn't candlelight. She gave a small shrug with one shoulder and returned to her soup. "No, nothing. But thank you for asking, niece. It's certainly at the forefront of my mind."

They continued eating in silence for a few more moments. A radio played in the drawing room, its tinny sounds tinkling across the foyer, reaching the pair as they dined. When they were done, Bridget appeared to clear the empty bowls.

"You know," Isabel said, "the New Yorkers have their own version of chowder that's red."

"Whichever version, it's delicious!" Emily said, and meant it. "Thank you, Bridget."

Bridget glided out under the weight of the tray and Isabel and Emily were alone once again.

Isabel clasped her hands in front of her. "What did you do, niece, on a day-to-day basis, at your farm? I'm curious about what your life was like before, with my sister."

Emily found that a strange way to phrase it—*with my sister*. "I had tons to do. A variety of daily chores, you might say. I had to take care of Juniper, my horse, and our other animals, making sure they were fed and clean. Then, depending on the season, I might go to school, or I might be out in the field doing things like weeding or detasseling or the hundred other things that always need to be done on a farm."

"Detasseling," Isabel murmured, her eyes wide. "Fascinating. So, you performed a lot of manual labor?"

"I guess you could call it that. We just called it work."

There was an awkward pause until Bridget swooped in again with her tray. As she served from the platters to the plates, Isabel pressed for more.

"What was your favorite type of job, if you had one? Maybe you didn't have one."

Bridget threw a guarded glance her mistress's way before continuing with serving.

"I suppose my favorite was when I was tinkering with any sort of machinery. You know, plows and scythes and the like, sharpening and cleaning and oiling, and then putting it all back together. I like that type of work." Emily was thoughtful, staring out the only window in the room into the darkness beyond.

Bridget put Isabel's plate before her, before setting one carefully in front of Emily as well.

"And your least favorite?" Isabel followed.

Emily stared in horror at the mess in front of her, at a complete and utter loss for words. If she could've created in her mind the type of food she might find most unappetizing, it would be this weird gelatinous mass. On one side of the plate sat a red, quivering, translucent blob that looked like pictures of pudding she'd seen (Constance never made anything like pudding), but instead of being served with a cherry on top or with whipped cream, it had chunks of peppers, onions, and sliced olives in it. And it *quivered*.

"I think my least favorite had to be sewing," she said, eyes still glued on the shivering red glob of whatever-it-was, "or quilting, or anything else that kept me inside." On the other side of her plate was a roundish, coral-colored object that had been broiled and browned on top. This must've been the pink goop she'd seen Bridget scooping onto sheet pans earlier.

"But you seem so adept at it! Sewing, I mean. Your dress is quite cunning, although simple, and Fiona mentioned your quilt. She said it was real art."

Emily glanced up, diverted from the task of eating what lay in front of her, pleased and proud that Fiona should've mentioned her quilt.

"She said that? Well, I may be good at it, but I don't enjoy it much. Um, what is this?" She gestured as politely as she could at her plate.

"Tomato aspic and salmon croquettes," Isabel said, blithely picking up her fork. "My fork is raised!"

Emily then picked up her own fork in solidarity. *Here goes nothing*, she thought as she sliced off an end of the red pudding and stabbed it, placing it with as much temerity as she could muster into her mouth.

Fortunately, she didn't have to chew much; unfortunately, this was due to the fact that the aspic immediately melted into warm tomato goo on her tongue and slid down her throat. Not for her. Not at all. She chased it with a sip of sarsaparilla. Maybe the croquettes would go down better.

"I don't remember my sister being that skilled at sewing when she was here, or ever sewing at all, for that matter," Isabel mentioned as she used her impeccably mannered motions to pick up small bites of this and that and deliver them to her mouth, almost as if she wasn't actually eating at all, followed by sips of a light-pink liquid in a fluted glass.

"She got a sight better, and taught me how to on top of that," Emily said, and wondered if Isabel was drinking wine. Actual wine. This was absolutely against the law, although lots of folks flouted the Eighteenth Amendment daily. Still, Em's parents were teetotalers, and never drank, so it was quite a curiosity for her to see someone drinking wine so casually.

The pink puff pastry—salmon croquette—was flaky and easy to get a mouthful of, although not quite as yummy as the chowder (she could eat that every day). The croquette had an overly fishy taste that Em didn't care for, and it was kind of sweet on top of that, but it was far better than the tomato-and-olive concoction taking up residence on the other side of her plate.

"Well, what do you think?" Isabel asked.

Emily looked up into her aunt's hopeful gaze, then took in the similarly earnest expression on Bridget's face. They'd put a lot of thought (on Isabel's part) and effort (on Bridget's) to serve her this food. She couldn't let them down. She laid down her fork and wiped her lips. "It's the most interesting menu I've *ever* eaten."

"Yes, but do you like it?" Isabel pressed.

Emily's jaw tightened. "The chowder was nicer than expected, and the croquettes were good, though fishy."

"And the aspic?"

Emily pulled at the hem of her sleeve. "The aspic? That was new for me."

They waited, Bridget presiding over Isabel's shoulder.

"You know," Em continued, "I found the aspic to be—"

Brrrrrrring, brrrrrrrrrring!

In the hall, the telephone announced itself, saving her from what would've been a terrible lie or an impolite truth.

"Save that thought, Frances," Isabel said, raising her hand. "Bridget, please answer that, will you? We'll gather her opinions on the menu later."

Bridget, disappointed, left the dining room to answer the phone.

Emily sighed in relief as she wasn't quite sure how to soften the edges of her opinion on the aspic. Glutinous death on a platter, is what she thought of it. Even the name was strange: *aspic*. It didn't sound like a food, it sounded like a cleaning solvent. She bet it had been challenging for Bridget to make, so soften the edges of that opinion she would, somehow.

"Hello?" said Bridget from the phone cubby. "Hello, Thankful . . . Yes, I'll get her."

Bridget returned at once, eyebrows raised as high as they could go, all thoughts of tonight's menu forgotten. "Mrs. Hewett, Thankful has Captain MacNamara on the phone for you."

"Captain . . . Captain MacNamara? Oh my." Isabel breathed, her hand clutching the pearls at her neck as she rose, setting her napkin next to her plate. As she moved toward the hall, she said without looking at Emily, "I'm sorry to cut another meal short, Frances, but I must take this. If you'll excuse me."

"Please don't trouble yourself, Aun—Isabel," Emily stuttered to her aunt's retreating back.

Bridget started clearing plates, all the while watching the door of the dining room. When Isabel spoke, she stopped piling dishes on the tray and leaned toward the door.

"Hello, Thankful. Yes, this is Isabel Hewett . . . Yes, I'll hold."

During this pause, Emily looked over at Bridget, inquisitive, and the older woman gave her a grim smile.

"Hello, Captain MacNamara, this is Isabel Hewett at Hydrangea House, how are you tonight? . . . I am well, thank you. I gather you have some news?"

There was a long pause, so long that Emily thought perhaps her aunt had hung up the phone again, or that the connection had been broken. The radio played blithely on in the drawing room, some cheerful jig countless couples had twirled to, no doubt. It was severely out of place in this particular scenario as Emily felt like she could slice the tension in the room as easily as the awful aspic on Bridget's platter. When Isabel spoke again, it was in a different voice—a lower, grating voice. Bridget sucked in her breath.

"Are you . . . are you absolutely sure it's her, Captain?"

Emily felt a weight come down on her shoulders. Ann Simpson.

"Of course I can. It's the least I can do. I'll be there first thing . . . No, I'm afraid tonight's not possible. I'll see you first thing tomorrow morning, Captain. John Patrick will bring me by to view the body."

Emily's mouth dropped open, and when she looked at Bridget, she saw the same horror mirrored there.

There was a clang as Isabel replaced the heavy receiver, and Bridget abandoned her post and rushed out of the room. Emily jumped up and ran to the door to watch Bridget help Isabel out of the telephone cubby, holding her steady. A few silver tendrils of hair had escaped and sprung around her head in odd little whorls and curls.

Isabel didn't look at Emily when she passed her by, but she spoke in that same low voice. "I'm afraid they've found her, niece, and she's not clinging to anything anymore."

With that, Isabel and Bridget turned and climbed the stairs. Emily stood in the doorway, watching them go, and then reentered the empty dining room. Not knowing what else to do, Emily finished Bridget's job out of habit—stacking plates and collecting the rows and rows of unused silverware. Hopefully Bridget didn't have to wash the unused ones as well.

Em felt intensely sad about Ann Simpson, even though she'd never met her. The smiling face from the photograph had seemed like such a beacon, a bright light of curiosity and bravery. It was horrible that it should be snuffed out too soon. And what was that business about viewing the body? What was that about?

Emily tried lifting the tray but had to reset her feet to accomplish this task. She may have been a brawny farm girl, but the tray was not for the faint of heart. She finally got it aloft and, feeling awkward but also glad to be useful, set off down the hall to put it in the kitchen. She wouldn't go so far as to start Bridget's dishes for her (every woman Em knew had her own methods and techniques), but she could do the heavy lifting while Bridget tended to Mrs. Hewett.

Bridget was probably an old hat at that by now, having lived through all the losses that had piled up at Hy House. Emily glanced at the three portraits as she tottered by with the tray. A bead of sweat tracked down the side of her face as she paused before the double doors and revolved under the cumbersome weight, pushing her backside into the kitchen first, and then swinging forward again to place the tray, with a fair measure of relief, onto the butcher-board counter.

"Phew," she said. That wasn't easy. She would have to help Bridget more often.

Emily set about doing what she could without being too intrusive, knowing that a woman's (or a man's, she amended) workplace was like a copy of their minds, where everything had its rightful spot. But Em had been hanging around this kitchen for two whole days without a lot to do and had observed some of the more basic chores.

Stoppering the basin on the left and twisting the hot-water faucet,

Em plunged the used plates and silverware into the water, filling the sink, and left the unused for Bridget to sort out. As she watched the level of the water rise in the enameled emptiness, she shivered, thinking of Ann alone out on a boat in that storm.

When the sink was halfway filled and Em had just located the dish soap, Bridget walked through the double doors and came over to her, placing a dishcloth in Em's wet hands before leading her to the corner table.

"Fancy some tea, m'dear?"

Emily nodded as Bridget filled the kettle, thumping it on the large squat stove before she lowered herself tiredly onto the bench seat across from Em.

"Was it Ann?" Emily asked.

Bridget shrugged, her head a drooping bloom on the stem of her neck. "Probably. A body that authorities are fairly certain is Miss Simpson's has washed up on Chappaquiddick." Bridget pointed over her shoulder, as though Emily had any corresponding map of Edgartown stored in her head to understand where she was pointing.

"What do you mean, 'fairly certain'?" Emily asked.

"There hasn't been a positive identification yet on the body as most of Miss Simpson's closest relatives live on the North Shore, on the mainland. They've asked Mrs. Hewett to come by in the meantime to identify the remains."

"Lawd sakes," Emily breathed, using one of Mama's favorites.

"You don't have to say that twice."

On the stove, the kettle shrieked. Bridget got up with a groan and made her way over with a little less agility than usual, taking it off the heat with her apron-wrapped hand. After dumping some tea leaves into a sturdy earthenware pot, she covered them with hot water. Bridget then dipped into the oven, pulling out a pie and plopping it onto the butcher block.

"Musn't let it go to waste," Bridget commented. "'Tis a shame to let a warm pie go cold. It's apple, the last of the canned apple-pie filling from the fall. Island apples make the best pie. Mrs. Hewett said to offer it with a slice of cheddar cheese, in true Yank fashion."

"Why would you want to do something like that to a nice piece of pie?"

Bridget chortled, a sudden croak of laughter, and Em joined in. It was good to laugh. There had been enough tension in the house to suck the life out of them all; Em couldn't imagine what it might've been like in the uneasy limbo after Emily the First disappeared.

Bridget smiled. "I, myself, enjoy my pie with some cream, or whipped cream if we have it, which we do."

She sliced two generous pieces from the tin, cinnamon-scented innards steaming, and slid them onto sturdy, simple kitchen plates. From the icebox she retrieved the whipped cream she'd made earlier. Skimming off the cream that rose to the top of the milk jug, she'd let it stand in the cool pantry to separate, then beat it with an egg beater, adding a little sugar and a few drops of vanilla as she went along, then beat it some more. All of this Bridget explained while plopping two spoonfuls of the sweet white froth from the glass bowl, cold from the icebox, onto the hot pie slices, where it promptly began to melt like butter in sunshine. Bridget transferred the two plates, and then the pot of tea and two mugs, to the corner table at which Emily sat with uncomfortably idle hands.

"Can I help?" Em asked, finally.

"Sure you can, Miss Frances. Please get the sugar bowl, and some milk from the icebox if you need it, for your tea."

"I'm fine with just sugar, thanks."

"Me as well. Then please get us each a fork, and we'll set about our tea."

Once they were settled, Emily tucked into the slice with her fork, the whipped cream a sweet, cold accent—thick with a touch of vanilla—delicious on the hot softened apples encased in their flaky crust. She was lucky she'd landed in a place with such an accomplished cook. After all the food she'd choked down from station to station—

sad-looking cheese sandwiches and watery strains masquerading as soups—it was a pleasure to eat at Bridget's table.

Bridget noticed Emily's obvious satisfaction with the pie and smiled. "There's nothing quite as New England as apple pie."

"Doesn't every place say that? Nothing quite as Nebraska as apple pie?" Emily was already scraping her plate with her fork. "This is delicious, Bridge, really. Won't Mrs. Hewett want some? Isabel, I mean?"

"I'll bring her up a tray after a while. She's not wanting anything at the moment."

Emily pushed her plate away and drew the brown mug in front of her, wrapping it with both hands to warm them, the steam coating her cheeks. The window next to their table looked out onto the driveway, offering a glimpse of the main street through the sycamores. The white shells in the drive glowed in the light of the half-moon.

"She and Ann were great friends then, were they?" Emily asked.

Bridget spooned sugar into her own mug and stirred. "Since they were very small. Miss Simpson and Mrs. Hewett came up together on the island, and in Boston, and they were well matched as friends from a young age. Both had spirit, as my grandmother would say"—Bridget's accent thickened— "and they took to one another from the start. Since Mrs. Hewett lived here and Miss Simpson over on Starbuck Neck, just across town, they were always within shouting distance of one another. Their mothers were also great friends, schoolmates from Walker's. I think Miss Simpson's mam was Mrs. Hewett's godmother, or the other way around, back when that meant something. They went to school together, were even roommates, but both went their own directions in adulthood. Miss Simpson's always traveled further, and into darker places."

"She never married?"

"Not after a fashion. She was slated to marry a boy—some son of a rich Knickerbocker—but he died when they were only just betrothed. Shame. Knocked something out of her when it happened.

"There were others, of course. You can't be the heiress to such a handsome fortune and not have a few Earnest Edwards at your doorstep. But now, none of it matters," Bridget said, staring down into her mug. "It's not like she lived a safe life. She was a fine journalist. Her war years were epic, and she was very much on the front lines. Once the war ended, she was able to find steady work as a reporter and wrote for loads of rags. But the last few years, she'd been secretive, moving here all by herself. Rumor had it she was onto something big. Explosive even."

Emily let out a long whistle.

"Poor Miss Ann. If it is her. We'll see tomorrow." Bridget stood, gathering up the plates and mugs and sweeping them into the sink.

Emily brought the teapot over and Bridget took it, turning Em toward the back of the kitchen and giving her a push.

"Go on, girl. You go get some rest. I know how exhausting this all has to be for you."

Emily was up the stairs before Bridget had to tell her twice.

Chapter 8

In the morning, Emily missed Isabel's departure into the gray mist a little before eight. According to Bridget, she had told Isabel that Dr. Slate's opened at nine, but Isabel had in turn insisted that Everett would open early for *her*, and neither Bridget nor Pat had been able to persuade her otherwise.

Isabel was long gone before Emily rose at 8:15 a.m., a shock as she hadn't slept past six since the age of seven or younger. She could barely believe she'd slept so long, and her woozy mood befitted the weather—an impenetrable sea fog and little to no wind.

As the hours dragged by, Emily helped Bridget in the kitchen, always with an ear tuned to the crunch of shells under tire signaling Isabel's return. After a while, she escaped with the excuse that she'd like to explore the grounds. She shrugged into her coat with a vague idea about a garden bed. The Hewetts certainly had land, though none of it was farmed, or of any use at all as far as Em could see, except for its decorative distinction.

Behind Pat's garage, a large double-door affair the same white clapboard as the house, was a plot of dewy grass, out of sight of the manicured lawns and well hidden from any window view. This particular patch received a good amount of early-morning light, perfect for what Em had in mind. She took the time to trace a rectangle in the wet grass with the toe of her leather boot, marking out where the most likely spots for rows of crops might be.

When she'd mapped out the rows (all the while thinking how

she might ask Aunt Isabel for this particular favor), she took a spin around the grounds, trailing away from the ghost of her garden toward the subtle sounds of lapping water. A pergola-and-gazebo combination were perched opposite one another across a twenty-foot pond, which flaunted an ornate water fountain in its very center. Today it was not on, and the sculpture, consisting of several tiers of large seashells topped with Poseidon himself brandishing a trident, was a crusty, ashy white. It looked as if, when on, water poured forth from the back of the sea god's head, creating a foamy crown, which Em would like to see in action. It might be a fine sculpture while active—and Em looked forward to seeing it so—but looked forlorn dried up like this.

After inspecting the fountain some more, Emily returned to her plot—did she dare call it that?—behind Pat's garage. She was there, climbing up the backside of the outbuilding to spy through one of the small triangular windows under the eaves, as a car rolled into the driveway, its crunching tires and growling engine tearing through the close confines of her fog blanket. She gasped and teetered on her perch, startled out of the fever of curiosity that had gotten her up there in the first place.

Emily wasn't really sure how she *had* gotten up there. She'd been deciding where she might put rows of corn or sunflowers so as to keep them best out of view when she'd spotted a stepladder leaning up against the back of the garage amidst assorted crates, ropes, and a broken wheelbarrow. A wave of curiosity had overcome her and she'd looked around, walked quickly to the ladder, and righted it. Then she'd climbed right up, with the immature and admittedly peevish intention of peeking in Pat's window.

And this is where she found herself, tiptoe on the second-to-top step, nose just above the sill, when the car slowed and pulled into the driveway of Hy House. The motor's rumble grew, clamshells grinding under hard rubber, and then stopped altogether. A door slammed, footsteps sounded, and another car door opened. Emily swayed on the ladder until her legs began to shake, so that she was forced to grip the clapboards, shoving her fingertips under the overlapping edges to hold herself still. She was breathing hard, clammy sweat beading her upper lip.

"Thank you, John Patrick," came Isabel's voice, stern, authoritative, slicing through the fog. The car door slammed shut.

It would not do for Isabel to find Emily clinging like a barnacle to the side of the garage, and she didn't want Pat to think she was spying on him. She'd hardly spoken to him, other than the odd pleasantries in passing. She hadn't forgotten Pat calling her his "poor little mouse" the night she arrived. It was the nicest thing anyone had said to her up to that point since she boarded the train in Omaha. Em was simply curious, and had spotted a perfectly suitable stepladder below an uncurtained window. For a moment, it all seemed so ridiculous she thought she might lose her relative composure and bark with laughter. To stop the errant laugh from escaping, she loosened one hand's limpet grip off the wall and slapped it over her mouth.

Their footsteps thankfully took up again, crunching the shells, growing slightly less crunchy the farther away from the garage they went.

"Madam, if I may," Pat began. Voices carried oddly in the fog, and his formal Mrs.-Hewett voice was less Irish and slightly higher pitched than the gravelly brogue Em was used to hearing. "I'm at your service."

Well, that was vague. What did that mean, was it Ann's body or wasn't it? Emily's fingertips ached, and her legs trembled. A lot. She couldn't stay any longer or she would risk falling, and she couldn't jump down for fear of being heard. Someone thumped up the stairs; her aunt, she imagined, even though thumping was not a trait one typically associated with Mrs. Isabel Hewett. And was that sniffling?

Keeping one hand on the garage and the other on the stepladder, she made her way down as quietly and carefully as she could. Opting to jump from the third rung to speed her descent, she leaped to the ground but pushed off too strongly and barely stuck the landing. The stepladder lurched back and forth. Frozen in a crouch, arms halfway out like a bird caught mid-launch into flight, Em watched the ladder sway lazily back and forth in the fog-drenched air. Luckily, it didn't fall, instead settling back in its upright position.

Silence. Emily couldn't hear them anymore. Had they heard her? Would she be found out? She held her breath, still motionless in her crouch, thighs burning, and waited for Pat's head to pop around the side of the garage.

"Thank you, John Patrick." From the sound of Isabel's voice, they hadn't come any closer.

Em exhaled explosively and straightened up at last.

"Well, ma'am," Pat said, footsteps pattering up the stairs, "is there anything I can do for you?"

"No, thank you. I'll be going straight up. That'll do, John Patrick."

"Yes, ma'am."

The front door shut with a firm clack and all conversation ceased. Em pushed the stepladder back into its approximate original position and trotted into the fog-swaddled grounds, following the pattern of her footfalls to the fountain and its attendant sea deity. Walking through the fog was like walking through a cloud, or cotton wadding. A blush burned her cheeks as she marched across the mowed expanse of lawn and over the trim stone wall edging the pond. Better they discovered her examining the water feature or underneath the willow, looking pensively into the pond's depths, than seeming to spy through Pat's windows.

A bench she hadn't noticed before appeared through the haze, close to the willow, and she took a seat, clasping her shaking hands between her knees and trying to slow her breathing. Nothing like almost getting caught to speed up the heart rate. The willow branches stroked the back of her coat as if consoling her.

Emily couldn't help but think, despite her pounding heart, that the body had indeed been Isabel's friend. Ann Simpson was dead. Isabel would be in mourning. Again.

After waiting for what seemed to be an acceptable amount of time, Emily rose and started back for the house, trailing her fingers through the willow's branches and thinking of a charming poem her mother had read to her when Emily was ill or couldn't sleep—"The Lady of Shalott" by Tennyson.

"The yellow-leaved waterlily," Emily whispered as she walked, "the green-sheathed daffodilly"—the white house loomed like a specter through the curtain of sea fog as she approached, trees bracketing it like dark wings—"tremble in the water chilly, round about Shalott."

That one had always been her favorite line, and her mother would goose her in a ticklish spot when she'd read "chilly." But here, in this setting, the lines only made Em shiver.

When Emily was only a couple of yards away, the kitchen door swung open and Bridget's head poked out. "Miss Em—Frances! Are you out here?"

For a moment, Emily stayed silent, adrift in the creamy miasma of the mist, wanting to stay lost. It felt good to be on her own again. She missed Juniper. She could almost hear her nicker behind her shoulder.

Em stayed this way for a few more seconds, and then she spoke up. "Here, Bridget."

Bridget took another step out of the house, one hand holding a dishcloth and the other shading her eyes as if the fog were the sun.

"Ah, there you are, Miss. Come on in. What are you doing out here all on your own? Exploring the garden? Not going to see much in this fog, I'm afraid." When Em reached her across the glowing circle of bleach-white shells, Bridget wrapped her arm around Emily's waist, like she had the first night. "Good morning—spot of tea?" Bridget bustled her inside. "I'm glad you've got your coat on; it fits you like a glove."

Inside, another tea tray sat, mid-assembly, on the butcher-block counter, the sweet, cidery smell of warming pie filling the tall-ceilinged space. It was blessedly toasty after the chill of sea fog. Emily slid out of her coat, hanging it over one of the chairs that stood by the corner table.

"And how are things here, Bridget?" Emily asked, rubbing her hands together to warm them. "How is Mrs. Hewett?"

"I'm not sure what went on at the doctor's; she hasn't said a word. Quite inconsolable. I don't know when we'll be seeing her."

Emily looked down at her feet. Another house in mourning.

"Did you see Seamus the Sea God? That's what we call him," Bridget said, scanning the tray for items to add.

"The statue with the trident? Seamus, is it? A perfect name for him. I found the little bench near the willow and sat on that for a while. It's peaceful there."

Bridget nodded, adding a silver pitcher to the tray. "That's Miss Emily's bench, the first Miss Emily, of course. Mrs. Hewett had it installed . . ." Bridget trailed off and walked over to a small butler's pantry, coming back with a cup, saucer, and small plate, the ones with the coral roses round the rims.

"I also found a place that might make a good kitchen garden, if no one would mind." Emily looked hopefully at Bridget.

"You'd like to put in a kitchen garden, Miss Frances?" She smiled and shook her head at the same time. "You shall never cease to amaze me."

"Do you think she'd mind? Isabel, I mean. Mrs. Hewett."

"That would depend on where you'd like to put it." Bridget poured hot milk into the pitcher.

"I was thinking behind Pat's, behind the garage. It's southeasterly, so it'll have good light."

Bridget refilled the sugar bowl. "That's a fairly out-of-the-way spot, then? Not smack in the middle of the mistress's view?"

Emily shook her head. "No, not at all. Not unless she's walking around looking for a secret garden."

"I can't see her doing that anytime soon." Bridget stepped back and appraised the tea tray. "As long as it's out of sight and does not intrude upon the view from either veranda or the bay windows in the parlor. I don't think it should be a problem." Her gray eyes bore into

Em's as she lifted the weighty tray. "I'm afraid you might have a bit of a dull day here in the fog."

With that, Bridget was gone, leaving Em in an empty but delicious-smelling kitchen. Sighing, Em glanced out the windows, staring into the white banks of nothingness, before making her way back to her room.

The rest of the day turned out to be fairly poor weather, once the fog lifted. Close gray skies hovered over Edgartown, giving her a claustrophobic feeling that kept her inside and in her room. She had tons to go through, anyhow. A whole pile it seemed.

The dresses that Bridget had been sorting while singing Al Jolson had once again taken up residence on Fiona's bed, this time newly cleaned, starched, ironed, or aired—a whole mound of taffetas and silks, satins and velvets. Truly, there were fabrics of types Emily had never before seen or touched, and colors so vibrant she could hardly look at them all at once.

These were the other Emily's dresses, and Em was going to have to make something of them for herself.

Grateful for a task that kept her to herself, Emily began sorting through the gigantic pile, holding the more complicated frocks up to study, and slipping on some of the simpler ones. There were quite a few that would only need a cursory nip in or perhaps a slight letting down. It seemed Bridget was right, she and Emily the First had almost the same figure. She found some favorites (almost against her will) and a few she would never wear in all her days. She was not one for frills or lace. She stared at the small pile of discards and retracted one—a black dress of washed silk.

There would probably be a funeral.

First, Em had to tailor the eight or ten dresses she'd chosen, starting with the simplest. She spread the dresses over every available surface and decided on a patternless tan one, mainly because it was in the least need of alteration.

Bridget had left her a well-appointed sewing kit, in which Emily found an enchanting pair of golden sewing scissors shaped like an ibis, each of the blades one side of a long, tapered beak. There was a normal-sized thimble along with a child's tiny one. Em couldn't help but wonder, as she threaded a needle with brown thread, if this wasn't another of Emily's possessions being handed down. Not that she minded using First Emily's things; it was good to put things to use, just like people. She was constantly amazed at the opulence and sheer number of possessions contained in this house, and wondered if other island homes held as many treasures.

Setting up a makeshift sewing station in between the beds, Em laid out her materials and got to work. With the curtains to the round window open, there was enough natural light to see her stitches as the needle darted in and out, flashing in the diffused sunshine.

As she nipped and tucked, pulling in sleeves and taking down hems with the tiny golden scissors, she worried about Isabel and Ann Simpson. It would certainly be a more silent and dreary time at Hy House if Aunt Isabel was locked away in her room. Pulling on the tan dress, Emily turned this way and that, testing the new stitches. Well, her wise inner voice (undoubtedly her lost mother's) told her that there was nothing Em could do about it one way or another, so she should just get on with it. She put the tan dress aside and took up another, a fern-green corduroy jumper with pearled buttons. She might as well keep sewing and see how many she could finish by tea.

The late morning waned and Emily sewed until her fingers and eyes ached. She did, however, almost fit herself out with a new wardrobe from First Emily's unused one. Isabel had been correct about finding an appropriate wardrobe—Em now felt she could enter these rooms with more confidence wearing the right clothes, if only a few seasons out of style. Disguise complete.

When she was done, Emily put away the sewing things and cleaned up snippets of thread and fabric. Her room thus straightened, she headed down in search of Bridget.

Em found her in the kitchen, facing a mound of potatoes with a peeler. "Do you want help, Bridge?" Em asked.

"No, Miss Frances, you're to meet Mrs. Hewett in the parlor." She had a potato in one hand and gestured with it toward the doorway. "She says she needs you."

"Needs me?" Em was confused. "Whatever for?"

"I have no earthly idea, but she's certainly got a bee in her bonnet about something. Best go see what it is." With that, Bridget started skinning the potato like she was flaying the devil himself, peels flying.

When Em got to the parlor, she stared, in utter shock, at her aunt. Isabel certainly had something of a bee in her bonnet, as Bridget had put it. She was standing, which wasn't that peculiar, but Isabel was also *moving*. Striding. She was pacing in front of the mantel with purpose, her skirts rustling as she turned back and forth. She was also drinking alcohol; Em could smell it from across the room, and the glass her aunt was sipping from was one-quarter filled with amber liquid.

Drinking alcohol was something of a prickly social anomaly in this day of 1929. In addition to being against the law, people felt strangely about Prohibition, probably as much here in the East as they had out West. Most folks she knew back home were Methodists, so they didn't drink, making Prohibition a nonissue for them, but there were plenty of Nebraskans who didn't appreciate being told how to spend their hard-earned husking money and made sure others knew of their displeasure.

As Em entered the room, Isabel stopped her caged perambulation to take a swift peck of her drink and replace it with a clink on the marble mantel, under which a feisty fire crackled. Isabel had begun to pace again when she spotted Emily staring at her cocktail. She stopped and nodded at the glass on the mantle: "*That* is a conversation for another day, niece. Today, I have something more pressing."

Just then, Bridget swooped in with the tray, deftly placing it on the table under the bay windows.

"Thank you, Bridget," Isabel said. She remained still, perched, tapping her fingernail on the mantel next to the glass, as Bridget laid out pie and coffee things. "That will be all. Please, leave us."

Bridget glanced at her mistress, one hand holding a saucer and the other a teacup, and gave Emily a quizzical look before placing both down and retreating from the room, closing the doors behind her to afford them more privacy.

It wasn't just that Isabel was up and about. Something about her flushed cheeks and sparkling eyes made her look more alive, more awake than she had during Emily's entire stay. (Not her stay, Emily reminded herself, her time here. It wasn't as if she was going home anytime soon.)

The older woman said nothing for many moments, so Emily kept her hands busy by making herself a cup of coffee from the tray. At last, Isabel ceased tapping her fingernail and turned toward her niece.

"Frances. I must tell you, I've had an extraordinary morning!"

From the way Isabel's eyes were lit from within like a jack-o'-lantern's, Emily didn't doubt it. She added two scoops of sugar and some hot milk to her coffee and stirred, waiting with raised eyebrows. It couldn't have been Ann's body then; Isabel's demeanor was far too cheerful. It must have been some sort of mistake.

"As you know, I was at Dr. Slate's this morning. To view a body. To identify it."

Emily sipped her coffee. There were still clear signs of her aunt's grief in her red, chapped nose, but her eyes were crackling. Maybe not cheerful. Vivacious, then, in the strict definition—*filled with life*. Lively.

"It was, unfortunately, Ann Simpson's."

Emily's mouth dropped open. For a few long seconds she couldn't find anything to say, her shock was so complete. Then she coughed out a response. "I'm so sorry, Isabel."

"Yes, a surprise to me as well. I hadn't expected it to be her. Well, that's not entirely true. I view myself as cursed, so I always, deep down, thought it would be her. Poor Ann." Isabel's face drooped.

Then she looked up again, eyes on fire, straight at Em. "But I know—and here's the rub, niece, I *know* it, in my bones. It took me a moment to think about it, *really* think about it, as my grief at losing my dear old friend was so great. But then I considered the scene again, and it all clicked!" Isabel's gaze was so piercing it was hard to meet her eyes. "Ann Simpson was murdered. I know it. And now that I know, I have to prove it." With this scorching admonition, Isabel took up her crystal glass and had a smooth, long swig of her Scotch.

Em almost spilled coffee all over the Persian rug. "Mur . . . murdered? Isabel, you can't mean—"

"I mean what I said. I know what I'm talking about. Ann Simpson was killed, on purpose, I am sure of it. She was murdered, no doubt in my mind."

This time Emily did drop her coffee cup. All over Isabel Hewett's gorgeous Persian carpet.

CHAPTER 9

There ensued a hubbub about cleaning up the spilled coffee, with Bridget rushing in and out, bringing rags to blot the stain with cold water and cleaning fluid before it set. Luckily the beautiful cup and saucer hadn't broken in the fall, cushioned as it was by the plush rug.

It was Emily who was most upset. "I am so, so sorry, Aunt Isabel . . . Isabel—"

"Do not worry, child. It was partially my fault. I should've prepared you for the shock and suggested you sit down, or to put down the cup at any rate. And that's the reason they weave such complicated patterns into these rugs anyhow, to hide imperfections. This also gives me an opportunity to ask Bridget for some small chips of ice. If you would, please, Bridget."

Bridget gave the rug a final scrub and stood up.

"I'm so sorry, Bridget, I didn't mean to—"

"Hush, Miss Frances, it was an accident. Nothing broken. Help yourself to another cup while it's still hot."

Emily did just that, pouring out new coffee for herself in the old cup with shaking fingers. Her mind raced. What could her aunt mean? Ann, murdered? Em sipped the black brew, grateful for the hot bitter burn down her throat. She needed to stay ready and alert.

Isabel waited until Bridget had left the room before she gestured to one of the red armchairs, pulling the other against the wall to give herself more pacing space. Em sat down and held onto her cup with both hands.

Isabel gazed into the hearth. "As I was saying, the body *was* Ann, my poor unfortunate. That was a shock in itself, to see her lying there, looking so small and so cold. But then I saw she had rope burns around her wrists, *both wrists*, do you understand? Not just one, but both of them. As if she had been tied up, like this." Isabel held up her own wrists, together, gold bangles sliding down her pale, speckled forearms.

For a few weighted moments, Em considered the idea that Isabel's mind might be crumbling under the strain of this new loss, and she was now seeing murders where they'd never happened.

But then a memory unlocked, flooding back to her. She and her mother and father had always gone to a neighboring farm to help with haying. One year, when Emily was about eight, there'd been a young man who worked in the fields with raw, red burns (rope burns, her mother had whispered) clean around his wrists, both wrists. Emily had wanted to question him about these, but Constance shooed her away, taking her spot and making sure no conversation at all occurred between that boy and her daughter.

On the way home, Em had asked her mother about the boy with the burns.

"He got dragged, Em," Constance had said. "Tied up by the wrists and dragged behind a horse. For a long while, looks like."

Emily hadn't thought about the boy and his rope-burned wrists from that day up until this moment in her aunt's parlor, but suddenly it all rushed back. Reflexively, she covered her own wrist with a palm.

Then she looked directly at Isabel, speaking softly. "She had rope burns on her wrists."

Isabel cocked her head, taking in her niece and looking all the more like a bird of prey, this time a very interested one. It wasn't unlike having a staring contest with a hawk.

"You may not know this—ah, Bridget! Returning with the ice."

Bridget entered with a small silver trough filled with chipped ice, tiny serving tongs atop the crystal hill, and a miniature decanter half filled with brown liquid to place on the mantel next to Isabel.

"Perfect, thank you." Isabel waved a hand in Bridget's direction and Bridget departed without a word.

"You may not know this," Isabel continued, picking up shards of ice with the child-sized tongs, pinky extended, and placing them deftly into her empty glass, "but sailors have a personal anathema against ropes, and we would never willingly"—Isabel released the tongs and stared meaningfully at Emily—"*willingly* wrap ropes around any of our limbs, especially not our wrists, and obviously not around both of them, especially whilst sailing."

Emily took another sip of her coffee and thought of working around Juniper, particularly as a foal. You never wanted to step into a coil of rope accidentally and have your horse bolt. "Recipe for disaster and broken limbs," she murmured.

"Right you are. Or drowning. Ann would never, *never*, have a rope wrapped around her wrist. And certainly not for long enough to leave such an ingrained mark, unless . . ."

Em thought of the dragged boy. "Unless someone wrapped it there for her."

"Yes, exactly right. So you understand my suspicions." Isabel poured a steady stream of amber over her chips of ice, replacing the stopper and taking a small sip from her glass. "Macallan over ice. The major would never approve," Isabel said to herself, then returned the glass to its post on the mantel. "Good thing he's not here."

"I don't know, Isabel, it sounds a little thready—"

"I'll have none of it!" Isabel abruptly took up her pacing again, this time all the way around the room. "It smells to high heaven! All of it. The timing, the fact she was out there *at all* with that squall coming through. Burns around both of her wrists? I don't believe it for one second and I am having *none of it!*"

After this outburst, the parlor fell into awkward silence. Isabel kept striding around the perimeter, her red woolen dress whacking the furniture as she passed. She revolved two more times and then stopped near Emily's chair. "And frankly, my dear, I don't need you to believe me." Emily stayed silent; Isabel smiled cheerfully into her stricken face. "I simply need you to find out who the murderer is for me. That's all."

Emily sucked in her breath hard. As if aware of how intense her stare was, Isabel didn't keep Em pinned with it for too long. She returned to her place by the mantel, picked up her Scotch glass, and played with it, rolling it back and forth between her palms. A log shifted in the fire, upwelling a cascade of sparks, followed by many minutes in which the only sounds were the sharp metallic tick of the small clock, the clink of Isabel's rings on crystal, and the merry flames crackling in the hearth.

Emily controlled her sigh. "This is a lot to take in, Isabel."

"Of course it is. I know that, I know that. And it's a lot to ask."

Now that the shock of what Isabel had suggested was subsiding, Emily's curiosity reared its feline and ever-present head. "What exactly are you asking me to do?"

"Well, you would never be in any danger, I would make sure of that."

Yes, Emily thought, *I'm sure you would*. Her eyes flicked to the bookcase and a black-and-white photo of Emily the First as a baby, a gorgeous baby, of course.

"I mainly need you to be my eyes and ears in places where I'm a little too . . . conspicuous. I'm well known about town, you see, having lived here off and on in the summer most of my life. If I turn up in odd spots, people might start to notice. And talk. You, on the other hand, are a virtual stranger."

Emily nodded. All this was true.

"As a young woman, I'm sure you have the ingenuity and adeptness to find what I'm asking for and to make yourself scarce when you need to." Two spots of color appeared on Isabel's high cheekbones.

Em didn't know quite what she meant by that and raised an eyebrow.

"That isn't clear, Frances? Let me be blunt. We will be hosting a series of events, beginning in three days." Isabel took a breath, and it hitched in her chest. "We shall be hosting Ann's family, with her sister Maisie and our cousin Ned dining with us on Thursday evening to start things off. Ann's memorial is on Saturday, and the reception afterward will be here. I need you, at each of these events, to use your wits, of which I suspect you have in abundance, to collect any information about Ann from the conversations while I'm greeting and nodding and making charming small talk."

Em nodded. So far, so good. This sounded easy.

"Ann grew up here during the summer," Isabel went on, "out on the point of Starbuck Neck. She even spent a year here before she went abroad to cover the war. Her father and sister live in Nahant now, and I'm the only family she has left on the island. Hence the hosting."

"What was Ann doing here? If her whole family was living somewhere else?"

"Her family has always had a place out on the neck. As of late, she'd taken to coming out and staying in the offseason. Mostly alone, from what I hear. Not even with regular staff."

"That must've been nice, to have your old friend back in the neighborhood. Did you visit?"

Isabel finally sat down in the other armchair. "We would see each other occasionally, but not very much, I'm afraid. I've been out of touch, as of late. She was working on something of which she was very pleased and secretive. She is a writer—*was* a writer," Isabel corrected herself, closing her eyes. "We'd only had a handful of engagements together since she returned last summer." Isabel's face faltered into familiar lines of grief. "That will always be one of my greatest regrets."

Em reached out and squeezed her aunt's hand, an impulse she almost quashed, but didn't. Isabel looked up at Emily's touch, astonished, but soon her mouth softened. She squeezed back and let go.

"I'm happy to eavesdrop at some of your parties, and whatever else we can dream up," Emily said. "And I'm sorry you lost your friend, and that you didn't get to spend time with her, but I'll only be your part-time investigator on *one* condition."

"A condition?" Isabel's eyes narrowed, instantly wary. "And what may that condition be?"

"That you stop calling me Frances." Emily could see the surprise and rebuke arise on her aunt's face and held up a hand to deter it. "I understand how my first name is painful to hear, but *Frances*? It makes me feel like a different person, and not one that I like very much."

Her aunt conceded this point with a small, reticent smile.

"How about 'Em'? Can you think of me that way?"

After a few moments of studying the carpet (taking in the new pattern that included Emily's coffee stain), Isabel looked up, eyes bright and—a wonder!—an honest-to-goodness smile on her face. "Em it is. I agree. Change of name in exchange for a part-time investigation. Fine. That will do for now."

Emily felt a wash of relief and leaned back, closing her eyes. "Thank you, Isabel."

They sat in companionable silence for a while. Then Isabel spoke up, staring at the jumping flames. "What was it that Doyle had his quirky detective say, Em?"

Emily thought for a moment. "Sherlock Holmes?"

"That's the one."

Isabel was in luck: Arthur Conan Doyle in particular, and mysteries in general, had been Constance's very favorite books. Em could almost hear the creak of the rocking chair on the wooden floor of their house and the pop and hiss of a cottonwood log in the stove as her mother intoned the words of an Englishman from across the ocean, her slippers whispering on the floorboards to the rhythm of her voice. "He said, 'The game is afoot.'"

Isabel smiled, showing a full set of perfect, gleaming teeth. It was a ferocious smile, somehow. She wasn't going to stop until she got it figured out; it was stamped in her expression.

"The game, my dear Em," Isabel said through her teeth, "is definitely afoot."

Chapter 10

When Emily left her aunt with her Macallan and waning flames, she didn't find Bridget in her usual place in the kitchen. Listening, Emily could hear voices coming from outside, either from inside the garage or near it. She plucked an apple out of a bowl on the corner table and, after considering, tucked a second into her pocket. Polishing the first on one of her Nebraska dresses—the one with the gray pinstripes—she headed through the kitchen and out the back door. Her feet crunched across the driveway, but Bridget and Pat took no heed, so involved were they in their conversation.

". . . she asked the girl to help her find the murderer!" Bridget was saying to her brother.

"What do you mean—she asked the lass to spy for her?" Pat's non-Mrs. Hewett voice was much deeper.

"Not to spy, exactly. 'Be her eyes and ears' was the way she put it." Bridget sounded indignant.

Emily decided she couldn't hear any more without being accused of eavesdropping, so she took a big bite of her apple. *Crunch!*

The conversation from the garage ceased and, a moment later, Bridget poked her head out of the open bay door.

"Well hello, Miss Frances! How are you coming along with the dresses?" Bridget asked, voice high-pitched, holding a basket of shoes.

Emily strolled into Pat's workspace and swallowed her bite of apple. "Hi, Bridget! Hello, Pat."

Pat rolled himself out from underneath the pristine car that took up half of the space. Its moss-green exterior gleamed in the garage's dull ambience, almost as if lit by its own inner light. Compared to the clunky truck, the Pierce-Arrow, like its owner, emanated class and elegance, down to its graceful hood ornament: a poised archer on bent knee, bow drawn. Through its open window, the plush buttoned seats beckoned invitingly, and a small empty vase sprouted from an armrest, waiting for a rosebud.

The truck that had brought her to Hy House was taking up the other half of the garage, and a door in the back of the garage was partially swung open, showing a slice of Pat's living quarters: the end of a cot, a hat on a hook, and a pair of brogues against the wall.

Pat sat up on the wheeled creeper, smiling at Emily, squinting through his mussed-up hair. "Hullo, Miss Emily," he said, taking a red rag from his shirt pocket and wiping his oily hands with it.

Bridget shot him a look to admonish him about the name, but Em just grinned more broadly. She reached into her pocket and drew out the apple, holding it out to Pat. His face lit up, and he nodded, holding his hands like a catcher's mitt. She tossed the apple and he grabbed it, swinging it up to his mouth in one swoop and biting off a large chunk. He raised the apple to her in thanks and nodded again, chewing with gusto.

"Great news," Emily said. "I've got my name back, sort of."

Bridget twitched her eyebrows at Emily.

"Isabel *did* ask me to be her eyes and ears, because she *does* think Ann Simpson was murdered." Em's voice became hushed on the last word. Pat stopped eating his apple. "I don't know whether she's right or blind with grief, but I'm willing to listen around for her. What harm could it do?"

Bridget and Pat swapped looks.

"What *more* harm could it do?" Emily amended. "And it means I get my name back, or a version of it. Isabel agreed to call me Em, short for Emily."

"Well, that's something," Bridget said. She did not sound sure.

Pat, from the floor, took up his apple again.

"Also, I got most of my dresses fitted. All but three."

Bridget's mouth fell open. "That many? It can't be."

"Sure did! Told you I was fast," Emily smiled, rocking back on her heels. "This is a neat spot you have here, John Patrick. Is it all right if I come help you sometimes?"

Pat, from his seat, looked at Bridget in amazement.

"I told you—remember the chicken?" Bridget said to him. To Em, she said, "You sure can, and start with these if you don't mind." She handed over the basket, filled with at least six or seven pairs of women's shoes—leather winter boots, Mary Janes, some cunning ballet flats that would have no business on a farm.

"Miss Emily's?"

Bridget nodded. "Yes indeed. She was a size seven. And yourself?"

Emily nodded. "Six and a half, but a seven'll do."

"I was just about to ask Pat for some shoe polish. He usually has some back here. And a rag."

Pat obligingly got up and made his way toward a worktable in the back, tossing his apple core in the rubbish bin before plucking a jar of Kiwi shoe polish from the shelf and grabbing an old rag from a bucket under the bench. He walked over and put them on top of the shoes in the basket. Up close, Em was struck by the contrast of Pat's coal-black hair and bright-blue eyes. He was, as her mother would've put it, quite a looker. He smelled like engine oil, tobacco, and sweat.

"Why don't you set up shop in the doorway here," he said with a friendly half smile.

"Clean 'em first, of course." Bridget glanced back toward the kitchen. "I've got to get back. Come in when you're done, Miss, but please wash your hands at Pat's sink, will you? I can't stand the smell of polish." Bridget crinkled her nose and started across the drive.

Pat pulled over a stool, gesturing for her to sit in the open bay, and then returned to the back bench, flipping on a small brown radio perched on his workbench. A tinny instrumental sound burst from it as he swung back down to the creeper and disappeared under the car. Soon one hand came out and fumbled for his wooden toolbox to pull it closer.

Em dropped the basket by her feet and stood up again. "I'm grabbing another rag, okay John Patrick?" she asked as she passed his booted feet.

"Sure, Miss Em."

She snagged one of the grayish rags from the metal bucket she'd spotted under the worktable and returned to her seat. "And John Patrick?"

"Mmmhmmm?" His blackened hand poked out from under the car to explore the contents of the toolbox.

"Can you just call me Emily, please? Or Em? All this 'Miss' stuff is for the birds."

There was a grumble under the car that could've been a cough or a guffaw of laughter, Em couldn't tell.

"You bet," he said, "Em. And I'm Pat. This 'John Patrick' stuff is fer the birds as well."

Emily spread the large rag over her dress and took up her first pair of shoes, the Mary Janes, rubbing the clear polish with care not to stain the silken interior.

They didn't say much, and they didn't really have to. The afternoon passed as the radio churned out jazzy ragtime melodies, and wisps of fog and mist floated across the open bays. Em was lost in a cloud of polish fumes and thoughts about Isabel's murder accusations. *Who did she think did it?* Em wondered, rubbing a dollop of polish onto the heel of the lace-up black boot. She'd been too shaken up to ask this morning, but as the afternoon wore on to evening, she couldn't help but wonder on whom Isabel's keen eye would fall.

Across the drive, Bridget's silhouette passed a kitchen window now and then, working away. As the pile of shoes in the basket diminished and the newly polished pairs set out in front of Emily grew, so did her appreciation of Pat's out-of-the-way position in the household. No closed-in rooms or stuffy parlor visits for him. It was definitely a great spot to do a bit of deep thinking.

When she was done with all the pairs, she wiped her hands and stood, cracking her back and wandering over to where Pat's bottom half stuck out from underneath the car, a bright-red bandana poking from the pocket of his oil-stained khaki pants. A steady muted clanging came from somewhere deep in the undercarriage.

"Need anything, Pat?" she asked. She'd often helped her dad on the farm in the shop. As she'd honestly reported to Isabel, tinkering with mechanical objects was one of her favorite things to do.

The clanging stopped and Pat wheeled out, squinting up at her. Sitting up, he pulled the bandana out of his pocket and gave the back of his neck a good rub. "I was just about to change the tire on Madam. You know what you're doing?"

"A bit. If I don't know, you can explain," Em said certainly. "Who's Madam?"

"S'what I call the Pierce-Arrow here," he said, giving the car's flank an appreciative pat as he knelt next to the left-front tire. With a small socket wrench, he began to unscrew the bolts that ringed a large central one. Em thought she'd been dismissed until he spoke up. "On the workbench, there's a Buffalo wrench. It looks like a socket wrench, but much larger—this big, in fact." He pointed at the big bolt holding the hubcap to the tire with one blackened finger.

"In your toolbox or on your bench?"

"In my toolbox . . . or I may have left it on the bench," he said. A ratcheting noise started up as he removed the smaller bolts one by one.

On the surface of the workbench, she found a wrench fitting that description sitting out on its own, not neatly nestled in Pat's toolbox with its cousins in apple-pie order. She glanced through the half-open doorway into his modest living space. Bed made perfectly. Not a wrinkle.

Emily took the heavy wrench back over and said, "Here."

He stuck out his palm, and she plopped the wrench into it.

"Thanks," he said, fitting the tool over the large middle bolt and starting to ratchet again, the sound growing louder as the bolt loosened.

Emily went back to her semicircle of drying shoes and moved her stool closer to Pat's work area, still with a view of Hy House through the bay. Ever domineering, Hydrangea House looked, at the moment and from this vantage point, almost cozy. Fog nestled in at the corners and the shells glowed as white as the clapboards, giving the illusion that everything beyond the doors of the garage had been carved from the inside of a cloud.

"Did I see Isabel . . . Mrs. Hewett drinking this morning?" Emily asked abruptly. She'd been mulling over the unusual series of events popping up since her arrival, creating whorls and eddies, currents and whirlpools all their own.

All sounds of work stopped. "I believe you did," Pat said in a measured voice, no accent at all. "She'd had a shock at Dr. Slate's."

"What about the Prohibition laws?"

The silence continued, and then the ratcheting began again. "I don't think Mrs. Hewett takes Prohibition into consideration when she has a spot o' Scotch for her nerves. And it isn't my place to tell her otherwise."

"There were folks like that at home, who didn't give a whit about Prohibition, or anyone who tried to tell them what to do. Is it like that here?"

"Fairly so," Pat said without hesitation.

She rose and walked back to the Pierce-Arrow. "How does she get it?"

He tugged the bolt off, plopping it beside him, and then pulled at the wheel, tugging it smoothly off its axle. Then he looked straight through her, giving Isabel's bird-of-prey impression a run for its money. "Looking to buy some pints on the side? Requesting a visit from Silk Sock Sam?" One side of his mouth rose.

"Silk Sock Sam?"

"Silk Sock pushes a baby carriage around with whiskey hidden in the false bottom. Quite inventive, really, since the baby—Sam Jr.—is usually *in* the carriage."

Em chuckled as she stacked shoes in the basket. "Back home, all the gossip was about where liquor was hidden and who had hidden it. A constant game of cat-and-mouse between those trying to enforce the law and the men who made money from smuggling."

"About the same here."

"Once, they hid whiskey inside the harnesses of pulling horses and, another time, they hid whiskey in pianos. There was even a place, folks said, that had a fake gas jet that dispensed beer. People in Nebraska are also very inventive."

Pat digested the wealth of information with a grin, studying her and running his hands over the smooth black rubber of the Pierce-Arrow's tire. He seemed satisfied that she wouldn't be siphoning off the Scotch in Isabel's pantry anytime soon, and he stood and rolled the wheel to his workbench. He returned to slowly fold the grasshopper-colored panels back over the immaculate engine with a velvety click. Then he walked to the other automobile, the dusty truck, such a stark contrast to the slick machine next to it, and opened the hood one side at a time with only a little less care, given the truck's work-worn appearance.

"Do me a favor, would you please, Em?" He smiled at her again.

She thought, in that moment, she might do anything for him.

"Get inside the truck, in the driver's seat, and give her a crank."

Emily scrunched her eyebrows together.

He made a twisting motion with his hands. "Turn the key in the ignition for me, but only when you hear me say so."

Emily nodded and hopped to, making her way to the driver's side. The metal lever on the truck door cranked down and it swung open. She climbed in, long legs folding into the cramped space. After a moment, she found the key jutting from the dashboard. Other than that, there was a steering wheel with circular dials behind it, a gear shift, three pedals, a parking brake, and not a lot else. *Not unlike a tractor*, she thought to herself.

"Now!" shouted Pat from the front, mostly hidden by the folded-up section of the hood.

Emily twisted the key, hard, and the truck made a grinding sound, lurching forward. Startled, she dropped her hand and the truck died in a dry rattle.

"Hold!" Pat said from the front. "Forgot to tell you . . ." He jogged around to her side and opened the door. "Put your right foot on the middle pedal and your other foot on the left pedal." He pointed into the darkness of the foot well.

"Like this?" she asked. The truck jerked forward as she depressed the left pedal, and she let out a whispery scream.

"Put your right foot on the brake. Like that. Don't worry, you're doing great. On my cue." He retreated to the front of the truck again, holding up one finger out from behind the hood. "Twist the key!"

Em nodded, more to herself as he couldn't see her, and kept both feet on the pedals.

"Now!" Pat yelled.

She twisted the key and the truck shuddered to life. This time, she didn't get frightened and let go. The engine caught as Em hung on.

"There she goes!"

She released the key from her iron grip and the truck continued its mellow rumble. *Like being inside a pleased metal lion.* She smiled to herself.

"Great! Now twist the key back to turn it off."

She did, and the truck guttered into silence as Pat came around to her side.

"You can take your feet off the pedals too, Em." He opened the door for her as she tentatively lifted both feet. As she unfolded herself, he gave the wheel a little pat. "Next time we'll go driving. Spare some of my uncle duties for the newest member of the household. I've always wanted to teach Fiona, but she isn't interested."

Her heart trilled at the thought of it.

He went back over to the Pierce-Arrow to grab his toolbox,

hoisting it to his workbench and unpacking its contents, putting the Buffalo wrench in a place of pride on the back wall, where it hung from a nail. "As to your question about where we get the booze, we don't use roads and rivers. We use the sea. And the best rumrunner in the harbor is Captain Butler. If you can't find him, you go to Starrin Perfidio. But Butler's who you want. He's got the fastest boat in the harbor. Rumor has it he replaced the engine with an airplane's to make it faster than any coast guard cutter." His hands moved quickly, tidying up the narrow workspace. "Now, some island folks think that hard boys from New York City gangs are moving in on the likes of Butler. If that's the case, no good is going to come of it, not for anyone." He tossed the rag into a basket under the workbench. "Why do you want to know?"

Em didn't know what to say. She folded and refolded her rag and then followed his cue, chucking it into the basket. "I just wanted to know what folks got up to for fun around here."

"At the fair age of sixteen and already looking for a spot of trouble. You better not be a bad influence on my Fiona, now." Pat glowered at her with a mock-stern expression.

Emily was appalled, but Pat just tossed his head back and laughed. "No, Em, you're not the criminal type, I can see that. Maybe the curious type, but not the criminal type. That's as plain as day. But curious still gets you into trouble. Even if the Mrs. asks you to do it for her."

Emily couldn't help but notice that Pat had more than just a passing resemblance to James Cagney, the stern-jawed, wide-eyed film star. She had never seen him in a movie, had never seen *any* movie in fact, but she'd seen pictures of him in Motion Picture Magazine at the train station, with the name *James Cagney* under the always-handsome, always-grinning front-cover photo. Pat was a dead ringer for him, but with darker hair.

Emily scrubbed up at the sink in the corner of the garage, per Bridget's request.

"As to what we do for fun," said Pat from his workbench, "lots of us go to Dreamland."

Emily paused while drying her hands. Dreamland—she couldn't imagine what it would be, but immediately wanted to find out.

"It's up in Oak Bluffs, and there's plenty to do up there on a day off. Mrs. Hewett lets me take the truck up there if she's of a mood. And most of the time she is."

But none of this enticing information gave Emily the faintest idea what Dreamland was. With the enigmatic name reverberating in her head, she picked up the shoe basket and turned to go.

"Seems like we might get a run of foul weather for the rest of the week. Fog. Clouds. A chill. If you ever need to find a place away from the house, you can usually find me in here."

She looked back over her shoulder and grinned. "Thanks, Pat. I shan't forget."

As she set out into the blanket of cold with her shoe basket, she inhaled the sea fog—thicker than regular air, flavored with salt and cedarwood. It seemed she had another out-of-the-way spot to escape to and maybe, just maybe, another friend.

Chapter 11

The next few days consisted of dense cold fog and little for Emily to do. In the mornings, Bridget would prevail upon her for some task or another, always asking her shyly and watching her go about it—kneading, folding, stirring—with a degree of skepticism and amazement that Em found perpetually funny, although she tried to hide her amusement so as not to embarrass Bridget.

Pat was less amazed at her capabilities, and more inclined to take advantage of them, once he got over the fact that she was a girl and related to Mrs. Hewett, his employer. She spent her time mostly in Pat's garage, whenever she could. They even went driving a few times.

Along with helping him around the shop, he added driving lessons as a kind of reward for whatever task they'd been about each afternoon. Every day was different—on one she organized his worktable; on another she helped him oil up and inflate the tires of a dusty Huffy bicycle she hoped would soon be passed along to her, like the dresses and shoes. Each evening they'd set off in the old truck for an impromptu lesson in driving, with Pat sounding off helpful lessons and hints as they bumped down Church Street and around to Main via Pease Point Way.

On Thursday night, the evening of the first dinner party, this included a ride with Em at the helm, around the block and a little farther, down Sheriff's Lane, where the dirt tracks petered out and Em almost dumped them into a ditch, pulling up short just in time, much to Pat's great amusement.

"And there you are," he'd said quietly to the windscreen as Em had fumbled around for reverse, the gear with which she had the most trouble.

Through a clutch of evergreens, a pond gleamed like a bright silver coin, sparkling in the rare sunshine breaking through the dense clouds. Another small pond shone behind it, and, beyond that, the indigo line of the sea. As if on cue, a pair of swans glided into sight.

"Here we are," Emily breathed.

After a few moments enjoying the last of the sun's rays before they were once more swallowed up by the bank of clouds, Pat broke the silence. "Do you remember, a few days back, me talking about Dreamland?"

She nodded in the darkened cab of the truck.

"After Mass this Sunday, I'm taking Fiona. Want to join?"

Muted into shocked joy, all Em could do was nod again. He smiled at her, the last illumination catching on his gleaming teeth, looking all the more like a movie star.

"Good. We'll go after Mass then. Put her into reverse slowly, Em," Pat said, by way of changing the subject. "Give her the gas, but slow, and don't forget the headlamp switch on your left-hand side."

Emily's hands trembled on the steering wheel as she made his suggested adjustments. Who wouldn't want to go to Dreamland with James Cagney?

The brief sunshine disappeared soon after they returned, and the fog closed in with the evening. Emily returned to the kitchen, thinking that Hy House looked like an aging lady drawing her petticoats in to keep out the drafts as the billowing mist crept around the corners.

Inside, she shrugged off her jacket, grateful for the warm stove that kept the kitchen and much of the upstairs toasty on the nights the sea wind was chill. Bridget was nowhere to be found, so Em thought she might steal some minutes away in the bathroom. She headed upstairs to see what could be done about the new dark smear on her cuff and the all-over grimy feeling from her work in the garage.

Bridget had given her an overview of the bathtub—how to work it, which knob was which—and Emily took her third indoor bath in the very large tub. After the chill of the garage, soaking in the hot water was a revelation, and she stayed in longer than she probably should have.

Back in her room, Emily realized she had a new task before her, a task that most wealthy women and girls of society had done countless times throughout their lives. But not Emily.

It was time to choose a dress.

Bridget had told her that two others would be joining for dinner tonight, and that Fiona would be coming to help serve. Emily was more looking forward to seeing Fiona than she was to meeting two new people, to whom she might or might not be related. She was sure that Aunt Isabel would set her straight on that account.

As the first tendrils of anxiety unfurled in the pit of her stomach, a cheery voice came from downstairs. She couldn't quite make out what was said, but she knew who it was. Emily grinned and waited, running her fingers through her still-wet hair. Sure enough, steps clomped up the stairs and the door to the room was thrown open as if by a force beyond the small shape now standing in the doorway.

"Moved into my closet, I see!" Fiona said when she spotted Emily by the open wardrobe.

"Well, it's not as if you had a whole lot in there to begin with!"

Fiona closed the distance between them to give Em a quick hug. "How are you holding up? I've heard the household's gone a bit topsy-turvy. Did the Mrs. ask you to be the Doc Watson to her Sherlock Holmes?"

"She did. It's not all that much, Fi, she just asked me to eavesdrop at her parties."

"Which you would be doing anyway." Fiona seemed quite interested in the dresses Em had recently tailored.

"I never was very good at social gatherings and such."

"May I?" Fiona asked, gesturing toward the dresses.

"It's your closet. Have at it." Em threw herself onto the twin bed and stared up at the slanted ceiling. "I was just talking myself out of escaping through the window. I have *no* idea what to wear. I thought the tan one? But now I'm not so sure. Can you help?"

"Are you joking? I would like nothing better! I've been eyeing most of these dresses all my *life*, and now to see them walking around?" Fiona thrust her hands into the fabric, pulling out a skirt here and a jacket there. "Mam told me it's a simple gathering. Casual, you know." She regarded an emerald satin skirt.

"Casual, sure. As casual as a state dinner," Emily said. Let Fiona pick out what she should wear tonight; Emily's decision-maker was all used up.

"Have you figured out the undergarments yet?"

"I've just barely figured out the bathtub—give me half a minute."

Fiona chuckled from inside the wardrobe.

After much debating, Fiona decided that Em should wear a red-and-light-brown dress made of silk. The underthings were a pain, and Em would've never figured them out on her own. She was glad for Fiona's help.

Fiona was helping her with the two cloth-covered buttons on the dress's high neck when Bridget's voice drifted up from downstairs. "Fiona, you up there, *cailín*? I need your hands!"

Fiona glanced hurriedly at the door and then spun Emily around, taking in the new look, including the knee-high socks that disappeared beneath the swishy fabric. It felt to Em like wearing snakeskin or fish scales.

"Shoes?"

Em pointed to the basket, which she'd deposited by the wardrobe and left abandoned; she only really wore her boots.

Fiona dove for it, throwing aside one polished choice after another until she found the dainty ballet flats. "Jewelry?"

This was such a foreign question to Emily that she didn't know what to say, but then remembered her mother's comb. She grabbed it from her shelf and held it out to Fiona.

"That'll do," Fiona declared. "It will give me an excuse to get your hair out of a braid."

Emily's sound of protest was instantly stifled as Fiona dragged the comb across her scalp.

"Let's do a half-up, don't you think?" Fiona stood in front of her, poking the point of her tongue out of the side of her mouth as she worked the comb so that half Em's hair was up on one side and the other half fell over her shoulder. "Beautiful," she said, leading Emily to the cloudy mirror. "Look."

The Emily looking back was far more sophisticated than the Em of a week ago, by a long shot. It took her breath away. "It's like I'm a different person," Emily said quietly, a strange, forlorn feeling overcoming her.

"You? A different person? Hardly. You didn't even let the old bat take away your name, did you?"

"Fiiiiiiii!" Bridget's call was much more insistent this time.

Fiona gave Em a quick squeeze. "You're going to knock their socks off, Em!" she said, and clattered out.

Emily was left with her more-fashionable self and an open door.

It took a bit of doing for Em to get herself down to the parlor. She'd rarely been in social situations in Nebraska, and her favorites had been the impromptu ones after a long day of helping out a neighbor. The only comparable formal occasion had been her cousin's wedding in Lincoln. Since Em had only been six at the time, much of that fine soiree was but a blur in her memory.

As she made her way down the back stairs, she felt a little queasy, not unlike her trip here on the steamboat, and put it down to nerves. The kitchen bubbled in a paroxysm of activity. Fiona was up to her elbows, mixing something in a bowl. She had a smear of flour on her face and gave Em a cheeky wink. Bridget stood over the stove, one hand holding a glass measuring cup of brown liquid, the other with a baster, squirting the juice all over the backs of whatever was roasting inside.

It smelled divine here. Em wished she could put up her newly combed hair, roll her newly buttoned sleeves up, and join them, helping to lay out the spread. But she knew she mustn't, and also knew now she shouldn't ask, to save Bridget the embarrassment of refusing her.

Instead she sailed through as if she knew exactly what she was about and where she was going. Bridget caught sight of her and spun, putting the gravy and baster on the butcher block and bustling over.

"Miss Em, you look stunning! Hold on just a moment." Bridget appraised her as Emily shifted from foot to foot. Fiona had stopped kneading and observed them with a proprietary smile. "I never would've known this wasn't your dress to begin with!" Bridget grinned. "And the shoes! Perfect choice."

Emily pointed her foot so Bridget could get a better look. From behind her, Fiona chortled. "I picked those out!"

"Well done, Fi," Bridget said as she caught Emily's hand in her calloused one. "And good on you, Miss Em. You look like you were to the manner born."

Emily glowed, reassured that she looked natural given that she didn't feel that way, not at all.

"Pat said he's taking Fiona up to Dreamland on Sunday," Em said, "and he asked me to join. Would that be all right with you, Bridget?"

Bridget dropped her hand and cut her eyes toward Fiona, whose smile disappeared. "Dreamla—Well, for Pete's sake. He's taking you up there again?" she asked Fiona, who was once more very interested in the contents of her bowl. She glanced up at her mother's question, all innocence.

"If it's all right with you, Mam." Fiona's green eyes were wide and her hands kept kneading.

"Last time wasn't so much of a success, was it?"

"It wasn't so bad, Mam! Only a little hiccup. And it won't be that way this time, promise!"

"I don't think it's such a good idea," Bridget said. Em's heart felt like it was splintering. She still didn't know what Dreamland was, but she wanted to go with Fiona, her new friend, and her new friend's James-Cagney-look-alike uncle so much the disappointment burned her throat like acid.

"Please, Bridget?" Her voice wavered. "We won't get into trouble."

"And it would be good for her to see other parts of the island," Fiona added from across the counter, "since she lives here now."

Bridget didn't say anything, just stood studying Em for a moment. Then she started sniffing the air, snorting like a horse. "Burning!" she shouted, then spun, throwing open the oven and thrusting an apron-covered hand inside. She yanked out a pan of biscuits that were just turning from golden brown to a darker shade and popped them on the counter, slamming the oven door shut again. With this accomplished, Bridget's gray eyes once again found Emily. "It's not my place to say whether you get to go or not as you will have to ask Mrs. Hewett. And good luck to that. She's never been a fan of the fights."

With this, Bridget once again turned her attention to the darkened biscuits, leveraging each one out of the pan with a butter knife. Emily stood watching for a moment before turning to go. She was glad she knew a bit more before presenting her plea to Isabel.

The fights, Em thought as she pushed through the double doors into the hallway. Dreamland was a boxing venue.

Em walked past the parlor and across the foyer to the open door that threw a slanted rectangle of light across the floor. Laughter tinkled through, both male and female.

All thoughts of boxing matches and James Cagney were knocked out of her head as soon as she entered the room. Lit by lamps and a small fire in the grate along with a few candles, everything glimmered and glistened with luminescence, even the three standing at the mantel—Isabel and two strangers.

Isabel was at her most elegant in a plum dress, silver hair piled high, and pearls layered around her neck in a choker. Standing next to her was a man of medium height with sandy hair swept off to one side and thick glasses. As Emily entered, the unknown woman in the middle was laughing, head thrown back. Her hair was shorn in a neat bob, and it shone like it was wet. A fanciful headband glittered against the slick black hair. The girl reached out one long white arm to the man as she laughed. Her dress, made up entirely of opaque crystal shards, glittered and shimmered as she spasmed with giggles. Even the candlelight glimmer was no match for the light this young woman threw off.

Emily coughed discreetly in the doorway and everyone looked over. So scrutinized she felt as though her heart would pound straight out of her chest cavity.

"Fran—Em!" Isabel recovered herself nicely, smiling with aplomb at her guests. "Ned, Maisie, I would like you to meet my niece, more recently my ward, Miss Em Cartwright."

Emily moved with as much grace as possible to the fireplace. Up close, the woman's gaze was intense, made almost predatory by the kohl liner tracing each of her pale eyes. She also had an entrancing beauty mark just above her upper lip, obviously fake.

"Em, I would like you to meet Ned Cooperson and Maisie Dahlia Gray."

Emily nearly curtsied, thought better of it, and extended her hand. "How do you do?"

Ned took up her offered handshake. "Hello, Em. I'm Ned. We're distant cousins or some such thing. Welcome to the island."

"Hello, Ned. Thank you."

He released her hand, and she offered it to Maisie, who took it and dropped it immediately—a limp, cool presence and then gone. "Hello, Em, pleased to meet you. I'm Maisie Dahlia, or just Maisie if shorter is better for you. My claim to fame is that I am Miss Simpson's little sister. Where are you originally from? Nebraska, isn't it?" Maisie's smile did not reach her eyes. "What do you think of the East Coast?"

Em nodded along to the young woman's quick cadence. "I haven't been here nearly long enough to form an opinion yet. But I can tell you it is the prettiest place I've ever been. Like a postcard."

Ned's open smile grew warmer. "It is, isn't it? I've been coming here all my life and every time I step off the boat, I'm gobsmacked."

Emily thought back to her own nauseated first moments, clinging to a piling on the wharf, and smiled politely.

"Is this one of your new dresses?" Isabel asked her, eyes sliding up and down the scarlet-and-tan material as if reading a newspaper.

"It is. I finished altering them. Fiona helped me pick this one." She swiveled, feeling Maisie's eyes on her.

The girl was stunning, and just enough older than Em to make her feel clunky. Maisie was like a will-o'-the-wisp, so thin she almost swayed with the currents of air in the room. Em imagined her getting sucked up the chimney in a *whoosh* of tiny sparks.

"Absolutely fetching," Isabel said from beside them. Maisie's eyes, however, said something else entirely. "Please, let's enjoy some hors d'oeuvres and cocktails."

Bridget had appeared with a tray in either hand, deftly placing one on the table under the windows and turning back with the other to offer them four glass mugs of something orange, an orange slice and cherry floating on top. "Mr. Ned, Miss Maisie, have a rum punch," she said, brandishing the tray. "Miss Em's is the one without the cherry."

"And also without the rum," Isabel added, and they all laughed, Em with an awkward chuckle she hoped sounded sincere.

They stood sipping the tangy punch as Bridget swapped trays to bring them appetizers, which looked like they'd been pried straight out of the ocean, ratcheted off a slimy sea rock.

"Oysters Rockefeller, everyone!" Isabel announced, and picked one up, the other hand taking a miniature fork, which she used to foist the grayish lump into her elegant mouth. "Lovely," said Isabel, discarding the shell on the tray.

Ned reached for one. "What's the birding like out there in Nebraska, Miss Em?" he asked as he fussed with his oyster, positioning his fork just so.

"The . . . the birding?" Em repeated. "The birds are quite . . . satisfactory, I assure you. They fly and do the regular bird things."

Ned laughed. "Hopefully they do! I mean, what types of birds are there?"

"Birds are Ned's special piccadilly," Maisie added. Em noticed she'd given Bridget a firm headshake when offered an oyster. Now Bridget turned toward Em, who wondered if she could manage to put her off with such a simple gesture. Em didn't think so. Special local menu and all.

"From what Mr. Audubon has described," said Ned, "many extraordinary birds make their home on the high plains."

Em took a warm oyster shell in one hand, a tiny fork in the other, suppressing an inward grimace at the gelatinous mass with its accoutrement of parsley sprigs. It looked no more appetizing up close. To avoid for a moment longer placing the thing in her mouth, she talked to Ned about birds. "These birds come through every spring, sandhill cranes I think. Loads of them. It's quite a sight; we rode miles to catch a glimpse of them nesting. It was quite something."

"Was it?" Ned asked in genuine awe.

"They're bigger than you'd expect, and they fly in groups, or flocks I guess. Formations. There are so many, and they fly in different parts of the sky. Some of them will be tiny specks hundreds of feet off the ground, and some will be coming in for a landing right in front of you, all at the same time. My mama and I rode out there every year we could. We'd pack a picnic and spend hours watching the cranes. She'd say they were one of the great wonders of nature."

"You don't say," Ned said in a breathy voice. "I'll have to go out there one of these days and see for myself."

Em nodded, glad to be of service, and noticed her audience's continued attention. Her oyster remained parked halfway to her mouth. *May as well get it over with*, she thought, and dropped it into her mouth.

With the breadcrumbs' crunch, the fresh tang of parsley, and a welcome dash of lemon juice, the oysters Rockefeller, like New England clam chowder, was better than it looked. It was not the *most* horrible thing she'd ever eaten in her life. The tomato aspic, on the other hand, remained squarely at the bottom of the barrel, right next to a snail plucked off a rock on a dare.

Emily chewed and swallowed, offering a smile to Isabel, who watched attentively.

"That one was a hit!" Isabel called over her shoulder to Bridget, who pretended to be busy at the corner table. "Put a check next to that one!"

"Whatever is she talking about?" Maisie asked.

"They've concocted a New England menu for me," Emily explained.

"Exactly so," affirmed Isabel. "We've tried clam chowder, a success, and tomato aspic, not so much. Let's go through to dinner, shall we? Bridget has whipped together quite a delightful repast for us."

Without waiting for anyone to answer, Isabel perched her mug on the mantel and swished across the blue patterned carpet, leaving the rest of them to follow in her elegant wake.

At the dinner table, Bridget served *Duck à l'Orange*, straying from the New England menu in favor of Maisie's favorite dish. Emily didn't mind.

"Isabel, it's always a pleasure to dine here," Maisie said, taking a sip of champagne, which they referred to as "bubbly." The tip of her nose was pink and her eyes unfocused. Her skin was so smooth it looked like milk. "You know, I don't think Prohibition has done a damn thing. All these curmudgeonly laws and the only thing to show for it is the extra work John Patrick has to put in to get the booze to Hy House."

"Don't be so coarse, Maisie," Isabel admonished.

"It's true, dear Isabel," Maisie simpered. "The only thing Prohibition did was make it harder and a bit more dangerous to get plastered. Everyone I know still drinks like a fish."

"That's not the only thing that Prohibition did," Ned added from the opposite head. "It took a strong criminal element and gave it an industry. It's not a light matter, Maisie. You realize how serious it is, don't you?"

"What do you mean?" Isabel asked as she fussed with the slices of duck on her plate.

"What I mean," Ned continued, in his element, "is that before the war, crime on the island was limited to a few seedy jobs—petty theft, a domestic row, drunken antics and their consequences—when it popped up at all. Since Prohibition, criminals have used booze smuggling to line their pockets with gold. And now the Mob has moved in with real strength and created an entire network, in fact. These new types of rumrunners are nothing to sneeze at, and they're everywhere, even places like Fisher's Island and, yes, the Vineyard."

The others stared at Ned in astounded silence while Bridget rotated between each guest, swapping the duck platter for a smaller dish filled with green asparagus spears.

"Ah, local asparagus," Isabel exclaimed as Bridget offered them to Ned. "For the side dish, we did stay true to our New England roots."

"Thank you, Bridget," Ned said as he scooped spring-green vegetables onto his plate. "Without the Woman's Temperance Union, Al Capone and his lot would have *never* been able to get their talons in a place like the island. Ach, clumsy," he admonished, blotting a new butter stain on his shirt cuff. "But now, those gangsters are running rum twelve miles out seven days a week. They even have speakeasies out there. Real speakeasies like you see in New York, with gambling and music and plenty of whiskey, all at sea." Ned waved a fork-speared asparagus for emphasis.

"I'm not sure I would put it in such drastic terms," Maisie said. She was attempting to cut the meat off the drumstick, but it was proving difficult. Wielding the drumstick by its natural end would've been a common response, but Maisie wasn't common, and she didn't seem like the type to willingly muss up her hands. *Duck à l'Orange* might taste marvelous, but it was messy to eat.

"Well, I would," Ned said as he worked on his own duck. "There is a rumor that the mobster Al Capone has an interest in some of the businesses out here. I don't know how much truth is in that, but it is *certain* that the rest of his buddies and bodyguards are doing a great job running their dark boats and having shoot-outs with the coast guard up and down the coast."

The glazed duck was cooked to perfection with just the right amount of crispiness. Bridget really was a master chef. Em would have to remember to tell her how good it all was. The asparagus reminded her of Constance. Every spring, she and Mama would ride miles on their trusty, rusty old bikes to Constance's secret plot of wild asparagus. This Vineyard asparagus was delicious too, she conceded.

"What would you have us do, not drink?" Isabel asked, taking a pointed sip of her champagne.

"No," Ned conceded, picking up his own delicate stem and giving her a half salute. "No, I wouldn't go so far as to *actually* bar drinking from those who wish to, but the consequences of the Temperance Union's good intentions are quite dire, more so than anyone expected."

"Is it really all that bad? All the way out here? Surely not Al Capone!" Maisie had her hands on either side of her face in mock shock.

"No theatrics, please, Maisie," said Isabel, taking a bite of duck with a slice of orange. "Not at the dinner table. I don't want to lose my appetite."

Em stifled a chuckle and began buttering her biscuit with the focus of a scholar.

Ned regarded Maisie with a stricken expression. "The runners carry submachine guns, and they have Gatling guns mounted on their decks. It's absolute madness!"

Maisie rolled her eyes at him but looked chagrined enough, apparently, because Ned shifted back to his meal.

"It may not be Capone, but we do have rumrunners like McCoy and Butler," Isabel said, "and they're enough."

"Why?" Em ventured. "What makes them so dangerous?" She

remembered Captain Butler from her first day at Papers, his rough hands rifling through the newspapers and his hat pulled too low to see his eyes. He cut a mysterious figure, to be sure.

"The rumrunners are dangerous because they transport illegal liquor in the dark by boat with no running lights whatsoever," Isabel said, sounding exasperated, her gaze flicking between each of them. "They are constantly shooting at one another or at the coast guard and smashing up something or other and being a great general nuisance. This is besides the fact that they are delivering what is, from my point of view, a necessary commodity." Bridget had poured them all half a glass of red wine to pair with their duck, even Em, and Isabel toyed with the cut-crystal glass as she spoke, making the liquid ripple. "It's as if one's milkman or the iceman went completely mad and smashed up the streets before making his delivery. An untenable situation. And one not easily remedied."

"No, not anymore. Even if they revoke the Eighteenth Amendment and overturn Prohibition, the Mob will just find something else to do on the island. The criminals are here to stay, I'm afraid," Ned said.

With this, the conversation simmered into silence, and Bridget returned to clear dinner. Emily had loved it all, even the dry wine, which tasted like fall at the orchard and enhanced the round, meaty sweetness of the duck.

Upon taking their after-dinner drink orders (cognac for Isabel and Ned, and coffee for Em and Maisie), Bridget returned to the kitchen, and Ned changed the subject back to one of his favorites. "The island is noteworthy for birding, and I may even catch a glimpse of a particularly rare bird tomorrow morning! It's a once-in-a-lifetime opportunity."

"Which bird?" Em asked.

"There have been sightings of barn owls in the area, and I'm going to try and see one out on the point!" he squeaked.

"How exciting," Maisie said with no inflection, slitting her eyes at Ned.

"I think it sounds marvelous. What are barn owls like, Ned?"

Emily asked. In Nebraska, birds were her constant little companions, twittering at her as she worked, giving her advice on the best way to do her chores; her tiny feathered advisers.

"Barn owls were spotted on the island for the first time last year, and they're about this big, bigger than a red-tailed hawk." He held his hands two feet apart. "A large bird with amazing facial markings—all white, but with a darker heart shape around the outside of the face. And, of course, giant eyes." He cupped his own eyes to illustrate, doing an excellent owl impression thanks to his thickly rimmed spectacles. He blinked a few times, making Maisie giggle. "I know where they've been nesting, out by Starbuck Neck. And they're nocturnal, so if I'm there very early, I might be able to see one."

"Something you don't know about Ned," Maisie broke in, looking at Em conspiratorially across the table, her catlike eyes very light in the thick black liner. "He has a pet owl, brings it to Christmas luncheon all the time, which you'll see for yourself since we always have the holiday meal at Isabel's. Has it sit on a wooden stick while we eat. It just stares. Unsettling, rather."

"Harriet is a member of the family, and she is a *she*." Ned was indignant. "She is not staring at you as you eat, Maisie. I always move her perch to the parlor, where she can reflect and admire the tree during Christmas lunch. And Harriet is never a bother, is she, Isabel?" Ned's voice had turned peevish.

"Of course not, my dear," Isabel reassured him. "Harriet is always welcome at my table. Well," she added thoughtfully, "maybe not my table, but certainly she is welcome in my parlor." Isabel's eyes suddenly gleamed with new interest. "Dear Ned, I've had the most marvelous idea! You say you're going out to the point to look for owls? Soon?"

Ned nodded. "Yes, an early-morning excursion tomorrow, with a start at four thirty, to arrive twenty minutes or so before sunrise."

"So early," Maisie groaned.

Isabel ignored her. "Why don't you take my niece with you?"

Em and Ned exchanged confused glances.

"She hasn't gotten out of the house much," Isabel continued, "and although it's early, it's a wonderful way for her to see that part of the island, especially after the sun rises. It will be enchanting."

"It's a nice idea, Isabel, and I would enjoy taking Miss Em on a birding tour of the island—"

Maisie groaned again.

"But I'm heading to the point by bicycle, and I don't think—"

"Tut, tut, Ned. Em has a bicycle that John Patrick fixed up for her. She will be ready when you arrive bright and early to pick her up."

"Don't you mean dark and early?" Maisie interrupted.

Although she seemed childish and a trifle vain, Emily was starting to warm to Maisie. She definitely added to the conversation.

"Are you sure it's a good idea, Isabel? What does Em think of it?"

"Of course it's a good idea. As a sturdy girl from the high plains of Nebraska, our Em is well accustomed to waking early and being active. Aren't you, Em?"

All Emily could do was nod.

"And it will give her the lay of the land. It's such an exquisite area, on the point. You said you're going out by Starbuck Neck?" Isabel glanced at Em.

"Yes. The point that juts out from the Simpsons' land, bordering it and running all the way back to Pease Point Way."

All of a sudden, it clicked: Isabel didn't want her to get the lay of any land, she wanted her to get a lay of the *Simpsons'* land. If Em had thought being Isabel's eyes and ears was going to entail waking up so gut-bustingly early and biking into the dark with a stranger (albeit a relative), she wouldn't have agreed so readily. But then again, she enjoyed any kind of adventure, even early-morning ones.

"Then it's settled," Isabel said, clapping her hands together. "Miss Em will come on your owl-hunting journey."

"It's not really an owl-*hunting* journey, per se," Ned said. "It's more of an owl-*observing* journey."

"What time did you say you were getting a start?" Isabel asked.

"Four thirty. The sun rises at about four fifty."

Em sighed, defeated.

"Then we shall see you here at four thirty sharp."

Again, all either of them could do was nod. Isabel, it seemed, was not the easiest person to say no to, not that this was a surprise.

It was at this moment that Bridget brought in the dessert, shuffling under the weight of the tray. Perched atop it was a pie made up of mounds of whipped cream or meringue; it was hard to tell which because, at that moment, it was on fire.

"Ah, dessert!" Isabel clapped her hands again. "And one of *my* personal favorites, Baked Alaska, or Bombe Alaska."

Bridget deposited the flaming platter as carefully as she could on the cleared space between Isabel and Em. She stood back, face glistening, as they watched the blue flames crawl over the surface of the dessert, turning it a charred golden brown.

Finally, the flames tuckered out and Bridget moved in with a pie knife and a stack of delicate plates, slicing four pieces and divvying them out. The smell of caramelized sugar hung heavy as Em made an attempt at the strangest-looking confection she'd ever seen—a browned crust hiding a frozen yet fluffy cake inside, along with multicolored meringue and a stone-cold heart of raspberry ice cream.

Ned broke the silence. "Isabel, you said the memorial is at the Methodist church, so who's coming here on Saturday?"

Isabel answered as Bridget returned with the coffee and cognac. "The usual crowd, unfortunately. Ann's father shall be in attendance, but her two older brothers, Robert and Douglas—the twins—were killed at the Meuse, both boys in the same battle. Her father is her surviving family, poor man, excepting present company." Isabel inclined her head toward Maisie, Ann's younger sister. Half-sister. Younger by quite a bit, too, from what Maisie had said at dinner. "Then there's the Whitlocks, the Bessers, the Eberhardts . . . all the Old Guard will be taking the boat from New Bedford to come pay their respects. Many of Ann's set will be there. Her new beau is supposed to come."

"Ann isn't having a service in Boston, just the one on the island, so it will be packed." Ned swished the amber liquid around in his glass.

"Daddy said he's on the 9:45 boat on Saturday morning," Maisie said as she sliced through her pie with the side of her fork. "He's a mess, poor soul. Even more so than when Doug and Bob were killed." Maisie shook her head; her headband sparkled in the candlelight, but her black hair didn't move, as if made of patent leather.

"After the service," Isabel rejoined, "I'm having a reception for those in attendance. And good thing too. Having everyone here will make it easier."

"Easier for what?" Ned asked.

"Easier to find the culprit."

Em felt a weight in her throat as she tried to finish her Baked Alaska; it wasn't going down but sticking there like a sugary hook. She swallowed several times. Isabel had that glint in her eye again.

"I'm sorry, Isabel, I'm confused," Ned said. "The culprit?"

"The culprit," Isabel explained, "of Ann Simpson's murder."

There was dead silence. Isabel took this opportunity to take a generous sip of cognac, still with the devil-be-damned look on her face. Ned stared at Isabel, thunderstruck, and Maisie was caught with her eyes wide, drawn-on eyebrows halfway up her forehead, coffee cup frozen en route to her mouth. Nobody moved. Em, slightly embarrassed, smiled a little as Ned stared at her in disbelief before shifting his gaze back to Isabel.

"You can't be serious, Isabel," he said finally.

"I certainly am." She put her glass down with a muted *thump*. "Ann *was* murdered, and I'm going to figure out who did it, and make them pay." The last three words dropped to a low growl.

"Why would anyone want to murder Ann?" Ned said. "I can't *believe* that anyone would want to murder Ann. I mean, she was a successful journalist, a prominent member of society, and beloved! She never rubbed anyone the wrong way."

Maisie snorted. "Sorry, Ned, I have to correct you there. Ann definitely rubbed some people the wrong way. Remember the head of the convent? What was her name?"

"Sister Marion Abernathy," Isabel said, her eyes drifting to the ceiling. "I shall never forget, Ann wrote an exposé on the sister's orphanage for her final thesis at Radcliffe and published it as an op-ed in the local paper, all about the atrocities that went on over there. She'd gotten herself a job at the place, and she put them through the wringer in her article. She even got them shut down. Did you know I was there when Sister Marion confronted Ann?"

Maisie shook her head.

"We were sitting at the counter of the corner store near campus, plain as day, when Sister Abernathy came in, shaking a copy of the paper like Moses's staff." Isabel's smile grew at the memory of her audacious friend. "Ann stayed calm as a cat, kept on eating her sandwich. When Sister Marion finished yelling—using language I thought bordered on un-Christian, mind you—Ann asked the soda jerk to put the lunch on her tab, and turned to face the furious nun.

"'I plead the fifth,' she said. And then she walked out. I, of course, scurried out after her. Sister Abernathy must've pleaded the fifth, too, because she didn't say a word. Just watched us leave. And Ann could barely be bothered."

"Exactly so," Maisie said. "The point being, Ann made enemies wherever she went. Lots of friends, but a fair number of enemies. Even nuns like Sister Marion. A lot of people had motive to kill her, or to at least get her out of the way. I mean, if we're talking about motive, even *I* have motive to murder Ann! Or had a motive, I suppose."

This was met with another thunderous silence as they all considered Maisie very carefully.

"I didn't," she amended hurriedly. "Of course I didn't! And she wasn't murdered; she died in a storm while sailing." She paused and looked around at the unreceptive faces. "I did *not* kill my sister!" She crossed her finger over her heart, making an X on her bodice. "I was just trying to prove my point: If I had motive then a lot of people did.

It doesn't matter, because she *wasn't murdered*."

"Financial motive," Isabel said over tented hands. "That's what you have."

"Yes, quite," Maisie answered, a droll smile on her red doll's lips. "Now I'm the surviving heir, and so I shall inherit it all. After the boys were killed in France, Ann was set to inherit, and now it's me. So you see? I would have had motive, and so would the people she wrote about, the people she exposed. There were quite a few. But angry enough to kill her? I don't think so."

"But why do you think she was killed in the first place?" Ned asked. "The doctor ruled it an accidental drowning at sea. You saw that storm—it was fierce. Not many sailors would've been able to face Neptune that day."

"Quite right!" Isabel exclaimed. "Why was she out there? Ann was a champion sailor, and a wizard when it came to watching the weather. Why would she place herself at such obvious risk?"

"Maybe she wasn't as vigilant that day," Ned countered. "It was a line squall, and they come at you out of nowhere."

"I doubt it. Not our Ann. She never missed, Ned, never. No, I thought it was all very strange, not suspicious mind you, but strange. Then I went to view the body."

"You had to see the body? How awful!" Maisie's face was stricken, eyes widened and mouth a sympathetic O.

"Not the first one I've ever seen, and probably not the last," Isabel said in a level voice. "It was a most informative visit, for it was upon viewing the body that my suspicions were aroused. Well, to be honest, it was only on reflection a little while later, after returning home. I was remembering her, so small and defenseless in that cold room." Isabel's voice got thready. "And then I saw them again."

"Saw what?" Ned asked.

"She had two substantial rope burns around both of her wrists, wrapped all the way around." Isabel let this sink in. Emily watched the others for their reactions.

Ned whistled long and low. Maisie looked from one to the other like she was following a tennis match. "What? That's bad?"

"Around both wrists? And the doc said nothing about it?" Ned asked.

"He maintained the burns could've been from a violent tumbling, like if you tried to sail a boat in a storm."

"I still don't understand," Maisie said, looking all the more like a stumped three-year-old at the big kids' table.

"Not a sailor?" Ned asked.

Maisie shook her head.

"It's the rope around the wrists. Getting your arms or legs tangled in lines is a death wish on board. You get yanked overboard or break a limb, or both. That does seem careless."

"Not just careless, deliberate." Isabel's fiery gaze was locked on Ned. "Both wrists, Ned."

"So, you see a rope burn on her wrists and immediately think murder," Maisie said in a monotone voice.

"And the timing of her sail."

"I don't know, Isabel. It's all a bit thin," Ned said, rolling the snifter in his palm.

"And why are you telling *us* all this?" Maisie asked.

Isabel leaned back at the head of the table. "Good on you, Maisie. Not so insipid after all. I disclosed this to see if, one, Maisie, you murdered her for the very motive you outlined here: the fortune you're now set to inherit."

Maisie blanched.

"I now know you didn't, as your reaction was not consistent with a murderer's and your knowledge of sailing is abominable. You couldn't have been on that boat. Did you grow up at your mother's?"

"I did," Maisie said.

"Off island?"

"Yes."

"Inland?"

Maisie nodded.

"It shows."

"Thank you," Maisie said faintly, still unmoored by the accusation.

"I also related my theory to you," Isabel continued, "because Em needs an accomplice to find out who killed Ann. Ned, you're perfect. So it's settled. Em joins you hunting owls."

Ned's eyes got even bigger behind his glasses. "Isabel, I've sincerely enjoyed your company, and always have a fine time at your table, but I hardly think—"

"Ned," Isabel interrupted. "You've been a dinner guest at my table for years, sometimes with Harriet and sometimes without, and I've always opened my doors to you, no matter what. What I am asking from you now is not that much in return, whether you agree with my theories or not. Take the girl around, make sure she's safe, but show her the layout before everyone arrives. You'll be going out to Starbuck Neck anyway, and Em will be a great help to you."

"Help?" Ned said, somewhat helplessly.

"Yes, as I've mentioned, she grew up on a farm. She's quite capable. As to any other doubts, I will hear none of it!" Isabel finished, her face serious and uncompromising.

The table was silent. It seemed that this admonition might put an end to the evening.

"Well then," Ned said, standing and scooting his chair back in a half bow, "I must bid you good night. It seems that you and I"—he nodded at Em—"have a very early start."

And that was that. Emily had her accomplice and a mission to get her started. She scooted her chair back from the table, thanked Isabel for a lovely dinner, and headed back to her room in a fog. That was quite the social introduction.

At least she'd gotten a bicycle out of the deal.

Chapter 12

As promised, when Emily arose in the pitch dark the next morning and threw on her clothes and coat, she was greeted by a sturdy, dark-blue Huffy bicycle awaiting her on the front drive. It was the same bike she'd seen in the garage, except cleaner and with freshly oiled gears. It was also much nicer than her old bike back home, just like everything else that had anything to do with Hy House. She studied it, thinking it was just about her size, as she sipped the mug of tea delivered by Bridget, a bathrobe thrown about her shoulders and her hair up in an old-fashioned cap.

The night was still close around Hy House, but the sky was perking up slightly—an almost-invisible shift, moment by moment, changing from inky black to lighter indigo, the stars winking out one by one. She could feel the sun coming, its presence a growing glow beyond the trees. Her aunt was right—it would be a stunning morning to watch the sunrise.

Her new mode of transportation had a broad leather seat and comfortable chrome handlebars that would provide her with easy steering. The pedals were wide enough for boots and would give nice leverage. Someone, probably Pat, Em thought, had attached a milk crate onto the back, which, when she inspected the inside, held a pair of binoculars in their sable leather case.

"Mrs. Hewett asked me to give you those so you could 'see what you can see,' as she put it," Bridget said from the doorway.

"Thank you so much, Bridget. And thank Pat for me, please."

"I surely will, but it wasn't a bother, Miss. Pat had more fun scrubbing up that bike for you than I've seen him have for a long while. And it kept him away from fixing the widow's walk's rotted rail. He's nervous when he's up high. He's been avoiding it for months."

"Thank him anyway," said Emily, smiling at the image of Pat being skittish about heights.

Bridget took the empty mug as Emily hopped onto her new steed to practice. On her fourth rotation around the driveway, the sound of bike tires crunching over shells announced Ned, appearing from around the corner.

"Good morning, Em," Ned said, throwing one leg over the side of the gliding bicycle and hopping off, trotting along beside it until it stopped. He was dressed in adventuring gear: tan breeches, a coat buttoned against the chill, and a brown fedora pulled rakishly across his brow. Emily had worn another old Nebraska dress for this adventure as she wouldn't want to tear or dirty one of the newer, fancier ones. Her cloche hat sat firmly on her head and the coat's horn buttons were fastened securely all the way up to her neck. She'd even flung on the scarf her mother had knitted her just last winter (which now felt like an eon ago) and jammed the matching mittens on her hands. Wearing her mother's last gift to her was a little like having Constance along, and her mother had always been game for anything. Although spring had sprung in New England, the predawn breeze had a wash of cold in it that made Em shiver when she wasn't moving.

"You're sure you're up to this, Miss Em?" Ned asked.

"Absolutely. I'm excited," she said, and she was. "Besides, I doubt Isabel would let me get away with staying, even if I felt like it."

They both looked up at the second-floor windows, where a wavering light bloomed in one. A curtain twitched as if someone had just moved it back into place.

"I suppose not," Ned said.

"And could you please dispense with the 'Miss' stuff? I'm just Em."

"Sure thing, Em. And I'm just Ned, in case you had a mind to call me Mr. Cooperson."

"I didn't, but thanks. Maybe Mr. Ned."

"Now that just sounds silly." He glanced over his shoulder at the eastern part of the sky. "We should get started. Time and tide wait for no man!"

Emily climbed onto her bicycle, pushing down heavily in her leather boots, gripping the handlebars as tight as she could in her mittens as she followed Ned's retreating form out the driveway.

"Good luck!" Bridget yelled after them.

Em raised one hand unsteadily into the air and made a wavering left turn, and then she was coasting down Main Street after her escort.

They picked up speed on the hill; the only real obstacles were the potholes. Their tires whispered along the shell-and-dirt road as Em and Ned sailed past the large white pillars of the Methodist church and coasted down the hill. She didn't even have to pedal. The stores on either side closed in on them, dark plate-glass windows displaying inscrutable wares. When they passed the Edgartown Market, a light flickered somewhere in the back. The grocers were beginning their day.

Ned's bell rang out, and Em could just see his left hand jutting straight out as he took a turn, leaving the red-brick bank to their right. Emily faintly remembered this part of the village from her first day walking about with Fiona, but they soon whizzed by the farthest she'd gone and were in new territory.

Stately white mansions behind picket fences flickered by as they picked up speed. Em chanced a look to her right at the great dark blot of the ocean and the harbor stretching away. Although hard to see, she could just make out the shapes of fishing boats on the water, and a faint suggestion of land beyond them.

As they rode, the number of boats on the black skin of the harbor dwindled and then disappeared altogether. Periodically, the lighthouse pierced through the darkness, beckoning them as they rode straight for it on a road that curved along the shore like a length of string. A trill of excitement went up Emily's spine as her heart raced along with the road beneath her tires. She couldn't see anything, but, judging from the brightening glow beyond the farthest hump of dark land, that scenario was about to be remedied.

Along with the consistent pulse of the lighthouse beam, revolving like a bright arm across their path, small lights blinked on here and there and sounds carried oddly in the windless air. Once in a while they could hear the bang of a door slamming or voices coming from an open garage or a dock as the Vineyard's early risers bustled about their tasks.

The road climbed a gentle hill, steep enough that Emily, unused to riding a bike given the past few months and unused to riding up hills at all, soon had to stop and rest, panting, heart fluttering like a trapped sparrow. She gasp-yelled at Ned so that he, too, brought his bicycle to the side of the road and paused, still mounted and twisting around to watch as she unbuttoned her coat and took off her mittens and scarf, stowing them hastily in the crate behind her. She gave him a small wave and they mounted up again, pushing hard to start their momentum on the slope. When they finally crested the top of the hill, Ned gave his bell a triumphant jangle.

A whale of a building grew in front of them, a large hotel of three stories not unlike a wedding cake. There were quite a few lights on behind the clapboard shutters. Ned softly called out "Good morning" to a figure pacing on the hotel's shadowed porch. The shadow raised a hand in silent greeting as they passed. It occurred to Em that she'd never met anyone quite like Ned—so warm and intelligent, so quick to greet a stranger.

Just beyond the hotel, the road veered sharply, and the view of the water disappeared behind an impenetrable wall of green branches as a thicket of hedges, grown to a height well over their heads, ringed a large gray house. Ned slowed his bike so that Emily came abreast of him as they made the turn. He then gestured to the imposing structure with one hand, the other holding his handlebars steady, as they rode close enough to the hedge that Em could've reached out and picked some of their tiny black berries.

"We're here," he said.

Ned pulled ahead as they rounded another corner in the other direction and then slowed his bike to a walking pace to turn into a driveway.

They'd arrived at Ann Simpson's house.

If the hotel behind was a wedding cake, this house was an austerely stunning fortress of wooden gables and turrets. It looked like the backside of a giant sleeping creature, crouched against the elements.

"We can park our bikes here while we go out to the point," Ned said as he glided to a stop, one foot on the pedal as if he was about to dismount a horse. A pretty nifty trick that Em vowed to learn soon.

Using her kickstand, she parked her bike next to Ned's on a driveway covered in the same white shells as the drive at Hydrangea House, hanging the binoculars in their case around her neck.

Ned wore a many-pocketed vest, and he, too, had a pair of binoculars around his neck, though his were much smaller.

"Those are some nice binoculars," he mentioned. "Are they yours?"

Em looked down. "No, they're from Hydrangea House."

"I bet they were Miss Emily's. She always had the nicest things. May I?"

Em nodded as she ducked her head under the thick strap and handed them over.

"Yup, look here." Ned came close and shone a flashlight onto the leather. There were letters embossed there: *ECH*. "Her initials, Emily Chace Hewett."

"Fancy," Em remarked.

"Always," Ned agreed. "I had such a sweet spot for her."

"Did you?"

"Of course! I was heartbroken when she disappeared, as was the rest of the island."

He handed back the case and started pulling various things from the saddlebags on his bicycle, stuffing them into his vest and then slinging an army-style canteen over one shoulder.

"Do you . . . do you want to use them, Ned?" Emily held the case out. "I can use yours."

Ned looked at her, almost startled. "Are you sure?" The darkness behind his glasses hid his expression, and Emily realized she very much wanted to see what it betrayed.

"Sure I'm sure! I'll use yours and you can use these fancy ones."

She smiled as he handed over his smaller binoculars in the dark. "Maybe just for this one time," he said as he shyly accepted, smoothing his hand over the supple leather and tracing the initials.

"You are the professional ornithologist, after all," encouraged Emily.

"I suppose I am." He slung the First Emily's binoculars around his neck with something like reverence.

After patting every last pocket, and adjusting his hat for the hundredth time, Ned pointed the flashlight toward the side of the house where a wall of bushes extended along the perimeter of the lawn. When Ned's beam landed on them, the shadows transformed into a narrow trail snaking through the dunes.

Em peered through one of the bay windows as they went by the house. "Do any of the Simpsons live here now?" she asked, a shiver going through her at the windows' empty glassiness.

"I thought maybe Alphonse would come down early to open the place up, but it looks like no one's in there at all." They passed the covered deck furniture. "When Ann came down over the last few years, she never brought any staff with her. She mostly came alone, or with friends. As of late, she'd come with a serious beau, Garrett. You'll meet him today."

The grass thinned out under their feet as soon as they left the lawn proper, and the path shortly turned to sand.

"She had beaus? Wasn't that frowned upon? Being unmarried and all."

"Well, sure, at first," Ned slowed down as they made their way into the bushes. "Watch these, they've got prickers," he said, gesturing with the flashlight and lighting up a snarl of bright-green branches. "People soon got used to it. And after the war, everyone was so happy just to have survived that a lot of those old social norms fell by the wayside. I'm sure the Woman's Temperance Union wouldn't approve, but as for the rest of us?" Ahead of her, Ned shrugged.

They broke through the bushes onto the beach of a large pond. Beyond it loomed another dune and past that a somber stripe of ocean. On this side of the brackish pond, the dirt and sand was spongy underfoot. Every step she took squished.

Ned stopped and surveyed their environs, aiming the flashlight's beam down at their feet, allowing their eyes to adjust to the semidarkness as he pointed out landmarks. "There's the lighthouse, obviously . . . to the east, the Simpsons' land. There's their dock, and you can just see the shape of *Charleston*, their skiff, at the end of it."

Sure enough, Emily could just see a light shape bobbing at the end of a gray strip in the water.

"This particular cove is excellent for boats. It's always protected, see? Both from sight and storms. And it's deep enough for small craft. There's a cut down by Fuller Street; a boat can get out to sea without going near the inner harbor or even the lighthouse. We're headed"— Ned pointed far to the left, where the gnarled scrub oaks transitioned into taller trees and became a thickened grove—"over to Eel Pond, where they sighted barn owls last spring." He glanced over at her, a shy smile on his lips. "You ready?"

Em nodded. Her fingertips prickled in anticipation.

"For an effective owl observation, you have to use both your eyes *and* your ears," Ned said as they started walking toward the taller trees. "Owls are forest flyers; they're good at flying in contained spaces, like from tree to tree. They are also quiet, as they need to sneak up on sensitive little creatures like mice, rabbits, shrews, and voles. Look for any swooping movements, and listen for the flap of their large wings, which also sort of whistle."

Emily had no idea what a wing whistle sounded like but decided that any unknown sound in the woods would be worth mentioning. Especially a strange whistling sound.

"They also have a particular cry—a high, raspy, shrieky noise. Like this." Ned covered his mouth with his fist and coughed a few times. Then he opened wide and issued the most bizarre shriek that Em had ever heard.

She burst out laughing.

"It's not supposed to be comical, Em. We shouldn't be dithering around."

Emily did her best to get serious.

"We must be really quiet . . . these creatures have unbelievable powers of hearing and sight."

She found this statement ironic, following his previous outburst.

As they walked into the deeper forest, he flicked the flashlight on the path ahead, periodically shining it behind him, gentleman that he was, onto the path just ahead of Em's feet. Emily followed, looking around in wonder at the trees towering twenty feet above her; she felt like she'd entered another world altogether. The sun had not yet come up, and the shadowy depths enveloped her inside different levels of darkness.

Emily hadn't been in many forests in her life, but she knew at once that she would like to spend as much time as possible in their leafy depths. For a girl grown among the tall grasses and bristly cottonwoods of the prairie, this place felt absolutely magical.

When she lowered her gaze from the obscured canopy to the path ahead of her, she just caught sight of Ned and his light disappearing into the undergrowth. She hurried to catch up and followed what seemed to be his route—threading along the hem of the forest. But a large stand of bushes had encroached, and Emily soon realized she'd lost him.

She triple hopped to catch up, feeling overwhelmed, alone as she was within the dark limpid depth of the trees. Spurred on, she beelined around a clump of scrub undergrowth and found Ned stopped in the trail, flashlight off. She froze and tried her best to calm her breathing.

A raspy trill arose from the dewy shadows, sounding like it came from everywhere at once. Ned stashed the flashlight in one of his countless pockets and raised a finger to his lips. She nodded.

Another shriek sounded in the vault of forest overhead, cascading through the branches. It sounded like a continuous rumble, as if the great bird were purring.

Ned beckoned to her, starting off on the sand path around the forest's edge. Emily peered out to sea through the fringe of trees but could barely see anything. Now the two of them were just across the cut, which Em gathered (being a landlubber) meant the passage from this smaller pond through to the ocean. Her guess was right. Here the softly glowing beach ended and the indigo of the sea flooded in, and with it, a shape, moving, blotting out the sand as it rounded the corner to the entrance of the cut.

Em squinted, looked down with eyebrows creased, then looked again.

The purr wasn't coming from an owl in the forest. It was coming from a boat with no lights, a dark shape just entering the cut and heading for Starbuck Neck. Shock and understanding jolted her, and she spun, searching for Ned. Once again, Ned had disappeared into the undergrowth in search of his elusive owl, and she was left behind.

But she wasn't alone this time. *It's always protected, see?* Ned's words floated back into her mind. *Both from sight and storms. And it's deep enough for small craft.*

The rumrunners had joined her in the indigo cut between Eel Pond and the vast, black sea.

Chapter 13

Emily made her way into the forest as speedily as she could, but the predawn trail was hard to see.

"Ned!" she called, peering intently around her while she blazed through the undergrowth, bushes tearing at her skirt and coat as she pushed through. "*Ned!*"

She could see neither hide nor hair of him, not even the watery beam of the flashlight. She stopped in the thick gray dawn, one hand on the lichen-rough bark of the nearest tree. The far-off rumble of the boat coasted by, probably on its way to the Simpsons' dock. What were the gangsters doing *here*?

Em sucked in her breath and gripped the trunk tighter, hurting her palm on the scraggly bark. The drive. Their bikes! The rumrunners would see the bikes in the drive and know someone was there. What would they do if the gangsters came looking for them?

Em shook her head, eyes wide in the near darkness (which made it much easier to imagine thugs pushing into the forest). First things first, she had to find Ned, and fast.

As she focused on the forest in front of her, either her eyes must have adjusted to the low light or the dawn was lightening the air around her, because she could see a definitive trail. Just beyond the last wall of brush, a shape moved, illuminated by a flashlight. Ned.

She took off in as fast a run as she could manage. Flying along, adrenaline and fear made her fleet of foot until she almost fell over a large stone in the center of the path a few yards down. Catching sight of it at the last moment in mid-run, she vaulted instead of tumbling over it, catching herself with an extra-long stride on the other side. Then, in her peripheral vision, she spotted a stock-still and very shocked Ned close to the trail holding up Emily the First's binoculars. She skidded to a stop and turned to meet him.

"Em, did you—" he began.

She silenced him with a finger to her lips. Then, cupping an ear, she leaned in the direction of the Simpsons' house. It was still there—the low grumble of the boat's motor.

"Ned," she said in a soft voice, "a boat with no lights on whatsoever came through the cut, or came in the cut, or however you say it."

Ned gawked at her. Em realized that day was about to dawn because the air around them had brightened enough to see one another. Lichen dappling the violet bark of the scrub oak stood out against the bright spring growth behind it, yet there were still no shadows in the angles and shapes of the forest. And, better still, no rumrunners looking for them or shouting at them. Their bikes hadn't been discovered, or if they had, the gangsters weren't searching the land around the house. Yet.

Ned looked worried, glancing toward the house while stroking his chin. Owl observation was off the docket for the moment. Em thought back to what he'd said the other night at the dinner table, about the gangster's boats and the guns bolted to their decks. Alarm made it hard to breathe.

"Did they see you?" he asked.

"No," she said. "At least I don't think so. But what about our bikes? They're sure to see our bikes in the drive!"

"That's true." Ned threw another worried glance over his shoulder in the direction of Ann's. "Cripes! What do you think they're doing here? Are they using the cove for a hiding spot? Do you think they're going to break into the house?"

"*Ned*," Em whispered fiercely, "how would I know the motivation of a band of rumrunners? Maybe they saw the bikes, realized someone's here, and left again. I don't hear a motor running anymore, do you?"

"We wouldn't, though, would we? Not if they've already tied up and are doing whatever it is they're doing there. What do you think they're doing?" Ned's eyes were huge behind his glasses.

"Again, Ned, I'm not a gangster expert."

They ceased their whispered discourse and looked at each other in horror. The forest became translucent as birds swooped from the tops of the trees down to the path, celebrating the impending arrival of the new day with a sandy dirt bath.

"I think we have to go see what they're doing, Ned." Em knew they couldn't stay here any longer.

Ned shook his head, vehemently and at once.

"All right, then. I'll go alone." She started down the trail, back toward the pond where she could catch sight of the dock. At the same moment, the sun burst from the horizon behind the trees and sorbet-colored light sliced through the forest.

"Hey! Wait up!" Ned whisper-yelled from behind her.

She stopped and whipped her finger to her lips. If their bikes had yet to be detected, it wouldn't do to call attention to their presence with sheer stupidity.

He trotted over. "You can't go alone," he said, keeping his voice low. "Your aunt would never, and I mean *never*, forgive me if anything happened to you."

She nodded, her heart loosening from its straitjacket at the thought. They both stood listening to the cacophony of birds as they eagerly greeted the dawn.

Then they set off, Ned in front, and wound their way back the way they'd come, through the grove of taller trees and then shorter scrub oak to the thicket of rose hip bushes, savage prickers lining their stems. The strong April sun beamed from the horizon in a torrent. Everything stood out clearly—each grain of sand, the ring of murky green seaweed around the brackish blue waters of the pond, the seagulls congregating along the beach, squawking loudly at one another as they fought over rotting fish and crabs. Ned stopped suddenly and put his arm up, barring her path. Em peeked around him.

They were perched on a little spit of land that pushed out into the pond from a clutch of scrappy bushes. Peering through the tangle of thorny stems, they could see the end of the pier and, beyond that, the Simpsons' house. Ned crouched down, craning his neck around the bush, and Em followed suit, lowering herself into the damp sand to peer around him.

Three men ferried boxes up and down the pier, stowing each carefully aboard. The bright morning light glanced off the back of the vessel, where it bobbed behind the Simpson family skiff. This boat wasn't white like the Simpsons', however. It was jet-black. *Better to blend into the shadows*, Em thought.

Ned half turned to her, pointing to her chest, and she looked down at the pair of binoculars hanging there. They both unsnapped their cases and slid the binoculars out. Magnified, Em could see things a lot better. From this angle, the Simpson house looked less like a gargantuan shingled sea creature and more like the estate it really was. Almost entirely made of glass, the whole east side of the first floor faced the ocean (and the sunrise, Em realized) and sported floor-to-ceiling windows, bordered by a stone patio; a sprawling weathered deck wrapped the house around its middle like a belt.

The men were using a door under the deck, moving boxes and whatever was in those boxes (booze most likely) out of the Simpsons' house and onto the boat. But why was it in Ann's house to begin with? Had she known about it? Surely not; it seemed out of character for her, what little Emily knew about her, to harbor rumrunners and let them use her house as a waypoint or storage facility. But that's exactly what it looked like they were doing.

Two of the men wore dark suits, which looked peculiar on a fishing boat amongst the nets and lines. Em wondered if they'd be attending the funeral the next day, and if their suits would smell like fish when they did. Then another man came out of the shadows beneath the porch, lugging a water-stained box, and she forgot about the other two men completely.

Em's mouth dropped open. She recognized him.

She knew only five or six people on this island, and one of them was crouched in the sand in front of her. The man now carrying the box down the stone steps and across the lawn, leaving footprints in the dew behind him, wasn't wearing a suit like the others but a muted-blue sweater, the same peaked fisherman's cap she remembered, and oily-looking trousers. It was Captain Frank Butler, whom she'd seen in Papers. She could almost taste that coffee frappé as she watched him make his way down the pier and clamber over the side of the boat with the grace of someone long accustomed to hopping on and off bobbing seacraft. He was the rumrunner Pat had told her about, the one who'd replaced the engine of his boat (that boat, she realized) with an airplane engine to outrun the coast guard cutters.

One of the other men came out from under the porch behind the captain. He wore a gray suit with a black tie, the matching fedora pulled low over his eyes. Em moved the binoculars over the man's shiny, impractical shoes, and was scanning back for Captain Butler when suddenly the round viewer was filled by Butler's bright-blue gaze, looking straight through the cylinders and into her soul.

She yelped, and Ned spun toward her.

"He saw me!" she said, scooting back in the sand. "He saw me!"

Ned glanced at the pier through the snarly bush. "What do you mean *saw* you?"

"I don't know, maybe a reflection on the lens? Maybe he heard something?" She held up her binoculars. "But he definitely looked right at me! Come on!" She got up and sprinted back down the beach, not even waiting to see if Ned was following her. She made a beeline to the trail back into the forest's dark heart. She'd be safe there.

Once they had dashed back into the depths of the trees, Em slowed by a deadfall covered in honeysuckle vines, then stopped, Ned beside her.

"Do you see anyone following?" Em whispered, leaning over, panting, hands on her knees, heart hammering.

"No, I don't." Ned was in the same panicked, disheveled state. "Do you?"

She glanced over her shoulder. No movement of large shapes beyond the brush. "No, maybe he didn't see"—then she froze.

A cautious shape shifted into view beyond the fringe of trees. He must've run very quickly to reach them so soon. The form moved a few steps, then paused, and moved again. She gripped Ned's forearm as they crouched in unison, watching the figure skirt the outside of their clutch of trees, only a dozen feet away from the large dead one.

Her grip on Ned's arm tightened. When whoever it was came around the log and bushes and saw the trail, they'd know where their Peeping Toms were hiding.

Just as Em thought they were going to be discovered, clutching one another, a horn sounded in the near distance: two short toots and a longer honk. The shadow paused, then turned. Moving an inch to the left, Em could see the shadow's blunt-featured face through a hole in the leaves. His gaze was at his feet and his head was cocked. He was listening, most likely for them.

Seconds ticked by. Birds called to one another, darting about, oblivious, enjoying the fresh new day. Em and Ned remained absolutely still, and so did Frank Butler. A trickle of sweat beaded down the side of Em's neck despite how cold her hands were. The signal sounded again, impatiently, two short and a longer blare.

The shadowed figure flapped a hand at the woods. "All right, all right!" he spat with impatience. They were close enough to see the anger and frustration on his face as he moved past their wall of woven greenery and vines. His fists were balled at his sides, ready to use.

He turned away, walking back the way he'd come. Em's heart lurched as he leaned down briefly next to the point where they had been. The captain looked back once more, and then disappeared behind the brush.

Emily and Ned exhaled a simultaneous sigh of relief. After a few moments, they stood and stretched, unclenching their jaws and unhunching their shoulders. Ned beckoned and they moved deeper into the forest. They walked as silently and quickly as possible for a few minutes, soon passing the boulder in the path, and then Ned turned left, pushing his way through the brambles and holding his forearms in front of his face. Emily followed, issuing breathy little gasps and shrieks as the prickers tore at her calves and scratched her hands. The sunrise painted the top halves of the trees in pink and orange.

After a few minutes of heavy going, they burst through a final thicket to find themselves beyond the hedges lining Ann Simpson's driveway. Her skin stung; her calves and the backs of her hands were now crisscrossed with tiny scratches in hatch marks. Her forehead and cheek throbbed where thorns had swatted her in Ned's wake.

Ned motioned for her to stay close as they skirted the protective ring of hedges. They crept in sight of the dock just in time to see one of the suited men cast off the stern line and leap clumsily into the boat in his slick shoes. Butler's face poked through the open window of the wheelhouse as the boat left the dock, taking care to avoid the much-smaller skiff still tethered there. The boat made a sharp turn into the inlet, opening up the throttle and kicking up a white purl of wake. The captain looked grim as the boat purred back through the cut and out to sea. No name had been painted on the hull, but a strange red shape hovered underneath the bow.

It was hard not to flinch as the men's stony gazes scanned the house and surrounding areas from the retreating boat. And it was hard not to notice the gun one of them wore under his jacket, which had flapped open as they picked up speed. At last they were blessedly cut off from view and the men were gone, their only trace the waves from their wake splashing up on the sand.

Ned and Em returned to their bikes, mounting them as fast as they could and trading glances but saying nothing. They rode back in a dead bike-sprint, hearts pounding and feet pumping as fast as the pedals would allow. Back at Hy House, they skidded into the driveway, finally feeling safe as the trees cut them off from Main Street.

Em dismounted and pulled the binoculars from around her neck. "Well," she said, "that was certainly the most exciting bird-watching expedition I've ever been on." Her heart still galloped painfully in her chest.

"Much agreed," Ned said, cleaning his specs. "But I think we got away scot-free."

"We might've," Em agreed. "Do you think they saw us? Would they even know who we are?"

"Saw yes, recognize no. How could he?"

"It was Captain Butler, wasn't it?"

"It certainly was." As Ned replaced his glasses on his nose, his eyes swam into view as he studied her sliding the binoculars back into their black case. Suddenly his face paled to the color of cottage cheese and his mouth dropped open as his gaze drifted down to the binoculars around his own neck.

"Oh, Em, oh no," he breathed. "The case." Ned held up his own binoculars and Emily's heart jumped back up her throat.

"The case? You didn't, did you?" But she knew the answer.

The smaller binoculars, Ned's pair, had a case whose top threaded through the strap, attaching it even when the binoculars had been removed, leaving the case laying clunkily across the user's chest. But Emily the First's pair were larger, fancier, and came completely free of the case when they were in use. Ned had taken these binoculars out of the case and put the case down—the case with Emily the First's initials inscribed in gold. He'd left it by the pond on the beach where they crouched while spying on the rumrunners. Emily and Ned stared at each other in terror, not finding any words.

Captain Butler hadn't needed to recognize them; he knew exactly who they were.

—

When Emily made it to the kitchen, she found Isabel and Bridget there, sitting at the corner table, each with a mug of tea steaming between their hands, talking about the next day's menu.

"Madam, if I may, Surprise Loaf is too festive a choice for something as somber as a funeral reception," Bridget was saying.

"Which is exactly why we'll be having it!" Isabel said in her no-nonsense voice. "And it's not an Irish wake, Bridget. Let's call it a celebration of Ann's life, and what's more celebratory than Surprise Loaf?"

As with many of Isabel's questions, there wasn't a real answer to this, because she didn't want there to be one.

The women looked up to behold Emily, who, she realized just as their eyes touched on her coat, her mussed hair, her trembling hands clutching her hat by the brim, must've been a sight.

"Miss Em! You're back so early!" Bridget was up and over immediately.

Isabel rose in a more stately manner and walked over to her niece, placing one cool hand on her forearm.

"Whatever has happened to you?" she asked, real concern gleaming in her eyes.

"We found the owl, out on the point, but then we heard something else. We didn't mean to bother anyone! Promise!" Em wailed. She had messed this all up somehow.

"Now, now, my dear, you've had a shock, that's all. Bridget, some tea, please?" Isabel took her in hand, leading her to where Bridget had sat just moments before. Emily sank down gratefully and soon Bridget deposited a hot cup of tea in front of her.

"Thank you, Bridget," Em said. She'd never been so happy to be seated in a kitchen with a cup of tea. So normal, so everyday, so *safe*.

"Now, start at the beginning. I was up when you left with Ned. I saw you ride out on your bicycles and head down Main Street."

The curtains twitching, of course. Em sipped her black tea and felt the sweet warmth go all the way down to the base of her spine.

She told them of their brief encounter with Captain Butler out on the point. It wasn't a long story, and she was only half done with her tea by the time she got to the part when they'd realized he'd left the case at the scene of the crime.

"Crime? What crime? You've done absolutely nothing wrong!" Isabel broke in in her most imperious voice. "It is they who have overstepped."

She stared out the window at the brilliant spring sky as Emily studied her profile. Although more subdued than the frenetic behavior they'd displayed at the sun's rise, the birds were showing a lot of springlike enthusiasm, frantically flying to and fro, building nests and hollering back and forth to one another.

Isabel looked angry, or maybe disturbed, but thoughtful.

"So, it's Frank Butler, that old cad. You know, he's a former schoolmate of mine and Ann's. I cannot believe he would have anything to do with her murder. We played on the beach together when he was still in short pants."

"We didn't see anything *that* conclusive, but it was suspicious. And taking place in a hurry, at Ann's."

"What did you really see?" Isabel asked. "Some men loading up boxes—"

"Undoubtedly liquor," Em stated.

"—from Ann's house to a boat."

"*His* boat."

"All right, his boat. Suspicious, yes," Isabel said. "But only of running illegal liquor, not of murder. And the fact that we've been friends for forty years might explain why he felt like he *could* use Ann's house for his operation."

"Illegal bootlegging operation is what it is," Bridget said from the stove in her most disapproving tone.

"But that's not the same as murder," Isabel said to both of them. "No matter *how* suspicious. I do hope it's not him. And you say he recognized you?"

"Not me; I've never met him. I saw him at Papers with Fiona but I doubt he'd remember that. But he saw *someone* watching him, and he followed us, but didn't find us. We hid."

"Well then, you have had an exciting morning."

"I'll say." Em slurped the rest of her tea, teeth aching with the unstirred sugar at the bottom. "And he found the binocular case. I saw him lean over. It had to be the case."

"Emily's case."

"Yes."

"That was foolish." Isabel cut her plum-colored eyes at Emily.

"Agreed." Em hadn't told her aunt that it was Ned who'd left the case. No point in telling her now. It would just come off as defensive.

"Nothing to be done about it, however." Isabel flapped her hand in the air. "Captain Butler is a rumrunner, that's certain. I have tasted some of his wares myself, so I won't paint myself too much into a hypocritical corner." She glanced over at Bridget, who was rolling out dough and didn't look up. "I do *not* think he is a murderer, although dipping one's toe into the criminal pool can sometimes lead to a full immersion. I could be bent to accept the fact that he might have killed *someone* in a shoot-out or in one of their ghastly late-night chases. But murder Ann? And for what reason?"

Emily looked at her, waiting to see if the pieces fell together. "To keep his operation under wraps is the obvious motive," she supplied. "He was using her place, she found out, he killed her to keep it up. Ned said it was the perfect spot—out of sight of the harbor, protected from view and the weather."

"Yes, that's true, it is fairly protected. But there are plenty of out-of-the-way coves and other docks and houses that go with them. It didn't have to be Ann's. This morning you must've surprised him."

"He did look rather surprised," Emily conceded, still feeling unsettled from the adrenaline of all the running and biking. "And angry. Very angry."

"Angry enough to kill?"

Em met Isabel's gaze straight on and thought about it for a moment. Then she shrugged.

"It can't have been the usual run they were on," Isabel said. "They must have been moving things in a hurry, probably because Ann's family is coming. And our good Ned, where is he?"

"He was going to come in and explain, but he checked the time and said he had to ride straight home. Some birding business he claimed. I think he was just embarrassed it all went so poorly on his watch."

Isabel glanced at the petite silver watch pinned to her green-striped morning coat. "Oh my! He's right! Tempus fugit! A quarter past eight already? My word." She rose and glided through the kitchen in her polished gold slippers. "We must stow this to dust off later, my dear. I'm off to dress. I'm sorry you've had a fright. Why don't you soak in the tub to soothe your nerves?" She paused at the double doors. "The game, Emily, is most definitely afoot. Let's keep an eye on our dear Captain Butler tomorrow afternoon, you and I, and see how he plays this out with me. Bridget, when you have a moment?"

And then she was gone, and the door swung closed with a definitive *swish*.

Bridget looked up from where she was rolling another lump of dough into a flat circle on the counter, her forearms covered in flour and a coil of reddish-silver hair springing from her head at an odd angle. Emily brought Isabel's discarded mug to the sink with her own. Bridget gave Em a speculative look, part wary, part kindness, but she didn't say anything to contradict her mistress, and neither did Emily.

Back upstairs, for once Em was in perfect agreement with her aunt. A nice soak in a hot tub of water sounded ideal. The water stung her welts and scratches, but eventually they subsided to a muted throb, and she relaxed for the first time in hours. It wasn't until she had been floating around in the still soapy water for fifteen minutes that it struck her—if she was right and Captain Butler was the culprit, then that meant he was willing to kill Ann Simpson because *she* knew about his rumrunning business. What would a person like that do to someone who was caught spying on them and knew about *both* crimes?

She sunk her head underwater, wishing it could wash her clean of this whole business. It sounded like Butler would do just about anything to keep his operation under wraps. Em let loose a tiny trail of bubbles, watching them float up and burst on the surface. The captain had looked surprised when she'd trained the binoculars on him. Surprised and angry. Maybe even angry enough to kill. *How can I know the motivations of a rumrunner?* she thought as she sat up, water sluicing off her head and shoulders. She hardly knew him.

Chapter 14

The following day—Saturday, April 27, 1929—at a quarter past ten, Isabel Hewett exited her house with Emily and walked the forty or so yards to the Methodist church. Em felt she was appropriately costumed in an emerald cotton dress (Em the First's) and unfamiliar patent-leather Mary Janes on her feet. The new shoes didn't pinch, but their soles were smooth and Em kept sliding around in them. They would've been worse in wet weather, although the day had decided to contradict the mood of a funeral.

Instead of the gloom and rain that had lingered all week, the surprisingly warm sun was making everyone uncomfortable in their drab funeral clothes. Em could almost hear the scraggly rose stems growing in the warmth, winding around the pickets of the white fences, and the new leaves unfurling from the apple tree's low-hanging branches as they passed. There were buds, and, in a few weeks, they would burst forth into splendid blossoms.

The four pillars of the church, like ancient oaks, looked even more massive up close, rising to support a broad clockface topped with four slender spires. As they neared the stretch of brick that fronted the church's white marble stairs, an older man in an ill-fitting gray suit and hat broke away from one of the various groups and pairs scattered about.

Isabel slowed a little, leaning in. "Here we go," she murmured to her niece.

As the man walked briskly over, his watch chain winked in the sunlight where it rode on his small, rounded paunch. "Mrs. Isabel Hewett, what an absolute honor," said the man, a wizened male version of the cheeky mountain climber in the picture of Ann in the Alps. "It has been overly long. Altogether *too* long." He was rumpled; his jacket wrinkled as if he'd slept in it, and his eyes were ringed with circles, the damp skin underneath purple with sadness.

"Oh, James, this is an utmost tragedy. My condolences are numerous and heartfelt, I assure you." Isabel clasped hands with Mr. Simpson. "This is my niece and ward, Em Cartwright."

"Of course, pleased to meet you," Mr. Simpson said, freeing one hand to doff his hat at her, showing his bald and liberally freckled pate. "Please find your way inside and sit up near the front, Isabel, with the close family and honored friends. Maisie will give you a program at the door." He held Isabel's hand a moment more, then dropped it, moving away.

Isabel threaded her arm through Em's as they climbed the steps, the broad pillars flanking them like ancient sentinels. The spring sunlight seared their backs as they took the steps slowly. Although the temperatures weren't particularly high, after a cold damp winter, the warm weather was stifling.

Inside, Maisie waited at the base of a set of double stairs, each leading away from the center to two sets of doors that opened into the church proper. She was poised where the staircases met in the middle, holding a stack of white paper, wearing an indigo silk dress with a dropped waist, a large blue silk flower pinned to her bodice, and a navy hat to match. Her eye makeup wasn't as intricate or bold as it had been at their dinner together, and her fake beauty mark had disappeared. She looked younger and, Em thought, prettier.

"Hello, Maisie," Isabel said.

"Good morning, Mrs. Hewett. Thank you so much for coming." Maisie wore a jeweled bracelet and a faint smile on her shiny lips as she handed over the program. "Hullo, Em. How did it go on the owl hunt?"

Em plastered a natural smile across her face and made sure that her voice was even. "Actually, we saw one. Or Ned did."

"Thank you for the program," Isabel said as she pulled Em toward the stairs. "We shall catch up with you at Hydrangea House afterward."

They mounted the right-hand stairs with Isabel in front as Maisie turned her attention toward an elegant-looking couple in their thirties, a child between them. When Emily and Isabel stepped inside the main hall of the church, Em's heart stopped, and then started again, double the speed. It was all so familiar but so strange at the same time. It had only been four months since her mother's funeral in the simple wooden Methodist church, all straight lines and practicality, but the two affairs couldn't have been more different.

The space was impressive. The ceiling stretched away above them, soaring almost fifty feet. Two aisles threaded through the pews to a simple stage with an even simpler altar at the back. For Ann's memorial, a wooden table topped with a giant silver punch bowl frothing with flowers took up most of the space, a spotlight trained on the blooms. Indeed, the fiery reds, sunny yellows, lambent corals, and violet-blues were the brightest things in sight.

There had been a big to-do about getting the flowers here on time. The whole household had been in an uproar for many hours while Bridget fielded calls from Thankful and sent Pat on missions to the poor florist downtown, who could not have possibly gotten this caliber of bloom on such short notice. No, these were Boston blossoms, and they'd come with a hefty price tag, since the florist's son had to ride all night like Paul Revere to get them here on time.

The church's first three rows were already filled up and almost half of the rest of the pews were occupied as well. Isabel set off like a great ship in full sail down the aisle, nodding to those she knew, Em at her elbow. At the front, they made their way to seats in the center. Isabel sat with a rustle as she clasped her purse in one hand and the program in the other. She gazed at the clutch of flowers sprawling from the punch bowl. On an ancient wooden easel perched a portrait of Ann, looking almost straight on. Once again Em was struck by the wide-eyed hopefulness and general mischievousness that grin exuded.

Em nudged Isabel. "How old was she there?"

Isabel glanced at the portrait as she snapped open her black purse. "I don't know, about seventeen or eighteen, I believe." She took out a pair of glasses and a handkerchief, stashing it up the sleeve of her black silk dress. She leaned over to push her bag underneath the seat and when she straightened, she needed to dab at her eyes with the handkerchief. "Oh, Ann," she said softly, replacing the hanky and putting her glasses on to read the program.

Murmurs filled the high-ceilinged space as Em looked around as inconspicuously as she could from the front row. The organ started up suddenly in the balcony, a low thrum reverberating in the deepest chord, the organist just letting them know he was there. Behind her and nearing the outer aisle, she spotted Ned and waved to him in a manner she hoped was subtle yet enthusiastic. He was wearing a tidy-looking tweed and looked less terrified than the last time she'd seen him.

"How are you?" he mouthed across the space between them. Beside him, a toddler squirmed in her mother's lap, trying to get Ned's attention.

Em held up her hand and made a seesawing motion to tell him she was all right. Then she nodded at him, mouthing, "You?"

He nodded, with a slight smile, and drew the back of his hand across his forehead: "Phew."

Em nodded, agreeing only halfway. He had left behind the case after all. Foolish, as Isabel had said. When Em turned frontward again, Isabel handed her the program.

It was only one piece of paper, a thick stock, with deeply embossed letters. *In Memoriam*, it read, *of Ann Eliot Simpson, 1872–1929*. Below this, Em was startled to see her own name staring up at her from underneath a poem.

> That is solemn we have ended,—
> Be it but a play,
> Or a glee among the garrets,
> Or a holiday,
>
> Or a leaving home; or later,
> Parting with a world
> We have understood, for better
> Still it be unfurled.
>
> —Emily Dickinson

The poem took Em's breath away in its simple elegance, as much as the celestial airiness of the nave had moments before. She'd come across some poets in her studies with Constance, but mostly English poets of a certain century that wrote about places far away and people long dead. She'd never had such slight words find their way so quickly into her heart. *Emily Dickinson*, she repeated to herself, memorizing the name to look for in Isabel's libraries later.

"I wish they'd picked a more recent photo," her aunt murmured from beside her. "It looks like we're memorializing a teenager."

Em looked around and realized that this is what they'd been doing for Isabel's daughter only five or six years ago, and probably in this church. She didn't mean to always be thinking back to Emily the First, she just came up all the time. Em studied her aunt's profile, the lines of grief that perhaps had softened some but never fully disappeared. The grief was there for good; a subtle type of haunting, to be sure.

The organ's low chords began to take shape, and soon the organist was playing a familiar hymn as the pastor made his way to the front. The church was almost full to bursting now, and the crowd's thrum petered out into anticipatory silence.

From the altar, the pastor began to speak, the usual lines about darkness and shadows, and losing a companion too soon. Then Mr.

Simpson joined him onstage, where he tearily intoned about his daughter, her public triumphs and private kindnesses, his pride and love of her, and his great, irreparable loss. When Mr. Simpson had finished telling them about Ann's bravery and temerity, Maisie helped him back to his seat.

Isabel was making great use of the handkerchief she'd brought, and Em could feel her shoulders shaking.

At the end of the service, the organist broke into the familiar chords of "Jerusalem" as people collected hats, purses, and children. As Isabel retrieved her purse and rose to leave, she reached for Em, who grabbed her hand, steadying her, and feeling glad she was able to do so.

"You all right?" asked Em. Her aunt's violet eyes were lined and red, her nose shiny like a ripe cherry.

"I'll be fine," Isabel returned. "Let's use the vestry entrance to get home before the horde descends."

Em couldn't have agreed more.

They pushed past Mr. Simpson and Maisie with a few murmurings of "pardon" and "thank you" and went down a set of stairs hidden behind the stage, crossing a polished wooden floor and exiting out the back of the church into a packed-dirt parking lot. Along with a couple of carts and a few Model As, a singular car sat awaiting its occupants.

"Will you take a look at that," Em breathed.

Chrome wrapped the snout of the car, gleaming in the spring sun.

Isabel, already at the gate connecting the parking lot to the gardens of Hy House, *ahem*ed to get Em's attention. "Waiting."

Emily took one more glance at the mysterious car and trotted to catch up.

"Good," Isabel commented as they climbed the front steps. "John Patrick swept the porch. Much better."

The reception was to start almost immediately after the memorial and go until around three in the afternoon. After leaving Isabel in the drawing room, Em visited the kitchen—a flurry of activity with

Bridget at the helm commandeering Fiona and two other young girls in starched white shirts and black skirts who listened to her every directive with round, obedient eyes.

"One pan of biscuits out, a new one in, Felicity," commanded Bridget as Emily pushed through the double doors. "My saints, you're back!" Bridget paused in her task of smearing white icing on three rectangular cakes. "That means the guests are coming." Her voice grew tremulous as she slapped down her knife, untied her apron, and rushed by Em and through the doors. "I must see what she'll be wanting before everyone arrives."

Emily came over to where Fiona was piping pink cream into pastry shells. "Hello, Fi!"

"Em, so much has gone on!" Fiona glanced up from the sheet pan and her fiery gaze crawled all over Em's face. "But what happened to you, got in a fight with a pricker bush?"

Emily's hand went to her cheek, to the painful ridges left from yesterday's dawn mission. "Oh dear. Something like that. I went owl hunting with my cousin Ned." She thought the cuts had gone down some. "Are they very noticeable?"

"Only to me. No one else will notice." Fiona grinned at her. "Owl hunting. Sounds exciting."

"It was."

"You must tell me about it soon." She laid the icing piper on the counter and opened up its back end, spooning in more of the pink mixture.

When she'd finished spooning, Fiona introduced the other two kitchen and serving helpers for the afternoon, Miranda and Felicity, different as night and day—the former a wisp of a thing with close-set green eyes, and the latter a woman approaching thirty with sable hair in a tight hairnet at the back of her skull.

"Can I help?" asked Emily, feeling out of place with empty hands.

"The best thing for you to do," Fi said, picking up the piping bag again and moving on to the last tray of pie shells, "is to enjoy yourself and keep an eye on Mrs. Hewett. You're joining us at Dreamland tomorrow?" Fiona asked as Em headed toward the front of the house.

"Wouldn't miss it," Em smiled, pushing through the double doors.

As Bridget bustled by in the hallway, muttering to herself, Emily realized she hadn't asked Isabel for permission to go to Dreamland yet. She hoped it wouldn't be a problem as the slick soles of her Mary Janes slid down the hallway.

When she popped her head into the drawing room, Connor had appeared at his mistress's side and sat expectantly on his silk cushion at her feet. Isabel looked the portrait of solemn respectability in her high-necked purple mourning dress. It matched her eyes perfectly, which, Em was certain, had not been a mistake.

"We must be vigilant," Isabel said as Emily crossed the room. "We have a few suspects to contend with this afternoon."

"Who?" Emily sat across from her aunt in the other armchair. Platters had been spread across most available surfaces, and Connor was not interested in a single one of them, proving once again that he was the most unusual dog she'd ever met.

"Captain Butler should be dropping by, and Maisie is still not off my list. It's a sizable fortune we're talking about. Neither is her favorite gentleman du jour, Daniel Sykes. And he's a sailor."

"All right," Em said. "Captain Butler, Maisie, her suitor. Anyone else?"

"You must remember, my dear, that everyone is under the assumption that Ann died by accident, not by someone else's hands. This may mean that the culprit, the real culprit, whoever they are, will be more careless than they would be if her death had been deemed an actual murder."

Emily was not about to point out that it was really *they*, she and Em, who were acting under the assumption of murder. It would be parsing the point too fine.

"We haven't much time," Isabel said, that familiar gleam lighting up her eyes. She glanced out the window, where smudgy dark shapes approached from various directions. "Keep a weather eye out for anything strange. John Patrick is directing traffic. He expects most to arrive by foot, but in case a few would like to park, he's ready."

"And so are we," Em said.

"Yes. We are," Isabel returned. And from her expression, it was clear that she meant it.

Emily was glad that at least one of them did.

Chapter 15

The first guest to arrive wasn't Em's personal favorite of the various islanders she'd met in her short time here. It was Mrs. Pritchard, the piano teacher. She hustled through the front door as soon as Emily opened it with the same unkempt owl impression she'd given the first time Em had met her.

"Who?" the older woman said, her white hair sprigging up in odd angles all over her head.

Em couldn't respond. So complete was the avian impression that she believed, for a second, that Mrs. Pritchard now only spoke owl. Then she understood the woman's meaning. "I'm Emily. Em, I mean. Em Cartwright. We've met once before in the Edgartown Market, Mrs. Pritchard, or just outside of it. Don't you remember?"

"Oh, yes, of course. I thought your name was Frances." The woman's hands clasped together in front of her and her thin lips poked out. "The hothouse flower's daughter?"

"Her name *is* Frances, Honoria, and it is also Emily," came a voice from behind them.

Isabel stood on the threshold of the drawing room, looking as patrician as ever. Connor's long snout peeked out from behind the jewel-toned folds of her skirt. She smiled indulgently at Mrs. Pritchard. "And so we've landed on Em. Haven't we, Em?"

Emily gave a small nod.

"Bridget has prepared refreshments, and they are in the drawing room. Won't you join me?"

At the mention of refreshments, Mrs. Pritchard stopped studying Emily with her saucerlike eyes and peered through the open drawing room door to assess the table.

"Shall we, Honoria?" Isabel swung her skirt in a semicircle and accompanied her guest through to the drawing room, Connor leading the way.

A few moments after Mrs. Pritchard's arrival, Maisie and Mr. Simpson approached from the sidewalk. Emily saw them and flung open the door, trotting down the steps to help Maisie lead Mr. Simpson inside. The older man was still on his feet, but barely.

"He's all done in," Maisie said across her father's bowed back as Em took his other arm. "After the service, we made the mistake of going out the front, and everyone wanted a word with him. He'll be right as rain in a moment."

Mr. Simpson perked up as the three of them started up the steps. He shook them off gently, resetting his hat and navigating the stairs and porch on his own steam.

"Why don't you bring him into the drawing room, Maisie?" Em suggested.

From her post on the front stoop, Em saw more people appearing around the tall sycamores of Hy House: Ned and a man in a hickory-colored suit looking sad, a woman with a toddler, a few others trickling in.

Emily held open the front door as Ned came bounding up the steps.

"Hullo, Em. How are you?"

"Fine, Ned, thanks."

"Better than the last time?" he said.

"Immensely."

There was an awkward pause as the other man took Emily in, and apparently found her wanting, because he threw his overcoat at her as if she were the help. Ned was astonished and quickly took the coat back from Em.

"Oh my, no. There's been a misunderstanding," Ned fumbled,

handing the coat back to the man, who looked confused and a little put out. "This is Em Cartwright, the niece of the house. Em, let me introduce Garrett Winterholler, the late Miss Simpson's fiancé."

The tall, spidery fellow leaned forward, taking Em's hand in his own. "Apologies, Miss." His voice sounded like it came from a throat lined with barbed wire. "Charmed."

Ah yes, Em thought, *Ann's beau*. "Margerie can take your coats for you." Em nodded to the young woman who had appeared behind her, the final complement to the staff this afternoon. "Isabel is in the drawing room where there are some things to eat, and there's more, I'm told, in the dining room."

"Thanks, Em," Ned said, as he led Mr. Winterholler away. Emily studied the back of Garrett's very finely tailored suit as the men found their way down the hall. Blandly handsome, she supposed, but certainly no John Patrick, and clearly more presumptuous. *There's no accounting for taste*, came one of Constance's favorite adages, and Emily wondered if she could hold on to them all her life. She hoped so.

Guests were arriving in earnest now, many of them pink cheeked and perspiring, fanning themselves with their hats or the programs from the service. The woman came in with her toddler, who was so adorably oblivious to the solemn circumstances surrounding the occasion that she danced around happily underneath the chandelier, making every gloomy face in the room smile at her pleased giggles. Emily directed the mother and daughter to the dining room first, to spare her aunt from the tiny Thumbelina's erratic movements and piercing questions about everything that came into view.

After these two, the onslaught of arrivals became torrential. As Isabel predicted, the horde descended. Mainlanders and islanders alike appeared out of the woodwork. Emily stood at her post at the blue front door, swinging it open with a smile when she heard steps outside. Once in a while, a fragrant gust of spring sea wind blew in behind the guests, clinking the chandelier crystals musically against one another.

She lost track of who came through as the crowd grew to around fifty people, Emily guessed, and then swelled to as many as seventy. Isabel had set out framed pictures of her friend—Ann in the Alps included, Em noted—in each room with a small lit candle near each as a reminder of the occasion. The ebb and flow of reserved conversation grew livelier as time wore on.

After about an hour as greeter, Pat came through the front door, looking sharp in an olive-green tweed jacket and a subdued blue plaid underneath.

"Hello, Em," Pat said. "How's the bike? Working all right?"

"Perfectly, Pat, thank you. Runs like a dream."

"That's how I like them. Speaking of dreams, you'll be joining us at Dreamland tomorrow, will you not?"

"I will," Em said, making a mental note to ask her aunt as soon as possible. "It's boxing, right?"

He grinned, transforming once more into his James-Cagney alter ego. "It certainly is, and we'll be seeing Aloysius Gonzaga, the Albany Albatross, versus Ed Garrigan, the Irish Hand." He danced in the momentarily empty entryway, pumping his fists like a boxer. She laughed.

"It'll be my first boxing match."

"You and Fi can watch or not. There's plenty to do in Oak Bluffs for a few hours, and it will be my honor to escort you." Pat stopped pretend boxing and gave her a little bow. As he did so, a lock of hair fell onto his forehead, and when he looked up, her heart raced. Steps clomped up the stairs outside.

"I'll take care of the front door, Em. Consider yourself at ease," Pat said, raking his fingers through his hair to put the errant lock in its place. "And we'll leave at one p.m. tomorrow, so be ready."

"Wouldn't miss it!" she said, relieved to be off duty. She headed to the dining room, ready for something to eat. The space had been rearranged to accommodate more guests, of which there were about fifteen or so perched or standing in various animated clusters around the room. The table had been shoved up against the far wall, covered in a spotless white cloth and festooned with all the silver platters and bowls Hy House had to offer. The bouquet from the memorial service, still in its punch bowl, now displayed its finery center stage, making even the silver service seem a little less grand.

Murmured conversation wound around Emily as she approached the table, picking up a plate from the stack on one corner. Before her lay treats of every shape and style—bowls of candied fruit, tiers of marzipan, a decadent glazed ham topped with honey-soaked pineapple rings, plates piled high with steaming boiled potatoes, brussels sprouts bathing in buttery pools, and steaming biscuits wrapped in tea cloths, nestled inside baskets.

At the center of the buffet sat three cakes, one with petals from the bouquet caught in its icing. They weren't complicated looking, just simple rectangles covered in pastel-pink cream. Em was surprised that there wasn't a fancier dessert on the table but was willing to give Bridget's creation a try. She picked up the silver serving knife and sliced into the cake's frosted exterior. When she pulled the piece away, a bright-green slurry spilled out from inside of the cake.

"Ugh!" Em gasped before she could stop herself, fumbling the serving knife, which evaded her grasp and landed with a clatter.

The green sludge could've been relish, or sauerkraut, or maybe even seaweed, and it oozed down the front of the cake like the viscous path of a snail. These weren't cakes, whatever they were.

Emily, thoroughly embarrassed and determined to seem at ease, decided to give it a try, in spite of its loathsome appearance. She scooped up the piece and plopped it onto her waiting plate, doubling down by spooning some of the green slurry over her slice as if it were caramel sauce or gravy. When she bravely popped a bite into her mouth, she immediately discovered that this was indeed a loaf, not a cake, and there was nothing sweet about it.

The icing seemed like a mixture of mayonnaise and cream cheese with a touch of tomato paste for color, she guessed, moving the stuff around her mouth, and the sponge cake, or what Em had thought was sponge cake, was actually sliced white bread. The real kicker, however, was the layer of green ooze in the middle, which revealed itself to be relish, equal parts tangy and sweet, that mixed with the other flavors in the most horribly surprising way possible.

As Emily chewed, concentrating on pushing the bolus of food down her throat, a tinkling noise drew her attention. At one end of the room, Mr. Winterholler stood with a cut-crystal glass, tapping it with a spoon: *ting ting ting*. One of Isabel's favorite paintings—a huge oil of a shipwreck—spread over the wall behind him. Conversations fluttered to a standstill, save the ambient noise drifting across the foyer from the drawing room.

"Excuse me, everyone," he said, setting his glass and the spoon down on a side table nearby. "I'd like your attention, please." As guests made their way to the edges of the room, creating space around him, Garrett smiled and put out his hands in front of him in what he must've hoped was a supplicating manner, but it made him look more like an usher than anything else. "I'd like to tell you about my Ann."

There was a murmur of appreciation through the crowd.

"If you didn't know Ann, you've probably heard about her, or heard one of her stories. She was a fearless spirit, one never to turn down an offer of adventure. This was coupled with her sharpness, a cleverness and confidence that she could use to unearth whatever it was that she was looking for. Unfortunately, she usually succeeded."

The appreciative murmurs turned to chuckles as people glanced at one another in agreement. Maisie dabbed at her eyes where she stood leaning against the doorway, and Em found herself softening to Garrett after the mix-up at the door—it had obviously been a hard week for him. She knew what it was like to lose somebody, after all. The fogginess it brought.

Suddenly, the front door flew inward and a trio entered the foyer—two men and a woman—filling the space in an instant. As Em studied them from her lookout in the corner of the dining room, an inkling of unease unraveled in her stomach.

"Many people haven't heard about how Ann and I met. Or remet, I mean," Mr. Winterholler went on, oblivious to the new arrivals. His voice was still raspy, like he'd just gotten over a terrible case of laryngitis. "As some of you know, it's difficult for me to speak for extended periods, due to the injuries I sustained in France." He coughed in his fist and forged on. "We knew each other thirty years before, Ann and I, but it was in France, in the Meuse, that we met again, on the battlefield. She was the ambulance driver, and I the wounded soldier. Imagine my surprise to look up and see a face from my childhood at my side."

The horrible bite of the cake-loaf-travesty sat in Em's belly like a brick. The three strange guests moved into the dining room together, and the two men's shoulders seemed impossibly wide as they just squeezed through the doorframe.

"My Ann was formida—" When Garrett Winterholler caught sight of the interlopers, his raspy voice failed into nothingness, and he had to start his sentence over. "My Ann was the bravest girl I ever knew, and without her, I wouldn't be here today." His broad, nice-guy-next-door face grew taut around the edges.

The tall man in the middle of the unknown trio, the one in charge, scanned the room with his chin angled up, eyes slits. When his gaze swept across her, Em didn't breathe, even though his dark eyes were barely visible under the shadowy brim of his hat. When he got to Maisie, he stopped, stared, and smiled—a long, slow grin. Maisie went pink and smiled back.

The brunette beside him had ruby-red lips and a brown fur jacket, too hot for the season and especially the day, thrown across her shoulders. When she scowled at Maisie, her mouth made an upside-down U. The main guy fastened his gaze on Winterholler, who was mopping his brow with a handkerchief, and made a little twirly motion with his hand.

Em thought of the men on Butler's boat, and the one wearing the wrong kind of shoes. She hadn't seen those men at the funeral, but Emily was pretty sure these were them. The bald one in the black fedora looked familiar, with his smashed-in nose and red ears.

"Ann was a shooting star," Garett continued with just one more moment of hesitation. He smiled, but it didn't quite come off as natural, and sweat gleamed at his hairline. "She was so curious and wise, an odd combination that got her into outrageous capers." Outright laughter greeted this proclamation. "She was . . ." Winterholler's voice was barely above a whisper and the crowd's chuckles drowned him out. "She was," he started again when they settled, "a brief burst of light and then gone. My muse. Please raise a toast to Ann, may she be with us always and may her memory be a blessing."

People raised their teacups and champagne stems in a unified toast, a few murmuring "here, here" in the audience. Em had nothing to toast with, so she stayed quiet and unobtrusive, watching the scene unfold. With a small bow, Garrett put his hand over his heart to the smattering of applause. The three strangers clapped as well, too slowly. Garrett immediately hustled over.

"Mr. Aringa! Rosso!" Garrett greeted them. "What a surprise!"

An excited whisper swept the room as people commented to their neighbors.

"Winterholler," the man said, reaching out to grasp Garrett's forearm. He leaned in, hard. "We thought we might find you here. We've come to check things. I hear there's been trouble?"

Winterholler paled. The men were around the same size—tall—but something about Aringa's bearing or maybe the cut of his suit made him seem broader, more powerful. He was definitely the one in charge, even from Em's vantage point tucked into the corner.

"Yes, a bit." Garrett put his hand over Aringa's and turned him toward the hallway. "But I'd be remiss if I didn't introduce you to your hostess first."

With one more appraising glance at Maisie, who simpered under his gaze, Aringa allowed himself to be led out of the room. The red-lipped woman followed, hissing at Maisie, trailed by the large slab of a man.

"Who were *they*?" murmured a middle-aged woman in a crushed crepe hat to her companions when the men were gone.

"I haven't the foggiest," her friend replied. "But definitely from away."

A third woman chimed in. "I've heard about the ringleader. I think they call him 'Rosso.' From New York."

"By way of Italy?"

The women giggled into their champagne flutes.

Em decided she didn't want to miss her aunt's introduction to the newcomers. She abandoned her plate with the half-eaten loaf on a nearby table and followed a curious group across the hall.

The drawing room was another picture-postcard: guests in well-cut cotton or tweed with teacups or champagne flutes and ornate plates were arranged against a background of teal and gold wallpaper and the ever-present art, like a tableau of how life should be, if they hadn't been celebrating on such a somber occasion. The large dark shapes of the three strangers once again stood in the center of the room, taking up all the oxygen, as Winterholler led them over to where Isabel perched.

A cellist played Chopin's "Nocturne, Es-Dur" at an appropriate distance to where Isabel was seated in her red leather armchair by an unlit fireplace. Connor, as well, had not changed position, but Em did see him snap up a dropped sugar cookie, proving he was a dog after all.

Isabel saw her enter, and her face lit up.

"Niece!" she said, extending her hand. "Allow me to introduce our guests, all the way from Sicily!"

"New *Yawk*, actually," said the gentleman, with his hat in his gloved hand, his thick accent making the name sound strange.

"Pleased to meet you," Em said. "Em Cartwright." She allowed herself a small curtsy.

"Charmed." The man's eyes barely touched her. "Mrs. Hewett, thank you for your warm welcoming. We're sorry to intrude on such a somber affair"—*somber* came out *sombah*—"but we were in the neighborhood and wanted to deliver a message. To you."

Next to him, Winterholler looked uncomfortable, his nervous gaze flitting from one face to the next. He excused himself, saying he needed to get back to the guests.

As Aringa spoke, Emily caught sight of another guest entering the room, and shock telescoped her vision into a swarm of shadowy black bees. It was Captain Butler, closing the front door behind him and scanning the groups of people, looking for someone.

"When I heard of poor Miss Simpson's unfortunate accident," Aringa said, "I felt I should pay my respects."

Butler saw the group in the drawing room and walked quickly toward them, taking off his hat so his coarse brown hair fell over his forehead. In his left hand he gripped the binocular case. A bowling ball settled into Em's abdomen.

"I have to tell you," Aringa continued, "I find this island full of people who like to put their noses into other people's business. I'm sorry for your loss. From all accounts, she was a good friend, even if she *was* a reporter."

Isabel didn't say a word, but Em swore her eyes got brighter by a few degrees. "Whatever do you mean, Signor Aringa?"

"Just that certain people should keep to their own, that's all," the tall man said, rocking back on his heels.

Captain Butler had been waiting to get her aunt's attention, shifting from foot to foot, light-blue eyes locked on Em, who squirmed miserably at her post next to Isabel's armchair. She felt a slight pressure on her leg and looked down, surprised to see Connor sitting next to her, leaning in—to give her courage perhaps.

"I say again, signore, to whom are you referring?" Isabel returned evenly, eyes still blazing.

Aringa cocked his head, not intimidated at all. "That's what Winterholler was saying, wasn't he? Before he skedaddled? That Miss Simpson was often precocious"—he drew out the sibilant sounds of the word like a snake.

"Isabel!" Captain Butler broke in.

Mr. Aringa's face spasmed, incredulous, and the big man behind him slid a paw under his jacket. Aringa stilled him with a cold look.

"Captain Butler," Isabel said, rising but still looking at Aringa, "you are interrupting our conversation."

"I apologize. I cannot wait any longer. I came to return this to you and to warn you." Butler looked hard at Emily, but his gaze softened as he glanced back at Isabel. "You must keep a better watch on your possessions, if you hope not to lose them. Again."

With that he spun on his heel and left as quickly as he'd come, leaving the front door open in his wake for the other guests slowly trickling out.

"My, my," Isabel murmured. "Everyone and their warnings." She handed the case to Em.

"I too will take my leave as I consider my message received, Mrs. Hewett," Aringa said.

"Yes, why don't you," Isabel agreed.

Aringa bowed his head, and then he and his two friends followed Butler through the open doorway and into the overly warm afternoon, the woman's heels *clacking* across the porch.

A moment later, amidst the interested mutterings swelling around them, Ned joined Isabel and Emily by the disused hearth, polishing his glasses as he walked over. When he put them on, his eyes snapped into focus and, at the sight of the binocular case, widened even more.

"Captain Butler just returned our binocular case," Em said, her voice wavering.

"Yes," Ned said, concern creasing his forehead. "I saw him leaving. I'm so sorry I forgot it out on the point. Did he think it was you?"

Isabel's face grew solemn as she looked from one to the other. "So it was *you* who left the case by the point, and not our Em."

For some reason Emily didn't mind when Isabel called her that.

Ned looked abashed. "I did, Isabel, I was so overwhelmed,

what with, first, seeing a barn owl and then all the fuss with the rumrunners—"

"Voice down, please!" Isabel said urgently, glancing around.

"I lost track of it," whispered Ned. "You know my binoculars have the case attached so, in just this type of predicament, the two getting separated isn't an option."

"Do better, Ned," Isabel said. "That was foolish."

"Yes, ma'am," Ned mumbled.

Isabel laced her arm through Em's and left Ned miserable at the fireplace as they made their way across the hall and into the dining room, Isabel nodding and murmuring to her guests. Emily felt vindicated. She brightened suddenly, knowing that this was her moment.

"Isabel, could I please join Fiona and John Patrick at Dreamland tomorrow afternoon?"

Isabel's face set into its stern lines once again. "Dreamland . . . isn't that a boxing venue?"

"Yes, we'd be going to a boxing match," Em said. "I've never seen one."

"Well neither have I. That certainly doesn't make it a priority."

"Oh please, Isabel. I'll be safe with Fi and Pat, and I could extend my eyes-and-ears area, if you know what I mean."

"It's rather a crude affair though, isn't it?" Isabel sighed and her shoulders almost imperceptibly sagged. "I suppose it's all right, if you really want to go. I'm not one to dampen anyone's adventure."

Em squawked, then attempted to compose herself. She leaned over and gave Isabel a quick squeeze before her aunt could protest. When Em released her just as quickly, the older woman had a warm glow across her face.

"That's settled then," Isabel said, and turned to the buffet. Her violet gaze landed on the loaf-cake-relish remnants. "And look!" she exclaimed, pointing. "My Surprise Loaf was a success!"

What a perfect name for that mess, Em thought, amused by her aunt's delighted visage.

"Did you have any?" Isabel asked. "Was it a surprise?"

"Yes, I did," Em said primly. "And . . . yes, it was."

"Ha!" Isabel clapped her hands together. "A success all round. I think Ann would've had a lovely time, don't you?"

"If you say so, Isabel. You would know best," said Em.

"Yes," Isabel agreed. "Yes, I would."

Chapter 16

The level of activity at Hy House had been so unusually heavy that afternoon, with steady streams of guests and constant rotating platters, that Em didn't think she'd be able to get a wink of sleep when she laid her head down. Especially because she was so excited about Dreamland. She realized the irony, of course—the metaphorical Dreamland keeping her from the real one—but once again, her body outsmarted her and she slept soundly and deeply until first light. Then she was awake and out of bed.

She was getting the hang of picking out appropriate dresses, and today it was a blue number with ballooned sleeves and a nipped-in waist. It was a little longer than was especially chic, but Emily had learned that New England weather was as fickle as Nebraska's—if you didn't like it, all you had to do was wait five minutes, both Western and Eastern old-timers often said. So even though the weather looked like a balmy day with a hint of spring tingeing the salty air, Em knew better. A longer skirt made of stronger stuff and a jacket to layer on top was advisable if one was caught in changeable April weather.

After washing and dressing, Em still had miles of time. She checked the clock on the church out her small window again and groaned. It was just eight o'clock. Five more hours to go. She sighed and left her room, notebook tucked into the unusually large pockets of her coat.

As boredom was often a fount for creativity, or so her father had told her, in about an hour Em found herself ensconced in a back library on the first floor tucked behind the dining room. The leather-bound books gleamed from the bookshelves like wet stones in a riverbed, and for the thousandth time, the vast opulence of all these books—all this wealth—made her eyes ache. Out of all the decadence at Hy House, however, her mother must have surely missed this library. From the evidence, Constance had loved her life out West, but Em bet she recalled these shelves fondly.

To her utmost delight, Emily discovered a slim book with *Emily Dickinson* written down its spine. Another Emily at Hy House. She found a rocking chair next to a window and opened the pages, getting lost in the surprising images that sprang from the poet's spare lines.

As engaging as the simple, short poems were, they only enchanted her for so long. Soon she was reading as she paced the room, and then she was only pacing. Out the window, it was a perfect day for going out and trying something new. The sky seemed to go on forever without a shred of cloud, and a brisk breeze was testing the strength of the freshly born leaves.

Lapping the library for the hundredth time, book in hand, she considered the odd afternoon the day before. As she rounded corners, she thought back to Captain Butler's rude interruption of the strange guests, to the strange guests themselves. In the mystery stories she and her mom had loved to read, the murderers *always* turned out to be the strangers who'd arrived in the ninth hour. But life wasn't like a book.

She decided to search out some coffee in the kitchen. A hot cup of something would make the time pass more quickly, and it would give her something to do outside this silent library, where there wasn't even a clock ticking. As a last thought, she tucked the book of poetry into her coat pocket with her notebook. She didn't think Isabel would mind her borrowing it as there were floor-to-ceiling bookshelves built into the walls, and she knew this wasn't even the only library in the house. There was another upstairs.

And besides, she thought, pulling the door to the library closed with a *ka-chink*, you really never knew when you might get a moment to read a few lines.

When Em poked her head out into the hallway, she heard no sounds. And no one was in the kitchen when she pushed through the doors. Nobody up and about. But there was a pot of coffee Bridget must have left on the stove that morning, for it was still hot. She sipped the black brew from one of the kitchen's mugs and made her way outside, across the shell driveway to the back of Pat's garage. The sun beamed against the back wall, and Em pulled over the barrel with the least amount of splintering slats to sit on, tipping her face to the sun and feeling it warm her through her coat as the mug of coffee warmed her palms. It was pleasant. As Em soaked up the sun, she squinted at the ground in front of her, to what might one day be her garden, trying to picture where she would plant what and how the beds and paths could be shaped.

Life at Hy House truly was like one of her mother's favorite murder mysteries, she mused as she put her mug at her feet and took out her notebook and pencil nub. Em didn't know whether she fully believed her aunt's steel-clad proclamation that Ann had been killed with intent, but she didn't *not* believe it either. The past week had been so strange—every person a new face, every meal something she'd never tasted before—that she almost didn't know what to believe anymore. Isabel's ideas seemed as real as anything else Em had experienced so far.

Emily's main motivation (that she could only admit to herself) was that she was going along with it all because it brought her closer to Isabel, and in this moment in time, one of Em's loneliest, she needed somebody, even a reluctant somebody. And, additionally, it made her aunt's eyes gleam with a youthful curiosity. Like everything else about Isabel, she was hard to say no to, especially when she was onto something. And she had been right: Emily was an ideal candidate for an objective eye in this extraordinary situation. It wasn't difficult for her to equally weigh all the suspects since they were all strangers to her. Even though the islander at the funeral had tagged the three from Sicily (or "New Yawk" as Aringa had corrected Isabel) from off island, so was Em. She was just another washashore.

In her sketchbook, Emily drew a rough rectangle and then began putting in lines where someday corn might grow, then a row of sunflowers, a row of pole beans, and perhaps some squash to spread their large leaves over the soil to deter weeds. She hummed and cocked her head as she drew, feeling the sun on the line of her part where her scalp showed through. She thought that Bridget might appreciate using fresh herbs in the kitchen, and mint would be lovely in so many drinks, especially in the summer.

As the coffee in her mug diminished and the outline of her simple garden grew, with isolated plots for mint and berry bushes creating a border around the whole thing, she found herself quite lost in the project. A peal of laughter broke her out of it, and when she looked up to see where it came from, the sun had moved a fair number of degrees into the sky and her sketch had become a detailed drawing of penciled-in vegetables, herbs, and flowers with small, cramped writing labeling each item around its edges.

When she popped her head around the corner of the garage, Bridget jumped as she, Pat, and Fiona crossed the driveway.

"Em!" Bridget said, hand on her chest. "What a fright."

Fi beamed at her. Pat gave her a nod.

"What've you been up to over there? Did you find the coffee?"

Em nodded and, when Bridget looked at her quizzically, handed over her notebook.

"Excited for Dreamland?" Fiona said, as Bridget studied the garden plans.

"You bet! I didn't think I'd sleep, but boy did I sleep soundly. I've been up for hours, just waiting."

"This is quite detailed," Bridget said, handing it to Pat.

He studied it through a hank of dark hair. "Well, aren't you a mighty marvel? Pluck a chicken *and* plot a garden, my saints!" He pretend fainted, hand to his forehead and leaning into Fiona, who cackled and pushed him away.

Emily glowed with his praise.

"Tell you what, I'll leave some string and stakes out here. If you show me where you want me to dig, I'll turn the earth over for you."

"Thanks so much!" Em was touched.

He handed her back the sketchbook. "Leaving at one!" he said abruptly before disappearing into the darkness of the garage. Em groaned as she glanced at the clock above them again—only 11:15.

Fi laughed at her grim face. "Come, me love," she said in a broad Irish brogue, threading her arm through Em's and sashaying across the shells. "We'll find something yet to occupy us!"

A wire basket sat next to the kitchen stoop, filled with ridged, circular shapes drying to ashen gray in the strong sun.

"Marvelous!" said Bridget as she caught sight. "Constanza brought scallops. We'll have them tonight."

Yum—another New England culinary adventure.

"Luckily there are muffins, and Mam will make hot coffee for us," Fi said, catching Em's look. "And you won't have to deal with those until dinnertime."

—

IN THE END, Em and Fi used the time before Dreamland to stake out the garden plot. They were just finishing off, Em thumping in a last corner stake with a mallet, when a loud metal rattling erupted from the garage.

Emily and Fiona exchanged excited glances and dropped what they were doing (although Em brought the mallet along to put away on Pat's fastidious worktable). They rounded the corner as Pat backed the boxy work truck out of the garage, being careful not to ding the gleaming car next to it.

Fiona hopped with excitement as the truck backed up in a slow circle. Em darted into the cavernous garage space, the temperature dropping a few degrees in the shade, and replaced the mallet on Pat's worktable.

"Em, you're up front," Pat told her when she came out, feeling the immediate shift to warmth as she stepped into the sun. He was leaning out the truck window, his dark hair even darker wet, his tan corduroy collar damp around the edges.

"Aww, Pat!" Fiona cried as the car jerked to a stop. "Why do I have to take the back? We can all fit!"

"So Em can see better," Pat said. "It was Mrs. Hewett's idea."

"I thought it might be a good idea if someone, *in addition* to John Patrick, who knew how to drive one of those things sat up front," came a voice from behind them.

Isabel and Bridget stood together in the drive. Fiona quieted but still grumbled as she climbed over the slat wood sides into the back of the truck.

"We've come to see you off," Isabel said. "Em, come over here, please."

Emily trotted over and Isabel produced a dollar and a small beaded bag. With her spade-shaped nails, she tucked the dollar into the coin purse and handed it to Emily.

"For you and Fiona," she said. "For something to eat."

"Oh, thank you, Isabel!" Em took the small turquoise satchel.

"You should try the fried doughnuts, Miss," Bridget said, dropping a saucy little wink. She looked out of sorts in her Sunday best and kept tugging at the high collar of her gray dress. "At LaBell's. Fiona knows where it is," she continued as Emily skipped around the front of the car and clambered into the seat beside Pat. She was getting used to getting in and out of these things with all her driving practice over the past few days, but this would be their longest excursion to date.

Pat gave Emily a quick grin as he worked the pedals and put the truck into gear. "Shall we?"

She closed her door with a *thunk* and gave Isabel and Bridget a last wave. "Yes, please!"

Pat coasted out of the drive, looking one way and then the other and slowly pulling onto Main Street. Emily watched, rapt, as he pulled at the gearshift and pumped pedals, taking an immediate left just after they passed the Methodist church. The car picked up speed as they coasted by, and once they were past it, she caught sight of Hy House's back gardens. The willow's branches cascaded into the dry pond, where Seamus—the resident sea god—was a still, ashen figure.

"Why isn't the fountain on?" Em asked.

"It's broken," Pat said, yanking at the gearshift again. "And because it was Miss Emily's favorite." Pat glanced over at her. "The *other* Miss Emily," he clarified.

In a few hundred feet, he pulled over, stopping the truck and turning it off. "You want to drive?"

She looked at him. "You think I'm ready?"

"I know you are," he said with an encouraging nod. "But the real question is, do *you* think you are?"

With only a little hesitation, Em nodded.

"All right then. Let's swap seats."

Pat hopped out and trotted around the front of the truck. Em slid over, very aware of the warm indentation where Pat's big body had just been. From the back, Em could hear Fiona's weak protest. Then the vehicle hawed to the right as Pat slung his bulk into the passenger seat and rubbed his palms together.

"She's been running a little, so she'll start up right quick. If she'd been sitting, you'd need the choke, remember?" he said, pointing at a black pommel on the dash.

After giving her a quick refresher, Pat sat back in his seat and Emily cranked the car over until it sprang to life. She yanked the spark advance, then closed the gas-adjuster lever until the engine purred. Just like they'd practiced.

"You're getting to be an old hand, Em," he said proudly, and Emily glowed, trying to concentrate on the instruments in front of her.

All the lessons Pat had been drilling into her head the previous few days swirled together. The truck puttered forward, first tentatively, then with confidence as Em goosed the gas.

"You've got it," he said, chuckling. "Easy as falling off a log."

"Says you!" Em glanced at the various buttons and levers, not to mention the pedals below. Juniper was much easier to navigate with only a couple of reins.

They drove on. As the avenue broadened into a wide road, the motor shifted from a high whine to a low growl, reverberations shuddering through Emily's body. They slowed down to steer around the occasional pothole, and when she hit one, the whole cab shuddered and jolted as if it was about to fall apart.

Juniper could just avoid those potholes, Em thought smugly. But then again, a car wouldn't get spooked by snakes, or mice, or shadows of mice, or rabbits, or gophers, or shadows of gophers. Good ol' Juniper.

"How long until we get there, Pat?" Em asked, glancing at Fiona braced in the bed of the truck. Fiona stuck out her tongue at her.

"A little under an hour, depending." The wind from Pat's open window was stirring his hair around, drying it to a shiny black. "It's almost summertime, you know. Traffic will pick up and parking will get scarcer."

It did feel like summer was around the corner. The strong sun warmed Em's face as they bumped along, and the tang of the ocean filled her lungs. In the sandy soil along the roadside, gnarled pines bent into one another and sparse oak trees stretched out spindly branches deep into the undergrowth.

Emily followed a slow wide turn and, as they came clear, the land opened into dunes and ponds and ocean beyond, a picture of blues and yellows and greens. Emily's jaw dropped; it was easily one of the prettiest sights she'd ever seen.

The wind was strong enough to tear numerous tufts of white off the crests of the ocean waves that swirled out, one after another, in long ridges. It reminded Em of the prairie when the grass was high and the sun low, except instead of red, all was blue.

They chugged along, alone except for the seabirds lifting off from the middle of the road and cawing their annoyance. A sleek white sailboat matched their speed for a moment before the skipper tacked northeast. Em could imagine what fun it would be to sail, harnessing the wind and racing along with the waves. Almost as much fun as driving, she reckoned, putting on a little more speed. Maybe she would learn how, here in her new home. A bittersweet jolt shot through her as she realized that this was her first time thinking of this place, this strange place, as home. Her home. She almost cried, remembering the shimmering waves of tawny grass coming up to her thighs as she and Juniper sauntered through them, grasshoppers and locusts surfing in front of them.

"Oh, and the most important part"—Pat said *part* like *parrit*—"other than the brake pedal, I suppose, is this right here." He leaned over her, punching at a black rubber bulb near the window. Instantly the cab was filled with the horn—*aaaaaOOOOOga!*

Emily shrieked and Fiona whooped with laughter in the back, thumping the roof of the cab.

"Can't forget the horn!" Pat yelled and cackled at her.

—

When the truck later crested the final hill, the shells and dirt of the beach road became a hard-packed, measured promenade bordered by a high seawall that blocked out the ocean. A few picnickers lay on the beach on striped blankets and towels, but mostly the sandy stretch was deserted.

On the other side of the road, rooming houses and hotels crammed one after the other, broad porches all looking out to sea. The houses in Oak Bluffs were more decorated than those in Edgartown (except the very large ones like her aunt's). The big houses lining this promenade were festooned with trellises, curlicues, and other wooden adornments, and were painted colors as gay as an Easter egg—candy-hued pinks and robin's-egg blues and saffron yellows.

As they topped the hill, Oak Bluffs proper spread out before them. Then the road curved around, cradling a bowl of grass, punctuated by a bandstand in the middle. A jaunty orchestral rendition of "I Just Roll Along" drifted through her open window and Em looked for the source, but the bandstand was empty save for a pair of kids playing hide-and-seek. A red-and-green mansion crowned the park with two circular turrets and two porches, one up and one down, overlooking it all. The band was playing on the upper porch, and a sign hung from a shingle off the lower one that read, *Open*. A few couples twirled in the cool shadows below as the brass horns gleamed in the sunlight. In the small area of the truck's cab, she could smell the spicy tang of Pat's cologne mixing with the ocean spray.

"We're almost there," said Pat.

They puttered up a hill, and Em put the truck in neutral to coast down the final slope to the ferry wharf. A small clapboard shack guarded the entrance to the wooden pier, and already, a line of people buying tickets for their ride home had formed.

"Bravo, Em," Pat said as she ground the truck to a halt at a stop sign. Pat gestured in front of him. "Welcome to Dreamland."

Thus far, Em had been very impressed with Oak Bluffs' sandy cliffs, watery views, jaunty bandstand, darling houses, velvety lawns, and live music, but Dreamland did not quite live up to its name. This Dreamland was no dream of Emily's, although it was, she supposed, a fair name for a man's dream.

Through the windshield, a squat building with double-bay garages and a wide set of stairs winding to the second floor stood in front of them. On the whitewashed wall, painted words read, *Automobiles for Hire, Daily, Weekly Rates*, with a line of gleaming cars parked at an angle fronting the establishment. Suited men in twos and threes, hats pushed far back on their heads, trotted up and down the stairs, with only a few women interspersed throughout. Em glanced at Fi in the back and mouthed, "Almost there."

Fi nodded and braced herself again as Em put the truck into gear, taking a wide left and staying in the outermost lane, and then swung a sharp right around the stocky building, leaving the main road as it carved around a harbor dotted with anchored boats of various sizes. Across from Dreamland, another street branched off—a short, steep hill with shops and buildings slotted in shoulder to shoulder.

Pat gestured for her to pull into the dirt parking lot. She coasted to a stop in the middle of the lot next to a similar truck, this one shabbier than theirs and loaded with fishing gear. With a fair amount of relief, she shut off the truck, twisting the key and pulling the hand brake with a jerk.

Pat and Em got out of the cab and reconvened at the back as Fiona jumped down.

"Nice job," Pat said, holding out his hand.

"Thanks," Em said, and dropped the key into his palm.

"You'll be a regular race car driver in no time." He tucked the key into the pocket of his rust-colored waistcoat.

"Hopefully without any tragic endings," Fiona said, brushing her fingertips through the bottoms of her curls, which had been whipped into a frenzy by the wind. "I told you it was no good for me to sit in the back. Look at this, Uncle Pat."

On the second level of Dreamland, a door banged open and two men stepped out onto the balcony to smoke. One of them, with a black beard and white streaks at his temples, raised a hand in greeting, and Pat raised his in return.

"All right, girls, what'll it be?" Pat asked them. He'd taken a black comb out of a pocket and was managing his unruly waves. "Do you want to stick with me at the fight, or do you want to meet back here after all is said and done?"

The girls only had to trade one glance before Fiona answered for them. "We'll see you back here after it's done, Uncle Pat. What time do you want us back? And right here? Back at the truck, just like last time?" Fi was hopping up and down from one leg to another, black curls bobbing on her bodice and mostly behaving.

"Yes, girl," Pat said, turning *girl* into *girrul* and looking fairly excited himself, his blue eyes sparkling. "Be back here at five sharp. It's a quarter after two now," he said, consulting a pocket watch, "so that gives you plenty of time to have a look around." He kept glancing back at the bearded man on the balcony. "You two stay together above all else. Mrs. Hewett gave you some pocket money, I saw. Best make it last."

"Yes, Uncle Pat," Fi said, tugging on Em's hand. "We understand."

Pat looked at Emily, brows beetled above his blue eyes. "And you, Miss?"

Miss? She'd thought they were beyond that. "I understand."

"Righty-o then," Pat said, shooing them away. "Off you go until five."

The girls squealed and clutched at each other, skipping across the parking lot in the direction of town.

"And girruls," Pat said from behind them. "One more thing."

When they turned back, Pat was doing his very best movie star impression, hands in his pockets, scarf wrapped around his neck, saucy grin on his face. "Bring me back a LaBell's doughnut. And one for Bridge, too. She loves them."

Chapter 17

The girls, arm in arm, crossed in front of a crowd of men loitering on the wooden steps of the joint dance hall and fight club. They darted through some sparse traffic on the busy street that fronted Dreamland, skipping in front of a clot of cars exiting the ferry terminal. Em pulled her hat more firmly on her head to ensure its safety from the feisty breeze coming off the sea.

With Fiona, Emily could be a true tourist and let herself be borne along by her tour guide, gawking at the sights. Fiona insisted on going straight to LaBell's bakery and yanked her along.

"We don't want the doughnuts to run out, so we might as well get them first," Fiona said. "They sell out so fast, you wouldn't believe!"

A strange octagonal wooden building was perched at the base of the main street, called Circuit Avenue. It was isolated from the other stores and shops lining the Circuit, as Fi referred to it, by the roads crisscrossing the busy intersection of Oak Bluffs. They stepped up onto the wooden sidewalk, but the building didn't give much of a clue as to what was in it until they approached the front. Music drifted down the wide set of stairs and through double doors that opened into an indoor carousel, the tune almost blotted out by the clanging of the ring arm—the long metal conveyor that swung out to tempt riders with rings almost within reach. The gleam on each ring was a still point in the rotating scenery. The horses whizzed by as children screamed, reaching their hands out to try and grab the brass one. A sign proclaimed that this was *The Oldest Carousel in the Country*, and

Em had no reason not to believe it. She caught a whiff of cotton candy and her stomach gurgled.

"Flying Horses is loads of fun," Fiona said as she tugged at the arm of Em's coat, pulling her away from the building, "but after doughnuts, please. And not too soon after."

The girls started up the hill of Circuit Avenue. Ice cream shops, paper stores, taffy-pulling places, and more lined the one-lane road, jostling for purchase amongst the tourists and their pocket money. It was fairly crowded, as it was Sunday, and quite a few couples and groups moved along the sidewalks, crossing the road at random and promenading. Oak Bluffs was more accessible from the mainland than Edgartown, with boats landing right here, Fiona informed her on their walk to the bakery, so the onslaught of summer visitors came early.

Emily could smell the doughnut shop even before they came upon it. The sweet scent of fried pastry drifted above a crowd thickened around the entrance, over which hung a sign shaped like a giant cauldron that read *LaBell's*. Fiona pointed at the sign and began shouldering her way through the crowd to get to the front.

When they got through, Em could see that most of the people standing around already had their doughnuts and were contentedly watching more being prepared. Inside, a woman in a stained apron lowered a grate of raw doughnuts into a giant copper kettle that took up most of the space in the front window. The gleaming kettle hissed as the girls stepped inside, and sugary steam enveloped the woman's broad smiling face.

She looked questioningly at Fi, who held up four fingers, and then deftly plucked a piece of newspaper from the stack next to her and tonged four golden doughnuts from those lining the front window as enticements to passersby. She put each in a paper napkin, sprinkled them with powdered sugar, and twisted the top closed, before folding the four in a newspaper cone and handing it to Fiona. The woman tossed her copper-colored hair over one broad shoulder, gesturing behind her with her chin to a tiny, wizened woman wrapped in about a hundred shawls, including a few on her head, perched on a stool in front of an ancient cash register.

Still inhaling the steam wafting from their doughnuts, Fiona nudged Emily in the direction of the crone, who looked up from her book to fix Em with a serious unblinking gaze.

"How much for four?" Emily asked, taking out the blue bag and the crisp dollar from within.

The woman didn't speak but took both hands off her book, with all fingers and both thumbs spread.

"So ten?" Em asked, handing over the dollar bill.

The old woman was missing half her ring finger on her left hand, but Em knew that didn't mean the doughnuts cost nine-and-a-half cents.

She received nine dimes in change and put all of them carefully in the small pouch, tucking it away. The coins weighed the pouch down in her pocket as she walked back to Fiona, and the two pushed their way out of the store and through the group of doughnut lovers hovering outside.

They rounded the corner of LaBell's, heading for one of the benches scattered in between the bakery and the neighboring building. The end of this makeshift seating area led to another road and, across that, the green bowl of Ocean Park. As always, Em could just see a spot of navy above the seawall—the ever-present ocean. Fiona sat down on a bench near one of the grassy patches coming up in the shadow of the souvenir shop next door.

A family of six ate a packed lunch with their doughnuts on a bench at the end of the lot, and a couple of kids played in the dirt close by, one around the age of four, the other ten or so, with an older woman watching them from a stool in the sun, her back against the brick wall of LaBell's. When Em and Fi sat down, the younger one, a girl, looked up with a shy smile, then went back to building her house of twigs. Her older brother, or so it seemed, helped by breaking up larger sticks for her to build with as the woman napped.

Fiona unfolded the end of the cone and lifted out one of the doughnuts, handing it to Em and taking one for herself. The little girl took a couple of sidelong glances at them as Emily sank her teeth into the still-warm, crispy skin. It wasn't too sweet and had the perfect ratio of moistness to crispness. After the Surprise Loaf, anything would be tasty, but this was a special treat.

When Em opened her eyes again from her gastronomic reverie, the little girl was still studying her with serious brown eyes.

"Serene!" her brother whispered. "It's rude to stare!"

The little girl went back to her stick house, but not before whimpering, "I know, but it's just I'm so hungry."

Emily and Fiona looked at one another.

"Could we give her Pat and your mum's?"

"We could tell them that they sold out?" Fi said with an innocent expression on her imp-like features.

"My thoughts exactly," Em agreed, and they both got up and walked over to where the two children sat in the dust.

Fi handed the newspaper cone with the other doughnuts to the boy.

"What's this?" he said as he looked up in surprise.

"We want you to have it," Fiona said, and Em nodded.

"No, we couldn't," the boy said, even as his little sister yanked at his arm.

"We insist," Em said, smiling down at the dark-haired slip of a girl and watching her smile grow in return.

"Nan?" The boy looked over at the older woman, who had awoken and sat up straight on her stool, using an umbrella to keep herself steady. She had a long, pointed chin and a sailor's tam pulled low on her brow, and she nodded at the boy, who grinned at Em as he took the cone. "Thank you so much."

"Thank you," said the little girl, parroting her brother.

He was very well spoken for a ten-year-old, Em noticed as she and Fi returned to their bench to finish their own doughnuts, so well spoken that Em suddenly suspected that he was really about twelve, not ten. The little girl was most definitely around four, from the unabashed way she devoured first her doughnut and then most of the second one when her brother offered her his. The girls enjoyed the rest of their doughnuts in silence.

"Wait a moment," Fiona said, licking her fingers. "Aren't those the men who came to your aunt's yesterday for the wake? The ones from away?"

Em's last swallow of doughnut stuck in her throat as she looked where Fiona was pointing.

Across the street, on the other side of Circuit Avenue, a pair of men were sauntering along the sidewalk. Unlike those taking the air on Circuit that afternoon, these men weren't wearing the light colors of leisure. They still sported the severe suits they'd worn to Ann's services. Emily checked their shoes. The shiny black leather looked like it would crack and blister after one day at sea. Definitely the men from the night before, Em decided, scanning their shadowed faces, but where was the woman? Her shoulders tightened. And why were they here? For the doughnuts?

The men crossed and made their way around the crowd gathered outside the bakery. Although they were walking casually, strolling along and whistling, Em had a sinking feeling that they weren't as relaxed as they wanted to appear. A breeze whipped between the two buildings from Ocean Park, flapping one of the men's coats open, the one with the boxer's face. Before he could rake the front closed again, Emily saw the thick metal of a gun in his waistband. All of her organs shrank up against her spine and she froze, head tucked down as the strangers closed in. As they approached, Fiona grew rigid beside her.

Em was staring so hard down at the toes of her boots that she was only aware the men had stopped in front of her when their pointed, shiny toes came into view. She looked up, taking in Mr. Aringa's double-breasted suit, red pocket square, and the mean slash of his face. The little hairs bristled on the back of her neck.

"Can I . . . can I help you?" Em said, standing up and fumbling for the words. Fiona stood up too, her small but firm presence just behind Em. The man loomed over her, too close, legs wide, hands clasped in front of his buttoned jacket.

"You know who I am? You remember?" Mr. Aringa said. The other man stood behind him, not looking at the girls but keeping his attention pinned everywhere else.

Em nodded, the sweetness of the doughnuts lodged in the back of her throat. "Yes, we met yesterday afternoon, at my aunt's, didn't we, Mr. Aringa?"

"Good, you do know who I am. That'll make this easier." He pulled at the lapels of his coat, straightening them. "I want to make sure that your aunt got my message yesterday, before we were so rudely interrupted."

Fiona snuck her hand into Em's and squeezed.

Aringa leaned in until he filled Emily's whole vision. She smelled sharp cologne and onions, and he was baring his teeth at her, showing their yellowed, uneven edges. "You tell your aunt," he growled, shaking his blunt pointer finger in her face, "to stop meddling in affairs that don't concern her." Then he poked his finger in her chest twice, hard, punctuating each word. "Or else."

"Or else?" Em said, her voice shaking like a palm tree in a hurricane.

"She'll know what that means," he said, finger still jabbing painfully into the spot right below Em's collarbone.

Fiona interjected. "Hey, mister, stop that—"

"Tell her from us," Aringa cut her off. "And if she doesn't—"

Suddenly, a big black umbrella came sailing between Aringa and Emily, cracking down on his forearm. He gasped and whirled. A tiny woman stood next to the bench, an indignant and rageful expression on her face. "Mind your manners, mister. What do you think you're doing with these girls?"

It was the older woman who'd been napping on the stool, the kids' Nan.

Mr. Aringa held onto his forearm with the other hand. "I hardly think—"

"You get lost, you big bully," Nan cut him off again, stepping in between Em and Fiona and the two strange men. She only came up to his pocket square, but she shook the umbrella under his nose with a fearsome rattle. "If you don't stop terrorizing these girls, I'll 'or else' you myself. These are island girls, and you can't come here and start scaring the bejesus out of the locals. We won't stand for it. Police!" On the last word, Nan cracked open her mouth and hollered so loudly that Aringa took a step back, and the other man looked around, startled.

"Madam, there is no reason to bother the authorities with such a mundane matter." Aringa took more steps back, bumping into his friend. "We certainly don't want any trouble—"

"I'm sure you don't!" Nan said indignantly, with more vicious shakes of her umbrella. "I know who you are, and you too"—she jabbed it at the other man, the one with the gun, who flinched—"and rumrunners like you never want to get the police involved. If you don't skedaddle and leave these young ladies alone, I'll beat you soundly with my umbrella, and then I'll call the local law to come and scrape you up." Nan raised her weapon, and both men took a giant step back. They didn't look scared . . . well, maybe the one with the gun did, a little, but Aringa looked absolutely mystified and a trifle impressed. He pulled at his lapels again and straightened his hat.

"C'mon, Harold, let's get out of here. We delivered the message." With one more blunt stab of his finger in Em's direction, he growled, "You remember." Then he spun and walked off, his compatriot following. Aringa, elbowing people carelessly out of the way as they crossed the street, strode back in the direction of Dreamland.

"Or else!" Nan yelled after them.

"You tell 'em, Nan!" whooped the boy. He was standing on her stool, very unsteadily, waving his fists at the men.

The tinkle of the band floated in from Ocean Park, the music finding its way through the cottages and narrow one-way streets to where the girls stood, clenched together, as Nan brandished her umbrella at the retreating rumrunners' backs.

Chapter 18

It was Nan, once again, who took the reins in the aftermath of this strange confrontation. Everybody else was frozen, except for the little girl, who was still constructing her dirt town against a sapling. She hadn't even looked up.

"Come on, you two," the old woman said after the men had well and truly disappeared down Circuit. "Let's get out of the crowd and get a spot of tea. Get a few breaths. We live right around the corner. Stuart, grab my kit, please."

The boy went over to the wall and retrieved the stool and a bag of knitting supplies, two needles sticking up through the cloth handles.

"Come on, Serene," Nan said, holding out her hand.

"You can call me Slick. Everyone does," Stuart said from a few steps ahead of them. Fiona and Emily walked arm in arm, but not in the same carefree, skip-to-my-Lou manner in which they'd parted ways with Pat. Now they clutched one another, trembling with adrenaline in the aftermath of terror.

"That's not true," Serene piped up from Nan's side, where she bopped along like a tiny friendly sparrow. "*You* call yourself Slick, but no one else does, and you must stop asking people to."

Em decided that Serene was also a lot more eloquent than any four-year-old she'd ever met. These kids were just exceptionally small, like their Nan.

The five crossed Circuit and through a gate between a hotel and grocery, following a brick path leading away from the business end of town. The path soon opened onto a green area, then splintered into smaller brick tributaries, ushering them into the most fascinating neighborhood Em had ever seen.

A maze of tiny dollhouses—cottages painted all colors of the rainbow—were festooned with rivulets of trellises and toppings of turrets. Still, Em couldn't help snatching glances behind them. The hair on the nape of her neck was still standing up, and her heart rate would not slow down. She kept expecting to see the men appear, but there was no one.

Ahead, Stuart and Serene were still arguing about his name.

"Who calls you Slick, then? No one at home," Serene said, every bit the accusatory starling.

"Hey," Em said, interrupting them as they turned right by a bright-pink house with red trim, "where are we?"

"The Campground," Stuart answered. "The Methodists live here in the summer."

"Em, who cares?" Fiona said. "Those men, they were so scary!"

"Hush, you two," said Nan, turning on them with a searing look from her black eyes. Emily could understand why the gunman had been frightened; she looked like a murder-minded granny. Nan's eyes shifted to the dozens of shelf-sized porches and curtain-festooned windows. "It may be Sunday, but there are eyes and ears about."

Deep in the heart of the Campground, Stuart turned by an unlit streetlamp. The proportion of the fences, cottages, and paths—and the diminutive stature of their hosts—made Emily feel like a giantess who'd stumbled into Pixie Land. A cheerless picket barrier ran around a patch of dirt and weeds, where an automobile tire sprouted a clutch of daffodils from its middle, and a swing (looking as if it could only bear the weight of a hummingbird) hung from a solitary tree. Nan stepped up onto a creaky back porch (somehow supporting a washing machine as well as a disused sink), and started up the double set of stairs that snaked up the back of the building to a second story swaying precariously above them.

Nan marched up the stairs with Stuart supporting her on one side, helping her climb while carrying her trusty umbrella.

Em tugged on Fiona's sleeve. "You sure?" she said, feeling unsafe all of a sudden. It seemed like everywhere she went, there was some menacing man in the near distance, staring at her. "You're sure we're safe?"

Fiona laughed. "Nothing's going to happen if we're with Nan and her umbrella. And besides, they're islanders. Me mam knows her, or of her. She's infamous."

Emily stared at the woman's back as she remembered the look on the gunman's face. Yes, they would be fine with Nan.

When they reached the second landing, Nan fiddled with the door until it jostled open. They all filed into the space after her—an attic apartment with a peaked roof. A round table held all sorts of bric-a-brac: pieces of pottery, jars filled with sea glass, and stacks of magazines. The dining table was solely an artifact repository, it seemed, with strips of seaweed layered to dry on newspaper, tingeing the air with the scent of ocean and decay. A pair of scissors lay open with scraps and shards of photos filling the spaces between the piles of stuff.

They moved into the room, and Serene skipped into the back of the apartment as Stuart stored Nan's kit in a basket under the bench. Nan moved with ease through the chaotic yet cozy decor—overstuffed armchairs sitting next to overstuffed bookcases, end tables, side tables, and stuffed birds and other creatures in all sorts of odd poses. Someone was an amateur taxidermist.

"Make yourselves at home, dearies," Nan said as she moved through her sitting area and into the kitchen proper. "Let's sit for a moment to breathe and let our trail go cold out there. Those men were very unfriendly." She unwrapped the scarf from around her neck and threw on an apron that looked like it had been sewn from a grain sack; Em had seen similar ones back in Blue Hill. "Fancy a spot of tea? I think I have a tin of biscuits somewhere. Take a look, would you please, Stuart?"

Emily glanced over at Fiona, who was gently moving some conch shells from a dining room chair to sit down. "Yes, please," Em answered for both of them, her voice still watery from fear, and sat on the nearest armchair, a bright-yellow affair with only three legs, the missing one replaced by a stack of books.

She lowered herself down, but as soon as her rear end touched the pillow, a yowl issued from underneath and it erupted in an explosion of fur, hissing and streaking underneath the other armchair, another well-loved maroon one.

"Watch out for Smidgen. He's small but feisty," Nan said as she flicked a wooden match along the side of a matchbox. "Sorry about the mess," she conceded as her eyes darted around, perhaps seeing it for the first time through the girls' eyes.

Em didn't mind the clutter. Actually, she felt more at home in Nan's house with her bits and bobs than she did in Isabel's grand dining room. It was comforting to be in a place that smelled like baking and pets and other people's clothes. Sure, it was a little strange, she thought, watching Smidgen creep out from under the armchair and make a mad dash for the back of the room. But it was a home, a real home—lived in, well used, and well loved.

Stuart brought in a tin of homemade biscuits and placed it on the dining room table.

"What was that all about, Em? Who were those men?" Fiona burst out, her eyes tense slits, her manner uneasy as she played with the frayed hem of her coat. "What if they're still out there? How are we going to get back to Uncle Pat? This is scary, Em. One of them had a gun. Did you see?"

"I saw, I saw," Emily said. She leaned back into the armchair and closed her eyes, trying to calm her heart rate, which had jumped painfully in her chest again at Fiona's questions. Emily could hear the sound of Nan pouring water for tea, the clink as she replaced the cover, and then the kettle went back on the stove with a clang. This had gotten out of hand, and rather quickly. She couldn't shake the image of Mr. Aringa's face, his large nostrils curled up in a sneer. "What are we going to do?" she whispered, more to herself than to anyone else.

"Here. Drink some tea. It's something to do."

She opened her eyes to Nan leaning over her with a mug, which she took gratefully. "Thank you."

The older woman nodded. "It'll be all right, don't you worry. My Stuart can get you to your uncle. Where's he spending his time this afternoon?"

Fiona took another steaming mug from Nan. "At Dreamland."

"Sure, he can get you there. Hear that, Stuart?"

Stuart had already pushed two biscuits into his mouth and was in the process of fitting in a third when the conversation, as well as everyone's focus, suddenly shifted to him. He stopped chewing and looked up guiltily, nodding. Em stifled a giggle and took a sip of the hot black tea, remembering that he had given most of his doughnut to Serene. He was good to his grandmother and little sister. Em decided she'd call him Slick whenever he liked.

"You get these girls back to where they're meeting their uncle," Nan said, returning to the kitchen area, "and you'll go the scenic route, you hear? Not by Circuit, but through the Campground. You must be quick about it; they'll be wanting to get home safe and sound as soon as they can." Nan's face was stern, but Em guessed it had more to do with the severity of the situation than with Slick.

"Yes, Nan."

"And offer around some of those biscuits, boy, before you finish them, or they finish you."

Stuart sheepishly offered the tin to Fiona, who declined, and so he held out the tin to Em, who also shook her head. Fear had made her stomach uneasy.

"Those men, they were rumrunners, but more like gangster types, from away," Nan said. Em noted this was not a question. Nan stated this as fact.

"Yes, ma'am. We think so." Em put her mug on a side table.

"Not all rumrunners are bad, you know? People were living real scrappy on the island when Prohibition came about. Lots of us run rum, my husband, Marvin, included, rest his soul. That there was his last taxidermy project." At this, Nan nodded in the direction of one of the oddest stuffed animals in the room, one Em had already noticed: a crow with a doll's straw hat sitting in a miniature sailboat. The curiosity sat atop the bookcase next to the kitchen setup at the end of the room, clearly a place of honor. The taxidermist had been quite clever, threading a thin rope through the crow's wing feathers and pointing his black beak toward the bow as if he were gauging the wind.

"There are plenty of island boys that turned a pretty penny running rum, and for some families, they went from not eating regular to eating every day. It's hard to say no to that," said Nan decisively, still gazing at the nautical crow.

Em, who'd had some experience with hunger in long lean winter months on the prairie, nodded.

"But now, there's a different type coming, you hear?" Nan continued. "Those men today, they weren't from here. They've come from New York and New Jersey. Big-city boys with big-city problems, coming here with their guns and their dealings. I don't like it."

"They were visitors at my aunt's, Isabel Hewett's," Emily said.

"I know your aunt. And I know your mum." Nan nodded in Fi's direction. "Nice ladies, the both of them. Will help a body out each in their own manner."

Em couldn't agree more with this assessment. "Aunt Isabel's friend, Ann Simpson, died, and Isabel suspects she might've been murdered. The Mob—"

Nan held up a wrinkled hand. "You can stop right there, missy. I don't need to know any more. I don't invite trouble." Her expression brooked no nonsense. "And you should be on your way, judging by the time." A brass clock under the crow skipper read a little after half past four. "Stuart?"

"Yes, ma'am," Stuart said, standing and putting on his plaid flap cap. The girls followed suit and stood.

"None of your tour guiding," Nan said as they moved toward the door. "None of your talking and walking backward, you hear? Straight there."

The girls thanked Nan profusely as she pushed a couple of biscuits into their hands and pooh-poohed all their offers of paying her for her kindness.

"It's the island way. I'm not going to sit there while some thug berates my neighbors. Not on my watch." They were clustered at the front door, and the umbrella had found its way back into Nan's hands where she once again brandished it like a sword. "And with Big Bertha at my side, I'm never scared!"

Fiona snickered. "Bertha? You named her?"

Nan turned her fiery gaze from her flapping black umbrella—almost the size of her and looking as much like a bird as the dead one on the shelf—to the girls in the open doorway. "A weapon as formidable and forceful as this fine thing? Wouldn't you?"

Chapter 19

It was nearly five o'clock when they made it back to Dreamland.

"We made it," Stuart said. "Where's your uncle?"

"I don't know," Fiona said, looking around.

"Maybe at the fight?" Em said. "Should we check inside?"

She surveyed the crowd, but Pat was nowhere to be seen. Going inside seemed like the only option, so Emily and Fiona set off for the entrance of Dreamland, Slick taking up the rear. They walked through the back doors of the establishment, which during the weekdays (Slick informed them) served as a garage and auto repair shop. It was clear this was the case, as broken-down cars and tools jammed the space in an orderly manner, and double bays, all closed for the night, lined the walls left and right.

The roar of a large crowd thundered down from overhead, the sounds of men smacking each other with boxing gloves, like fists hitting a side of meat. Emily didn't really want to go up there and search for Pat in that crowd. What if Aringa was there? After the recent turn of events, she realized Nan was right. She just wanted to get back to her room, safe and sound. But what else could they do? They needed to find Pat.

She was sure Slick would be game to go looking for Pat on their behalf. His eager gaze seemed ever ready for adventure. But their new pal didn't know Pat from Adam, as her father would've said. He wouldn't be able to pick him out of the crowd.

She sighed as the three bunched uncertainly in the middle of the vacant garage, both Fi and Slick looking to her for instruction even though it seemed she should be looking to them.

"Well . . . I guess there's no two ways about it," she sighed again. "We'll have to go upstai—"

A door to their left was thrown open with a bang, raucous laughter and men's voices streaming out as one of them took his leave. With the murmur and roar from the crowd overhead, and the squeak and creak of the floorboards beneath the ring as the boxers danced around in their pugilistic tango, Em hadn't realized that men were gathered in a room close by as well. The man stumbled and swayed past them in a liquored haze, eyes bloodshot, then threw himself through the door to the outside. When he got out, he made a beeline for the weeded part of the lot and started retching, horrible barking sounds that stopped, mercifully, when the door swung shut again.

From inside the room, a familiar voice brayed, "Well, then I told Captain MacNamara that he could sod off with his billyboys and go a-hunting elsewhere, I says!"

Em and Fiona looked at one another in horror and tiptoed to the doorway, which was still ajar, and peeked into an office of sorts with a file cabinet, a round wooden table, and four spindly chairs pushed up against the walls to make room for the men clustered around a far corner with their backs to the girls. Some had their jackets and hats still on, but most were in varying states of disarray as they played a game, their yelling and hollering hammering around the room with each toss of a pair of dice. Then her eyes found Pat, who wasn't playing, but rather sitting on a chair skirting the group of men, leaning too far back and studying the ceiling while he talked in a loud Irish accent.

"So Captain MacNamara says—"

"John Patrick MacInnes O'Callahan!" Fiona stood in the doorway doing her best tiny-tempest routine, hands on her hips, face on fire. "Where have you *been*?"

Pat took one look at the furious Fiona and said, "Bridge?" rather unclearly just before the legs of his chair slipped out from underneath him and he went over backward.

At the crack of Pat's head against the wall and the smash of the chair against the floor, the men took notice of the intruders in the midst of their craps game. Most laughed and pointed at Pat, now unmoving on the floor, while some gave the young women curious glances. A few of them hastily stashed bottles in their pockets. Em even recognized one: Garrett Winterholler, who gave her one guilty glance and looked as if he might address her, but chose to make his escape with a few others instead, thinning the crowd down to six, newcomers included.

Fiona sighed and marched over to Pat's sprawled body. He still wasn't moving, though he snored loudly, his untucked shirt showing a blotchy patch of stomach, his face bright red and shiny.

"Ah, Uncle Pat, not again. Not now!"

"What's happening?" Em said.

"He's drunk, that's what," Fi said with disgust, toeing Pat in the ribs.

"Dead drunk," Slick clarified.

Pat didn't budge, but his snore paused and started again, even louder this time. Before long, the rattle of dice against the corner drew the men's attention away and they stopped paying attention to Pat and resumed their crap-shooting banter.

"How are we going to get home?" Panic seeped into the edges of Fi's voice. "He can't drive! Look at the state of him!"

As if to illustrate this point, Pat took an unsteady snore that sounded like a boat's motor. Then he wheezed it out again like a deflating tire. It was his most un-movie-star-like impression yet.

"What if those men come back?" Fi said, her voice high-pitched and thready.

Emily studied Pat. "I think," she said slowly, "I can get us home. As long as we can get him into the truck. Can we do that?"

"I don't know, Em. He looks heavy."

"Ahem!" Their new friend stood at attention at Emily's elbow. "If I may be of your service. I have an idea."

Emily and Fiona traded looks. What did they have to lose?

"Have at it, Slick," Fi told him.

Slick disappeared into the cavern of the garage for a few seconds and reappeared, rumbling a luggage cart in front of him, the sort used to transport bags for customers.

"Brilliant," Em breathed as he rolled up.

As they rolled Pat onto the cart, a voice came from behind them, "Hey!"

Emily looked over, tension constricting her chest. A man in suspenders and a white undershirt walked over, tore off the top sheet of his pad, and stuffed it into Pat's chest pocket. "Tell our drunken pal to check his pockets when he wakes up, then come see me."

"Who . . . who are you, sir?" Em asked.

The man didn't answer, just walked back to the game.

—

IT TOOK THEM almost an hour to get back to Edgartown once they'd hoisted Pat in the back of the truck, thanks to Slick's help. As Em had driven away, giddy with nerves, he'd run beside the vehicle, cheering them on. Fi had waved at him eagerly, smiling a big smile that quickly evaporated, her fear at Emily driving them home clearly surfacing on her face.

"Fi, are you okay?" Em had asked.

Fi nodded, nervously.

"Come on, not even the slightest bit fun? Where's your sense of adventure?"

"Nebraska," Fiona said, a chuckle bubbling up.

They had laughed in breathy snatched gasps as the sea breeze from the open windows swirled in and around them, Pat sleeping perhaps too peacefully in the back.

When they'd finally made it home, a feat that made Emily almost dizzy with joy and pride, the long line of familiar sycamore trees appeared on their left, and Emily yanked at the gearshift, putting the truck into neutral, spinning the wheel in an almost-perfect arc and using their momentum to crunch into the driveway.

"Look!" Fi said, pointing. "He left the bay open!"

As carefully as she could manage, Em aimed straight into the garage bay.

"Stop!" Fi whisper-yelled from beside her.

Just before the truck bumped into Pat's workbench, Em pounded on the clutch and the brake, yanking the hand brake for good measure. She twisted the key again with her feet still mashed on both pedals and the engine sputtered to a stop. It was only then that her heart really unclenched.

They sat in silence as the truck ticked and settled.

"Phew," Emily said.

"Phew, indeed," Fi chortled. "Em, that was marvelous. You saved us! Especially Pat back there." They both turned and looked at Pat, still dead to the world.

"I don't know about all that," Em said, getting out of the truck. "And we're not there yet."

When the girls unhinged the tailgate, Pat's legs sprung out like a busted puppet. They each grabbed one and tugged, but the big man was heavy, and it soon became clear there was no way the two of them were going to budge him.

"Not a chance," Em said.

"Do you think we could use the blanket?" Fi asked, tugging at it. "Like a sling?"

Em pulled the blanket out from under Pat's legs and wrapped him up in it, or as much of him as she could. Now that Slick was gone, there was no way they were lifting him on their own. "I think dear old Uncle Pat can have a restful sleep out here in the truck, and if he doesn't like it, he can get up and move. We've done our part."

"Agreed," Fiona said with a pert little nod. "He made his bed, as they say."

"Yes, and now he'll sleep in it."

The girls laughed, feeling easy for the first time since they finished their doughnuts back on the Circuit.

"I'll close up out here so nothing's amiss," Fi said, "and then I'll head back to the Howsons'. Tell Mam I'll see her tomorrow."

Em gave Fi a quick hug goodbye before scurrying off, already looking forward to hot tea, a bath, and maybe a leftover scone or cookie from the kitchen.

The garage bay door rattled down behind her as Em crossed the driveway. Halfway to the kitchen door, the sound of a car emerged beyond the thick tangle of the sycamores. She paused as the engine's growl grew. A vehicle slid into view at the driveway's end, a sharp-looking car, sleeker and more polished than most island cars.

Aringa's car.

Fear clutched an icy hand around Emily's throat as the back window slowly rolled down, revealing nothing but hollow darkness. Suddenly, the red coal of a cigar glowed as a gloved hand slid out like something subterranean and cold-blooded. The black car glided by, and a hand pointed, took aim, and shot directly at Emily. Then it retracted like a snake into its hole, disappearing into the shadows of the back seat. A growl of laughter blended with the sedan's steady rumble as it slid out of view and down the hill to the harbor.

Aringa had taken his aim, and Em was in the crosshairs.

Chapter 20

Emily knew there would be a good deal of explaining to do and couldn't fathom how exactly her aunt might react to the new developments—that the Mob was indeed sending threats through her teenage niece—but as it turned out, she didn't have to explain anything at all. When Em had creaked open the kitchen door, it'd been odd, but also a relief, that there'd been no one about upon their return from Dreamland. Considering the circumstances, she wasn't about to tattle on Pat, but she didn't like lying either, and probably, under an onslaught of pointed questions from either Isabel or Bridget, wouldn't have done so very well.

So when she'd slipped through the door the previous night, her chest had loosened considerably at the sight of a plate with a flowered napkin laid atop it, and a note in Bridget's cramped, laborious writing. *Em*, it had read, *Mrs. H in her chambers. I'm at dinner down the street, back at 9, supper under cloth. B.*

Emily had lifted the dishcloth to reveal one of the most normal-looking and genuinely appetizing meals she'd had to date in Hydrangea House—cold chicken, potato salad, peas. After a solitary repast, Em had found her way into the bath and then straight to bed. Although her day had been packed with one exhausting adventure after another, Emily did not drop swiftly into sleep, but spent most of the night tossing and turning with Aringa's sneer perpetually hovering in the background.

She could still feel the bruised place below her collarbone where he'd jammed his finger.

In the morning, still groggy after a restless night, Em sat on the edge of the bed, brushing her hair and preparing her statements to Isabel when the Methodist church struck the hour with eight peals. She sighed and replaced the brush on the shelf. It was time to tell her aunt about Mr. Aringa's message and how he'd delivered it, but at least she would be able to do so over a hot cup of coffee.

She was surprised, once again, to find the kitchen deserted. There were signs of Bridget's recent occupancy, however, as a hot coffee pot awaited on the stove. Em poured a mug and sat at the table, waiting for someone to appear. After a few minutes, Bridget bustled through the double doors and swept into the kitchen, a broad tray littered with dishes and a wine glass balanced on her shoulder.

"Ach! There you are! We missed each other last night." Bridget was all smiles. "How was your time at Dreamland?" She placed the tray next to the sink and began to unload its contents into the deep enameled basin.

Em studied Bridget's profile, but Bridget seemed totally undisturbed this morning. Emily assumed that this meant Pat's subterfuge still held. No way was she going to ruin it for him if she didn't have to.

"We didn't go to the fights with Pat. We went for doughnuts." Em clamped her lips shut to stop herself from prattling on, as was her wont when she was embellishing the truth.

"And you had a grand time, riding there and back with Pat?"

"Oh yes," Em said, studying the contents of her mug. "He's an excellent driver."

"Well, good." Bridget was scrubbing the inside of a large pot and didn't turn around.

"Aunt Isabel?"

"You know, dear, it's strange. There was a box delivered from her lawyers late yesterday afternoon. Two actually, a big one and then a small one on top. Strange, as it was Sunday. And I've not seen hide nor hair of her since she got them. She asked for dinner upstairs last night, and the same for breakfast this morning. She's reading, reading, reading, papers everywhere, about what I couldn't tell you." Bridget shook her head. "I don't like seeing her this agitated, I really don't."

"She was agitated?"

"It seemed so. Excited, maybe. Interested, definitely. Keen. I asked her if she wanted to see you, and she said after lunch. So, we'll leave her be, don't you think? For the morning at least."

"I have a rather pressing message for her."

"Message? Whatever it is, it'll have to wait. The Mrs. gave me express directions that no one, not even you, was to disturb her." Bridget rinsed out her pot, balancing it on a drying rack nearby. "If you'd like something to occupy your time until then, Pat's cutting through the first layer of your garden behind the garage. Why don't you go give him a hand? That is, if you don't mind getting your hands dirty." Bridget was studying her, perhaps misconstruing Em's torn expression as a reluctance for hard labor. That, of course, wasn't it.

"That sounds fine, Bridge. I'll go help Pat."

"Bring him one of these," she said, wiping her hands on her apron and picking a basket off the counter. She whipped back a maroon dishcloth to reveal a pile of corn muffins. "And take one for yourself. Fresh this morning."

Em took two. They were still warm. As she put her mug by the sink, she wondered what she was going to say to Pat once she got out there. "Thanks, Bridget."

Stepping out the back door, Em was surprised by the turn in the weather. Unlike the picture-perfect conditions they'd enjoyed the day before in Oak Bluffs and the warmer weather at Ann's services, today the island was trapped beneath a dense layer of clouds, with a strangely chilly breeze rustling the tender new leaves and the few early apple blossoms.

Crunching across the shells, Em looked toward the road, where the high line of trees ended, instinctively searching for Aringa's car. There was no sign of a vehicle, and no one cagily watched her from the end of the driveway. Suddenly she froze, struck by an idea.

Previously, she'd assumed that Aringa's message was referring to her own sudden appearance at their booze storage facility—the Simpsons' compound on Starbuck Neck—but what if she was wrong? What if the message was actually about Ann's murder, and not the day-to-day operations of rumrunners? Maybe the meddling Aringa referred to was Isabel and her theories of foul play that she'd been spouting off to anyone who would listen. Em's blood turned as chilly as the wintery breeze, making her shiver. Perhaps the Mob *had* killed Ann, and now Isabel was getting too involved for the culprit's comfort. Maybe it had been Aringa himself who took care of Ann. She shivered again, crossing her arms tightly across her chest.

Emily hustled toward the garage, but not without another glance at the empty road and one up to the second floor of Hy House. She half expected a twitch of the curtains betraying her aunt's presence, but there was nothing. She knew she had to deliver the message to Isabel sooner rather than later, make her understand the danger, that these warnings were real, and somehow get her aunt to tone down her investigation.

As if that was easy, or likely, or even possible. She took a bite of the muffin and went to find Pat.

He was bent over a spade, slicing through the top layer of soil in the rectangle that Em and Fiona had staked out the day before. He wore a T-shirt, the same waistcoat he'd had on the previous night, and his scarf. His wet hair moved heavily in the wind. His face was no longer red and blotchy as it had been yesterday evening but a nauseated mask of yellowy tan. Purple half circles hung like wet hammocks underneath his eyes, and every few seconds he stopped to spit and wipe his forehead with a bandana.

When Em came around the back corner of the garage, Pat started and stared at her, an expression equally baleful and guilty. "Miss Em," he said, his handsome face all sorrow, "I'm afraid I don't remember a thing about my night. How did we find our way back? Did you . . . did you drive us back here?"

Em nodded and held the muffin out to him. He took it, looked at it with little interest, and put it on a nearby barrel.

"You drove then? How did I . . . how did I get back in the truck? I was in the truck when I woke up this morning." The hangdog look on Pat's face was almost enough to make Em feel too sorry for him to be mad, but then she thought back to the hectic events leading up to their escape from Dreamland, and the rage burned back, even brighter. They really could've used him, and Em told him so.

"You were a mess. We got you in the truck. We had some help. Not your friends, ours. But one of your friends put something in your pocket and told me to tell you to check it when you woke up." She nibbled smugly on her pastry as Pat rummaged through his pockets, finally finding the slim slip of yellow paper and reading it with a growing expression of unease.

"Everything all right, Pat?"

He tried to smile, but it looked more like a grimace. "Seems as though I were a bad escort, a bad driver, *and* a bad gambler last night." He waved the folded slip in the air and tucked it back into his pocket. "I truly apologize, Miss Em. I was in a terrible state."

"You were," Em said, "and it was terrible. You should be sorry." She lasted a few more seconds while he ground his toe into the dirt, looking like he wanted to melt into the hole he'd just made with the shovel. Then she relented—she couldn't help it. "But we all make mistakes, just not such noisy ones." She wiggled her eyebrows at him as his expression switched from abashed to aghast.

"What do you mean, noisy?"

"Well, with all the snoring, burping, and farting, you gave us quite the concert last night."

"Us?" Pat's voice rose a few octaves, and his curdled complexion turned pink. "What do you mean, us?"

"Oh you know, Fi and me, our new friend Slick, all the guys you were gambling with . . . who else? Probably some others out in the lot behind Dreamland, I can't recall." She grinned as he squirmed.

"Good Mary and Joseph," Pat intoned. "Never again!" He made a sign of the cross, kissing his fingers and rolling his eyes skyward. "Never another drop."

Emily dusted her fingers free of muffin crumbs and studied him wryly. "That's what Fi said you said the last time this happened. Just stick to it this time, all right, Pat?"

The big (still handsome) Irishman nodded, one hand inspecting his bristly jawline and the other holding tight to the flatheaded shovel.

"All right, water under the bridge," Em said briskly. "I'm here to help. Let me get a shovel. And Pat?"

He looked up, bracing himself.

"Get some of Bridge's muffin into your belly. You look terrible."

—

THEY HAD BEEN at it for about an hour, the nine o'clock bells ringing only minutes before, when the front door of Hy House banged open and a very distraught Bridget came barreling out.

"Pat!" she hollered. "Em!"

"Here!" Em called back, straightening and pushing the damp hair out of her face, sweating in her thin dress. Even though it was a good ten to fifteen degrees cooler than it had been the day before, it was tough work, for they had to slice through the stubborn layers of intertwined roots just below the surface of the grass.

Bridget came around the corner, still in her apron, but without the carefree air she'd met Em with that morning. Now she was pale, and her freckles stood out starkly on her ashen skin. Her gray eyes were very wide and switched frantically from Pat to Em and back again. In her hands, she held a piece of paper and an odd-looking rose. It was all black, the petals made of shadow.

"She's gone! I don't know where to, but she's gone! Look!" Bridget thrust both pieces of evidence at them. Em took the thick monogrammed sheet, which she recognized immediately as the stationery from Isabel's desk, on which she wrote all of her correspondence. It read,

Dear Ones –

    I have discovered who is to blame. I am bringing them to justice. I did not want to endanger Em and so have gone on my own.

-IH

Emily was thunderstruck. Her eyes raced all over Isabel's elegant lettering. There was no need for a message from Aringa—Isabel had uncovered the culprit and now she'd set off to single-handedly take down the Mob. Emily put a hand to her heart, feeling so helpless she didn't know whether she wanted to cry or throw up or both. She stood studying the curlicued initials embossed at the top of the page. Despite the whirling questions, she thought it sounded just like something Isabel might do. But alone? Without help? Isabel hadn't heard Aringa's dire threats; she didn't know.

"And it was with this!" Bridget brandished the rose at Em, who handed the paper off to Pat and took the flower. Bridget snatched her hand back. "I think that came separate from all the papers, in a special little box. I don't know. Once I read the note I went . . . I went a little berserk and came out here!"

It was an odd thing, the black rose. Its petals were a dense matte, still furled tightly into a bud that nested in the green of the sepals. She looked at the bottom of the cut stem and could see the tightly packed veins, all ebony. Em had never seen a black rose like this in nature. Maybe someone had taken a white rose and put it into a glass of ink for a day, but who would do that? And why? Whoever it was, it didn't matter. It wasn't the look of it but its meaning that was the point.

She held the flower out to Pat, who recoiled as if she were handing him a poisonous serpent.

"What is it?" she asked, rolling the cold stem between thumb and finger, in between the thorns. "And where did you find it, Bridge?"

"When I went in this morning, that rose"—each word dripped with dread—"was sitting atop an open box, just its size. It looked like one of the boxes that was delivered yesterday. Oh, Mrs. Hewett!" Bridget was overcome, holding her apron to her face, and Pat looked stricken as well, his large eyes stark in his bottle-sick complexion, staring at the rose in her hand as if it could bite him.

"Some of the boys," he started, and then fell off, coughing. "Some of the boys I play cards and dice with, they've talked about the black rose. They say it means nothing good."

"What do you mean 'nothing good'? What, like poison?" Emily took a sniff of the bloom, shoving her nose into the velvety blossom, and both Bridget and Pat gasped. She looked between them, disbelievingly. "You can't be serious."

"They say," Pat said, eyeing the pitch-colored petals, "that those who receive a black rose don't live long." Pat leaned hard on his shovel, all the strength gone out of his legs. "They say that the rose lasts longer than the recipient."

This was met with absolute silence all around, and Emily looked down at the flower in her hand with more wonder and respect. Quite a powerful message for such a frail thing.

"What about the box, Bridget? The one that came with the rose?"

Bridge lowered her apron to reveal red and glistening eyes. "I'll show you. Oh, the Mrs.!" she said again and turned toward the broad porch of Hy House. Em and Pat ditched their shovels and followed.

At the threshold, Pat and Em made sure to wipe their shoes before walking across the pristine foyer floor, but they needn't have bothered. Once inside, it became clear that the chandelier was having some maintenance done as it was down at half-mast. The trio skirted a drop cloth with a stepladder set up under it, screwdriver at the ready on one of the steps, while above, the glimmering glass tinkled as they rushed up the staircase, Pat taking them two at a time.

Pat and Em paused at the threshold of Mrs. Hewett's bedroom while Bridget plunged ahead. Em hadn't been invited in here during her time at Hydrangea House, and Pat certainly would not have been invited into her aunt's inner sanctum.

The room, or rooms (for Em could see an adjoining suite or maybe a dressing room through an open doorway), smelled like Isabel, looked like Isabel, felt like Isabel, and even sounded like Isabel. Pat stayed at the threshold for the duration of their visit, but Emily abandoned him to step into the light-imbued blue-and-gold room as if walking into a dream.

Although every room in this house was a revelation to Em—a new scene she had to get used to and stretch her imagination to understand—this one was so personal, so intimate, so entirely Isabel, that Emily forgot their troubling circumstances as she moved through the space after Bridget. A clock chimed twice, a polished alto *ting ting*, from the other room as her feet whispered across the deep-pile Persian carpet.

Tall windows buffeted with organdy curtains spanned two walls, one set overlooking the grounds and gardens out toward the Methodist church, and the other with a view of the sycamore trees in front. Em could make out other shingled roofs beyond the dense trees, widow's walks peeking up over their angled crowns of new leaves.

The rest of the room seemed to be dressed in the colors of the ocean, with gold and bronze accents. It looked like the bedroom of a mermaid queen, Poseidon's wife perhaps, or some other aristocratic naiad. The centerpiece was the combination of the bed, wardrobe, and dresser, a matched set, all made of deep mahogany with gilded edges; the four-poster was draped with a hanging cloth which hid the bed completely.

On the other side of the room, open curtains afforded a splendid view of the gardens to the occupant of either a yellow wooden desk that sat in front of one window, or the leather opera chair and ottoman in front of the other.

There were fewer paintings in here than in the parlor downstairs, but the ones hanging in Isabel's boudoir were undoubtedly the best in her collection. And *boudoir* was certainly the only name for a bedroom as opulent as this one.

On the wall in between the two windows near the desk and the opera chair hung a gorgeous painting that instantly made Emily feel both sad and curious—an oil of a copse of trees at sunset or sunrise, the light barely there, the echo of a path boring into the shadows. Closer to the bed, beautifully matted and framed, hung a portrait of Emily the First. It was less formal than any of the others in the house, and Em immediately liked it the best. It showed, with just a few lines to indicate an eyebrow here, a cheekbone there, the impression of a face, with coppery curls surrounding the same dark eyes as Isabel's. But Emily the First's mouth was different, completely. In it lurked the suggestion of a clever joke, snappy repartee caught just behind her parted lips. (Or maybe, the difference was that Isabel's mouth had stopped smiling around the same time this mouth had.)

The room was richly appointed and impeccably tidy, not a slipper out of place or a paper tossed aside, until Em came around to the front of the armchair. A whine issued from the adjoining suite as Connor slipped in to stand just behind Bridget's skirts.

"This is where I spotted it," Bridget said, standing near the armchair and pointing. "This is where the rose was."

There, in front of the armchair, a strong box sat sprung open, its contents strewn across the upholstered stool and chair—photos, handwritten letters, important-looking briefs, and even more letters. On top of the nearest pile of papers sat a wooden box, about the size of a man's wallet. It was open, and on the yellow packing straw lay one single black petal.

Em leaned down and picked up a paper on top of the pile, scanning it. It was a letter from someone, but she couldn't tell who.

It was a few pages in, and it started mid-sentence. The top line read, *out of character for someone with such an upstanding moral character and background to get mixed up in this!* Each pen stroke cut into the paper. *Not only to be complicit in such illegal affairs*, the letter went on, *but to double-cross criminals. How careless and irresponsible! What am I to do?*

Emily pawed through the papers, looking for more of the letter. A page with an embossed symbol at the top, like the one on Isabel's note, caught her eye and she snatched it up, running her finger over the embedded script. It was a monogram done in a deep inky blue. There were smaller letters, an *A* and an *E*, on each side of an ornate *S. AES*: Ann Eliot Simpson. These were Ann's letters, from who knew when, which had somehow arrived at Isabel's doorstep.

A book, blue marbled cover and brown leather spine, lay face down on top of the pile of papers gracing the ottoman. It was open to a middle page, the top of which read, *Dear Diary*, written in the same jaunty handwriting which graced the letter. There was also a date, years before. It continued in Ann's quick script.

Dear Diary,

I met the most marvelous man today, all the way over here in France. What are the odds, I'm wending my way from triage tent to battleground and there, lying on the ground, is a fellow from my own neck of the woods! Not blown to pieces, like most of them, but raving from gas, so I only found out he was a Yank later on. They say he was lucky to make it out at all. He keeps calling me his muse. Diary, he's handsome, educated, funny, and he's a sailor too! What are the odds . . .

This went on for pages, Ann's writing changing pen colors, but for the most part staying true to its spiky, confident tone. She wrote with so much enthusiasm that the nib had pushed through the thin paper at multiple points in the cramped paragraphs.

Em scanned the words, picking up what she could, flipping the pages and checking for photographs or any other clues that might waft out of the journal and onto the carpeting. Nothing dropped out of Ann's diary, however; if there were any clues, Isabel had taken them with her, wherever she went.

Emily looked up. "Do you know when she left?" she asked Bridget, who shook her head violently.

"That's just the thing, Miss. I saw her last night when I brought up dinner, and it was then she asked me to bring her a morning tray as well, that she would be dining in her chambers again. That wasn't so odd. Before you came, she would eat most meals in her chambers." Bridget's hands twisted the apron so hard her already-red fingers turned purple. "But this morning, when I brought her some tea at seven, the door to her bathroom was closed, so I just thought she was dressing or bathing and left her the tray, took the one from last night, and went on my way. The chandelier is always a beast to clean and I wanted to get started." Bridget glanced at the papers strewn across the floor.

"So what you're saying is that Isabel could've been gone a while."

"Yes, that's what I'm saying. Maybe all night!" Bridget cried miserably. "When I came up just now, the tray was untouched, just as I left it, and the door to the bathroom was still closed. It gave me the shivers. When I knocked on the bathroom, no answer. I went in and found the note on the sink, with the rose." Bridget ran out of breath, her voice catching in her throat. She pulled her apron to her face again, wiping her nose on one corner of the stained brown cloth.

"Gone all night," Em breathed. She realized that she was still holding the rose and put it down quickly on top of the papers. She looked from Bridget's streaming eyes to Pat, who looked both immensely uncomfortable and terrified at the same time. His forehead was a crisscross of wrinkles, and the blue bruises underneath his eyes stood out sickly against his curdled complexion.

Much like when she, Fi, and Slick huddled in the bottom of Dreamland, Bridget and Pat observed her hopefully, as if she was the natural choice to take all of this in hand. And maybe she was—who was to say she wasn't?

"All right, then," she said. "Let's go downstairs and figure out where she went, and how we're going to get there."

Pat turned from Isabel's boudoir gratefully and started down the hall.

"I've got a pretty good idea where she's off to, Miss," he called from the hallway. "If she's after who I think she's after, she'll be heading out to the *Atlantis*." His voice echoed in the empty space usually occupied by the chandelier as Bridget followed her brother out.

Just as Emily was about to cross the threshold, Bridget waiting to shut the door, something on Isabel's sophisticated dresser caught her eye, something sitting amongst the many perfume bottles and silver trays. What she saw stopped her dead. An electric shock ran through her and her breathing ceased for several moments.

On the dresser's surface, a silver seashell held four blunt bullets, looking out of place between the silver-backed brush and comb, dishes of bobby pins, and red leather jewelry boxes. The sight of them there was so jarring it was like finding broken glass in a baby's crib.

Chapter 21

Emily didn't mention the bullets to Bridget and Pat when they congregated downstairs to construct a plan. The words lodged in her throat as the two pattered on to one another in ever-quickening Irish accents. She would have to tell someone, and fairly soon, as the situation was more than out of hand, and had been for quite some time now. But Bridget was already so upset at the idea of Mrs. Hewett gallivanting out to the floating speakeasy, Em knew sharing that she'd gone armed wouldn't help in any way.

The three formulated a course of action fairly quickly when they got to the kitchen. Bridget was to stay home, and Pat and Em were off to look for Isabel. Bridget didn't like it, not one bit, and she let them both know audibly and multiple times.

While she was waiting for the errant Isabel's return, Em suggested that Bridget ought to talk to Thankful Downs, the island telephone operator, to see if she knew anything. In return, Bridget suggested calling the police in at this point, as the threat to Isabel's life was growing by the second, but Pat immediately, albeit gently, suggested otherwise.

"May I remind you, Bridge, that there hasn't been any crime committed, and calling the authorities to go retrieve Mrs. Hewett from the *Atlantis* will make many a rumrunner angry."

Bridge winced as she considered that particular point of view and, grabbing a scratch pad and a pencil, she made haste to the telephone nook to call Thankie.

Em and Pat left the house, but not before Em had shrugged a coat on over her thick dress. Inside the garage, they hopped into the trusty truck, a familiar beast at this point, with Pat in his rightful spot as driver—but not before Em made a crack at his expense.

"You're sure you're comfy there, Pat? I could set up a place for you in the back and take the driver's seat?"

"Ha ha, Em, very funny," Pat said, red flushing his cheeks as he backed the truck out the garage bay and threw it into first to take them away from Hy House. But as he chugged around the shell semicircle of a drive, he was smiling.

Emily followed the reversing-to-forward process with interest as they went out the driveway and onto the road. Then she remembered: "Hey, Pat. There were bullets. On her dresser."

Pat glanced over as they began to coast down Main Street. "Bullets?"

"Yes, bullets. On Isabel's dresser. I saw them."

His face went still, and then suddenly he pounded his palm against the steering wheel, anger and sadness flashing across his features.

Em hesitated. "That's . . . not all. Yesterday in Oak Bluffs, Aringa and his guy came looking for us. Or maybe they just happened upon us and saw an opportunity, who knows. They told us to deliver a message . . . to Isabel. About meddling, and not to do it." Emily put a hand over the spot where Aringa had poked her; it still throbbed.

They sat in tense silence as the truck rumbled down Main Street. It was a perfectly ordinary Monday for most, and Edgartown bustled with commerce, a smattering of very early summer people strolling and gazing at the sturdy gray clapboard houses or zinging by on bicycles.

They took the left by the Edgartown Bank, heading out toward the lighthouse.

"What if . . ." Emily paused, terrified to lay out all her fears and suspicions but desperate to do so at the same time. "What if Isabel is right, and the Mob *did* murder Ann. That means—"

"That means she's gone out there with her accusations to confront some very dangerous men on their own turf." Pat gave her a look that was as sick and horrified as she felt. Em's stomach did a full somersault.

Pat ground the truck into a higher gear, and the stately brick buildings and white summer cottages whizzed by. They hit a pothole with a shuddering *clunk* that made it feel like the truck's end was going to drop off. A wash of cold swept over Em, and she stuck her trembling hands between her knees.

Pat downshifted and made an abrupt turn, fast, down a short hill toward the water. Before Em could ask where they were, a sign flashed by—*Harbormaster*. Pat put the truck into neutral as they coasted to a halt in a puff of dust in front of a fishing shack. The road continued, angling down a slick wet slope into the bottle-green water of the harbor, cradled by a dock on one side and a line of pilings on the other. A lively trade of fishing boats with motors and sailboats darted back and forth on the waterway, and a cluster of moored craft bobbed just past the end of the dock.

Em followed Pat out of the truck and up onto a splintery wooden porch.

"Our ride isn't here yet," he commented, looking out to sea, and gestured to the chairs rocking in the steady breeze. "Take a seat." Pat disappeared inside the shack, and his muffled "hello" was cut off by the slam of the screen door.

Emily sat down in a rocking chair and watched the crisscrossing boats of all sizes and shapes zip around on the skin of the harbor. It was fascinating, a whole different world on the water side of town. Edgartown Harbor was a gem because it stretched from the outer harbor at the lighthouse into the seclusion of Katama Bay, making it one of the most protected nooks on the Eastern seaboard. Judging from the lighthouse on her left and where town sat behind her to the right, Em guessed they were just about at the neck, where inner harbor met outer.

As she watched the graceful dance of the boats, one of them peeled away from a group to motor toward the public landing, its snout pointed her way and its loud motor reaching her even from a distance. She sat up and looked harder, but there was no mistaking that boat for any other on the water. She glanced around for Pat, but he was still inside, chatting with another man, voices of different timbres rumbling through the thin walls.

It was the same boat she'd seen on the owl hunt, Captain Butler's boat, its flanks washed with ink, and, as it coasted closer, she could see the red eye shape painted over the flaking black paint just below the tip of the bow. The craft nosed up to the dock in front of the harbormaster's office, bumping into the pilings with a wooden *thwack*.

Emily gulped, gripping the arms of the rocking chair and trying to appear normal.

As the boat pulled up alongside the dock, fenders were flung over the side, bouncing on the outside hull on their short tethers. The engine swung into a different guttural growl as the boat reversed, foam churning at its stern, and two lines quickly lassoed around the tall pilings, almost simultaneously, forward and aft. The fishing shack door thankfully swung open and Pat popped out, grinning, as he spotted the black boat. "Our ride!"

"Of course it is," Emily muttered to herself, wiping her sweaty hands on her wool coat. She wasn't exactly sure how one was supposed to comport oneself in front of a person one suspected of Murder, capital M, and actively ran from only a few days prior.

"Ahoy, Butler!" Pat called to the boat, and received a calloused wave out the wheelhouse for his trouble. "Don't look like that, Em. This is brilliant. He has the fastest boat in the harbor. We'll be out there in no time!" Em sighed and followed Pat down the steps and into the dirt patch that made up the parking lot. Pat danced backward, finding his James-Cagney grace again. "I'm amazed Butler was free to help us on such short notice—"

"I wasn't free," a voice growled from beside them. "I dropped everything and came when Thankie found me."

Em turned, startled, to regard a pair of the bluest eyes she'd ever seen.

Captain Butler stood in front of her, in a navy peacoat and a jauntily perched fisherman's cap, as he studied her with an evaluative look, employing the same amount of focus with which she regarded him.

"Hello again, Miss," he said, and then he did something truly surprising. He smiled.

The smile faltered when Butler turned it on Pat. "Are you sure this is wise, man? Does she have any experience on the water?"

"Some," Pat lied. "But here's the thing, Butler—Em is a very capable companion. Why, I'd want her around in a pinch more than anyone else." He threw her a wink. Em thought he might be recalling their excursion to Dreamland and, specifically, the ride back. And maybe it was true, she was a good pal to have in a pinch. "She'll wear a life jacket, won't you, Em? You'll see, she's very light on her toes and quick to learn." Despite her misgivings, Em glowed with Pat's praise.

Captain Butler remained unconvinced. "Is she even armed? What will she do if something, you know, comes up?"

"I haven't armed her." Pat looked stumped. "It didn't even occur to me."

Butler gave them both an exasperated look before digging around in his coat pocket, coming up with a folded rigging knife. He held it out to Em, but before she could grab it, he yanked it a few inches out of reach.

"Wait a moment . . . do you have a penny?"

Emily creased her brow but obediently dug around in her pockets until she found a copper coin. Butler took it and dropped the polished knife in her waiting palm.

"It's bad luck to give a knife as a gift, so you're buying it from me for one penny."

"That's a new one for me," Em said, but her anxiety subsided the slightest bit when she slid the reassuring warmth of Butler's knife into her pocket. "We don't need any more bad luck." Her mind flicked back to the dull finality of those four bullets on Isabel's mahogany dresser.

"Now that that's settled," the captain said, "it seems I'm to be your helmsman this afternoon. Won't you join me on the *Nola*?"

He held out his arm and, although it had been only a few days since she'd been terrified by him, she took it. There was something about his demeanor that convinced her that he was on their side—hers and Isabel's—and, besides, she really wanted to see him smile like that again. The woolen sleeve was rough like driftwood under her palm as he led her, gently, down to the dock, Pat following.

Pat and Captain Butler both swung onto the deck of the *Nola*, one after the other, with the innate grace of longtime boat people. Pat held up a hand to help her step from dock to rail and down. The *Nola* was a small fishing boat with a snug wheelhouse and a ladder leading up top, a bow and a broad stern from which to throw fishing nets or chum, and not a lot else. Like her outside, everything on board the *Nola*—the wooden deck, the long benches in the cockpit with a toe rail running up to the bow—was all painted black. Thankfully, Em didn't see any guns bolted to the deck. Captain tipped his cap her way as he disappeared into the wheelhouse.

Pat looked over. "You all right?" he asked over the sudden burst of life from the engine.

She nodded as the motor reverberated through her chest cavity like a dragon's growl. The *Nola* had quite a bit of power, apparently. Pat nodded back and, with more verve than he'd shown for most of the morning, leaped to the dock, untying the fore and aft lines and throwing them on board. The boat coasted away from the dock, engine's growl growing and gap widening. Pat jumped back onto the stern of the *Nola* at the last minute as the boat made a tight turn in the small slice of harbor in front of the marina. Then he made a clever bow from his perch atop the rail before he sprung onto the deck.

The *Nola* straightened and chugged through the moored skiffs and sailboats, a zigzag course until they got to the darker blue of the channel. As they wound their way through the anchored seacraft, Pat handed her a life jacket and demonstrated how to put it on by pulling on one himself. She donned the scratchy horseshoe-shaped device over her coat and clumsily tied it behind her back. It was bulky, but she wasn't complaining; although she was a strong swimmer, this was only the second ocean boat she'd ever been on, counting the ferry over to the island. Boats took some getting used to, Em decided, looking into the glassy depths of the water, and she didn't want to go swimming.

Captain Butler slowly blended the *Nola* into the flow of other boats, pointing her bow out past the lighthouse. Em found a seat on one of the long benches running aft; Pat made sure she was settled and then paid Butler a visit in the wheelhouse. Em hugged the scratchy, hard life preserver and hoped her stomach wouldn't be as queasy on this trip as it had been on her passage from the mainland.

The *Nola* put on more speed and soon the boat's entire bow lifted out of the water. Emily spread her arms out along the rail and gripped the wood, enjoying the chaotic howl of wind streaming by her ears. Above them, curious seagulls wheeled and cried, waiting to see if any fish scraps would be thrown overboard, before sailing off in search of easier, slower prey.

It wasn't the smoothest ride—the cold temperatures and burly breezes made for sizable swells once they got outside the harbor's safety zone—but Em reveled in the feeling of speed. The *Nola*'s stern settled into the sea as her bow lifted, taking each wave with ease. It was the most extraordinary feeling, a combination of power, uncertainty, and danger all wrapped into the roar of the engine.

The cold wind whipped Em's hair around, pulling it out of its braid and sticking it to her cheeks as they barreled through the waves. Along the starboard side, a stretch of beach spread along the shore, dotted with bathing cabanas and little else. Sandy cliffs rose and fell, tapering to a point upon which one lonely cottage sat. After that, the land ceased completely and there was only water.

Pat had told her that the ride would take around forty-five minutes to get the twelve miles offshore where the *Atlantis* plied her trade free of legal repercussions. He'd also reminded her, once again, how lucky they were for Captain Butler's involvement and his little-to-no insistence on payback for the amount of fuel he was using on both this leg and (hopefully, if all went well) the return too.

Emily closed her eyes, letting the sound of the motor and the wind blasting by her ears lull her into a reverie. She was having a dream in which she toppled off the boat and into the ocean, but instead of hitting water, she fell down a hole that suddenly appeared, and then turned into a tunnel, through which she wasn't even falling, more like flying or floating, and then the floor—Aunt Isabel's black-and-white parquet floor from the foyer of Hy House—came rushing up with scary speed to meet her. She had just put her hands up in terror when *bang!* she was wide awake again, sitting straight up and trying to find her bearings amidst the bucking boat motions and unfamiliar ocean terrain.

Emily stood, finding her footing as she stumbled toward the wheelhouse. The panorama of nothingness wasn't an entirely foreign sight to her; there had been plenty an afternoon in which she and Juniper had just gotten lost, adrift for hours amongst the prairie grass, showing them where the wind hit the hills. They would find some spot in the shade and share an apple or two, guess cloud shapes, watch the shadows race across the land, and exist without a care in the world until the sun started to go down.

Em grabbed the doorframe of the wheelhouse to steady herself and knocked. The two men huddled around the wheel in the dark cramped space were peering through the windshield. Pat glanced back at her and Captain Butler waved her in.

"Hello, Em. Got what we call cowboy coffee over here in the thermos," Butler said, the pipe stamped between his jaws, making his words come out half muffled. "But it probably ain't nothing like what the real cowboys drink, and I'd bet my last dollar you'd know the difference."

Em nodded, shivering under the heavy life jacket; any kind of coffee would warm her up some.

Pat handed her a tin cup and unscrewed the top of the oversized thermos, using both hands to pour as they rolled over the waves. She smiled and nodded, cupping both hands around the cup as she kept her balance. Getting her sea legs, Pat helpfully informed her.

When the coffee had warmed her up a little, she asked them, "Where are we?"

Captain Butler took the pipe out of his mouth, pointing its stem through the windscreen. "We're eleven and a half miles offshore, half a click away from the *Atlantis*. Question is, what are you going to do once we get there, which, by the way, will be very soon." He popped the pipe back in his mouth, plucked a pocket watch out of his plaid waistcoat, opened it, and considered its face. "Half past one, or almost. Business will be slow on the *Atlantis*. You'll be noticed, whatever it is you plan on doing."

Neither Em nor Pat spoke.

"A plan," Captain Butler repeated. "Tell me you have one?" One look at Pat's face seemingly told Butler all he needed to know. "Damn, Isabel hasn't a chance."

"That's not necessarily true," Emily piped up. "She has us, and we're here. So she has a chance. No point in being negative."

Butler conceded this with a *harrumph*. "We have a quarter of an hour to put together something as it will look very strange indeed if we show up and bob around off their starboard bow."

"Em," Pat said. "You'll stand out like a sore thumb if you come aboard, especially if there aren't a lot of patrons. You'll stay put with Captain Butler, and I'll go aboard the *Atlantis* and look for Mrs. Hewett."

"No! Pat—"

"He's right, Miss," the captain agreed. "You wandering around on board will draw more attention than anything else: a young girl, walking around that floating den of iniquity? You'll have no shot at helping your aunt like that."

"What about Aunt Isabel? She's on board."

"Isabel Hewett," the captain interjected, "has managed in more difficult situations than you can imagine."

Emily surrendered, grumbling to herself and hiding it in her coffee mug. But they were right, and she knew it.

As the *Nola* climbed one wave after another, the three explored a myriad of ideas in the poky space of the wheelhouse. Em found a seat on the bunk bench next to the steering column and drew a stiff plaid blanket across her legs to keep from shivering.

"Why are you doing all this, anyway?" Pat asked Butler after a few minutes. "Who's Isabel to you?"

Captain Butler looked over at him with such intensity that Em could feel the force of his gaze from where she sat tucked into the corner.

"I've always had a fondness for your aunt, Miss Em," he said in response, looking over at Emily and then back to Pat. "My loyalties run deep, especially for those who have been dear to me since childhood."

This dried up further conversation. Emily's courage was flagging. Perhaps this wasn't the right thing to do, coming out here on their own. Maybe they should've left it to the authorities. She hoped that Bridget had finally phoned the police.

"Let's stick with the simplest plan," Pat said, taking over. "The one we started with. I'll go aboard and find Mrs. Hewett. I've dealt with some of these guys before, granted, usually at the wharf or the shanty and never out here, but I can make some excuse for it, I'm sure. I'll chitchat with Aringa and his lot, set up a deal for some liquor further on in the week, and then I'll ask him if he's seen Mrs. Hewett."

"As to our part," the captain said, "we'll circle around, keeping far enough away so as to remain inconspicuous. Thanks to *Nola*'s muted dressing, we can do that neatly. At five thirty sharp, we'll come back for you, so be ready, hopefully with Isabel."

"Five thirty," Pat said, taking out his own pocket watch to check.

"And thar she blows," Captain Butler said softly, leaning forward and looking through the windshield.

Emily hopped up to get a better look at the shape looming toward them through the smudgy glass. All she could see was a chunk of a boat, a small steamship, much smaller than the vessel she'd made her original crossing on but larger than the *Nola*, bumping up on the horizon where, a moment before, there'd been nothing.

"That's it?" she asked. They were approaching from the stern, and all Em could see was the boat's boxy rear.

"That's it—Martha's Vineyard's answer to Prohibition: the *Atlantis*, serving all and sundry a variety of beverages and other diversions, twelve miles out."

"Any other traffic?" asked Pat, peering through the oily swirls at the windshield's edges. He gave up and left the wheelhouse, Em at his heels.

Outside, the air immediately dropped fifteen degrees and smelled much fresher. Dark clouds lay close, and rain spat intermittently as the wind blew sea spray sideways. Pat found a pair of binoculars inside a toolbox and pulled them out, swaying side to side as the *Nola* climbed one gray swell after another. Em's stomach was fine; she was too keyed up to be nauseous, but her heart raced as she kept one hand on the edge of the doorframe, finding the rhythm in her legs. Pat handed over the binoculars and she pulled them to her face with her free hand.

The *Atlantis* loomed large into her view: a top deck with a wheelhouse crowning it, generous windows, and a mezzanine deck running around the edges. Two metal staircases, fore and aft, led down to the main deck, which was mainly occupied by an interior area with still more windows, save for some deck space in the bow.

With its white hull and black trim, it looked like it was dressed in a dapper dinner jacket. On the stern, in fancy script, read *Atlantis*, and below that, when the waves didn't heave into view and block it, a black rose underlined the curved letters.

Emily shuddered.

At least they knew they were on the right trail.

Chapter 22

Captain Butler carefully nosed the Nola alongside the *Atlantis*, using the docking station that sat on the port side. A section of railing was missing from the main deck and a stiff walkway jutted awkwardly into the waves, terminating in a narrow float only a few feet across. It was this narrow float, bobbing on the waves, upon which Pat had to step at exactly the right moment, and then scurry up the gangplank to the main deck. Waiting there on the deck stood a man, head and shoulders above Pat, very much wearing a dinner jacket, white with black trim, just like the *Atlantis*.

Emily watched through the dirty windshield (both Pat and the captain wanted her to stay hidden) as the man in the dinner jacket held out his ham-sized hand to stop Pat from stepping onto the steamship's deck. Pat talked and gestured wildly, and, after a few seconds of listening, the stony guard broke into a cheery grin and let Pat through.

Soon after, the *Nola* made a large turn and plunged off to the northwest, traveling with the swells and riding them like the rare sledding expeditions Em had experienced in her flat life in Nebraska. They coasted until the *Atlantis* was a mere smudge on the horizon. Then Butler ratcheted down the throttle, letting the boat ride the waves naturally.

"Now we wait," Butler said, and settled back on his stool, wedging his broad shoulders into the corner and focusing his gaze out to sea.

Em found out that Captain Butler was not talkative in his most natural habitat—the wheelhouse of his own boat—and for this she was thankful. Her mind was churning and she felt panicked; she'd been like this since Bridget had thrust the rose at her. With a pang, she thought the last time she felt this way was the terrible endless night of her mother's passing, the tortured wracking coughs and too-few breaths in between. She sighed, pulling the ragged blanket up over her knees. She couldn't lose Isabel so soon after her mother; she'd only just found her.

It was quite boring on the boat, and without knowing what was happening on the *Atlantis*, it was the most torturous boredom Em had suffered in quite a long time, at least since the train ride. After about forty-five minutes of amiable silence, in which Em danced around with her racing thoughts, it occurred to her that, if Captain Butler had grown up with Isabel, "known her since childhood" as he'd said, then he would've also known Constance.

"Captain Butler?" she said, breaking the long silence.

Butler's head snapped up and his pipe drooped. "What is it?"

"I was just wondering: Did you know my mother? Constance Hewett?"

Butler cracked the window next to him open, letting a gust of icy, salty air blast through the close space, and knocked the tobacco out of his pipe's bowl. "I certainly did. My condolences."

Em offered a small smile. "Thank you. What was she like, my mama, when she was young? I've gotten some conflicting reports since arriving."

Captain Butler grinned, his teeth white in the gloomy interior of the wheelhouse. He repacked the bowl of the pipe from a leather pouch and found a box of wooden matches in a pocket. "I'll tell you a story about your mother that no one else will."

Emily's eyes grew wide in the semidarkness.

"I don't know if you know this, but Isabel and I used to go out walking together, and sometimes I'd come visit her when she was minding your mother, her little sister, in the gardens of Hy House.

Her father didn't exactly approve of me, so we were always secretive. And your mother helped us many times." His smile grew at Em's astonished expression. "She did."

Butler took a moment to strike one of the matches on the side of the box and touch it to his pipe bowl, illuminating half his face. The flame went out as he sucked in, a red cherry blooming in the pipe bowl. "You know that weeping willow out back?"

Em nodded.

"That's where we'd meet. And your mama loved to climb trees, not the willow, but the others, the apple and the dogwood closer to the house. We had a system that if she saw Bridget's mother or Dr. Hewett coming, she'd make a birdcall from her perch in the tree to signal us and I would scram or hide behind the fountain statue."

"Seamus."

The captain guffawed a cloud of smoke. "They still call him that? I'll be." He took a moment to restart his pipe. "Constance was usually calm about it, and good at the birdcalls, sounding just like them. But one day when I was there, she was sitting up in the dogwood tree when her father came home at some unexpected time and marched directly across the driveway and into the gardens, foregoing the house altogether. Constance absolutely panicked. Most of the time her line was a simple blackbird's call. You know, four notes—two low, one lower, then one high?" He pulled the pipe out of his mouth and whistled loudly in the small space.

Em nodded, smiling—she knew the call, and he did it well.

"When Constance saw her father, every thought left her head. From what she said later, she tried whistling, but her mouth was too dry. Then she tried again, but by that time he was almost to the willow. Finally she just hollered out, 'For Heaven's sake, cock-a-doodle-doo! Cock-a-doodle-doo!'"

Emily burst out laughing and Butler smiled at her through the smoke.

"Of course, that stopped Dr. Hewett in his tracks, leaving me plenty of time to get away. Constance got a real scolding for it. Seems he was directly underneath her when she yelled. He may have even fallen down."

Em ruminated on this scene as Captain Butler contentedly pulled at his pipe and made small adjustments at the wheel. "That's not even the end of it," he continued. "For the next two months, she made us call her 'our hero' anytime we addressed her. It was something else. *She* was something else."

Emily smiled, gazing out at the waterscape barely visible through the windscreen. She liked thinking of her mama like that, hollering so loudly as lookout that she alarmed her otherwise grave father. She pictured her mother laughing her head off in the high branches, as silently as she could, until she was found out and called down to the ground.

IT WAS PAST five thirty and something wasn't right.

Captain Butler didn't say as much, but the force with which he ground his pipestem between his teeth increased, as did the number of times he consulted his pocket watch.

They'd puttered back toward the *Atlantis* through the swell and increasing foul weather, climbing one large moving hill after another, until they were just off the starboard bow. Butler steered them around to the port side to see if Pat and Isabel Hewett were nicely chitchatting with the giant guard Pat had sweet-talked before.

Nobody stood at the top of the gangplank as Captain Butler maneuvered the smaller boat around the larger one. The weather and visibility were deteriorating quickly.

The large boat was eerily deserted. Emily popped her head out of the wheelhouse and watched as the *Atlantis* loomed up next to them. Its oval windows were lit from the inside, most with thick curtains pulled across them, obscuring the view into the interior. Emily grasped the thick transom wire with one hand, the bulky life preserver rasping her cheek. She pulled herself up onto the rail to get a better view, just as she had when climbing fences and roofs back in Nebraska. Across four feet of turbulent water, the docking platform bobbed just off the *Nola's* bow. Em glanced back into the dark doorway of the wheelhouse.

"Don't you dare!" Butler barked from the shadows, but he didn't pull the *Nola* away; he kept her steady, as if considering.

The wind yanked at Em's body, as she stood, bobbing on the rail. "I have to!" she yelled into the wind. "There's no one there! Something's wrong!"

She didn't wait for his response but turned forward again, focusing on the bobbing platform and the irregular waves and the wind and trying to time it all correctly. Right before she was about to spring, Butler bellowed from the wheelhouse: "You can't do this!"

Em was indignant. Honestly, why did they keep doubting her? "I've roped calves, jumped gorges, and rode through the worst thunderstorms you've ever seen. I've even faced down a three-year-old bull with a highly irritable disposition!" she yelled back with a fury matching the wind and waves. "I can do this!"

His shadowy form was just visible in the darkened wheelhouse, holding tight to their course. She thought he was going to forbid her from jumping aboard the *Atlantis* when his gruff growl sliced through the wind again.

"All right," he said. "You got my knife?"

She nodded.

"Use it if you have cause to," he said, and then disappeared to keep the *Nola* steady while she jumped.

Em watched the waves, trying to decipher some predictable pattern, then, not finding one, she held her breath and jumped over the four feet of ocean to the dark square bobbing above the churning waters. Both her hands flailed at the float's wet rope and her feet skidded on the slick surface when she landed and, for a brief moment, she thought she had overestimated and was going to tumble into the waiting waves. Then her hands got a grip and her feet stuck, and she was on the platform, sea legs sorely tested. Rain needled her face on one side as Emily took a few large steps, using the wooden ridges lining the gritty gangplank for traction and squinting her eyes against the elements. The wind and rain were no longer separate, as if they'd been blended together in one of Bridget's kitchen gadgets; now it was just a fast-moving mist.

She reached the top of the gangplank and crouched, feet braced and grip tight on the cold wet post sleeve. No one was about, but instead of setting her mind at ease, this made Emily go colder than the metal beneath her palm. She crab-walked forward and onto the main deck a few feet, scurrying over to a rounded doorway that was shut tight against the weather.

Peeking through a porthole fixed in the center, Em cranked the handle to swing the door inward, revealing a stretch of dance floor with an abandoned bar glistening along the mirrored back wall. The room was empty, but a radio played from a small stage that had been made to look like a shell—a rounded front, scalloped details standing out from the walls, and a painted seascape at its edges.

The room looked like a dance hall, with tables and banquettes set around a broad open area in the middle. In between the oval windows, inset lanterns glowed weakly. Other than these and the backlights on the bar, everything appeared hazy and dim.

From another room, a sharp voice suddenly cut into the jaunty dance music, and then another one, louder, angrier.

Emily froze.

The voices seemed to be coming from a half-open doorway to the left of the shell bandstand.

Tiptoeing across the bouncy wooden floor, Emily scampered toward one of the black-and-green leather banquettes on the opposite side, sliding in as if she were taking a seat.

Suddenly, the half-open door next to the stage swung open. Light and shadow spilled across the dance floor. Em threw herself down on the bench, out of sight she hoped, and drew up her knees, screwing her eyes shut. The radio sang on. "*I can't do any more, I tried so hard to please . . . But let me thank you for those tender memories.*" Through the tune, she could hear a man's steps, getting closer and closer, and then, thankfully, retreating.

Em made herself count to sixty three times, her right hand pressed to the reassuring bulge of the knife in her pocket. After her third time through, she sat up and looked around. She was still alone; nobody loomed over her. She scooted over to the window near her table and saw a glint of white near the gap in the railing on the main deck, where the dinner-jacketed guard had taken up his post again.

Creeping to the stage, Em quick-stepped across its raised surface, feeling exposed, expecting a harsh yell at any moment. The shell shape took up most of the back wall but actually stood independent from it, creating a lucky hollow behind. Em tucked herself into the dusty space, just feet from the open door, and waited, listening.

The men's voices weren't as loud anymore, but she could still make out their tense, unsettled energy from her hiding spot.

"It wasn't your place." He trilled his *r* in a familiar way. "You shouldn't have made any kind of move at all and yet here I am. *Here I am!* And here we *all* are."

The sound of glass breaking was followed by a few breathy gasps and a shrill cry that made Emily's heart clench. That sounded like Isabel.

"Listen, Aringa." This other man had no accent, and his voice sliced through the noise like a hatchet. "I hate to inform you, but no one tells me what to do, least of all you."

Behind Emily, the radio announcer came on, followed by a big-band song that drowned out some of what she could hear. Her pounding heart added to the din, and she was terrified she was going to sneeze from all the dust in this cramped space.

"Sir, I have to protest!" a woman said in a shaky voice. Emily's heart stopped. *Oh no*, thought Em. Isabel.

"You put yourself in this position, you silly woman!" the stranger brayed.

There was a thump and then a yell that could've been Pat or could've been someone else.

"You've been too nosy for your own good!" hollered the stranger. "I think we should leave her a reminder, don't you, Rosso? I mean, more than just a flower delivery. Something permanent. So she'll stay out of our business."

Dead silence.

Behind Emily, the band played on. Time slowed down and stretched like cold molasses. Whatever she was going to do, she'd have to do it now or Isabel was going to get hurt. Emily slipped the knife from her pocket to her hand. She'd wielded knives before, though rarely in defense and never against other humans (not even at family reunions when the cousins would wage war on one another). She wanted to get it to Pat somehow. She shuffled forward a few feet, crouching to make herself smaller.

The sound of scraping chairs and a growl of protest made her flinch.

"Don't you move!" the strange voice said in a snarl that Emily could barely hear. "You see me, you see what I got!"

Another breathy shriek, more like a gasp, from her aunt. It was now or never. She took a couple of quick breaths to steady herself. Her mother was right: Bravery wasn't about not being scared; it was about being scared and doing it anyway.

Her aunt shrieked. "Don't you dare!"

Em jumped through the doorway, immediately assaulted by a hectic visual tableau.

The room was a cross between an office and a storage room, boxes and boxes of booze lining every available space except for a path to a circular clearing where a table and a few chairs were lit from above by a single swinging lightbulb. Around the table perched Aringa and his man, the one with the puffed-up ears. Next to this pair, who Em noticed had odd, pinched looks on their faces, Garrett Winterholler sat in a kingly manner, looking intently at Isabel, who was as wan as clotted cream with one hand spread on the table. Her opal, winking fire, was the most colorful thing in view. Pat sat at the head, tied to a chair, twine so tightly wound around him that it got lost in the folds of his shirt. His familiar bandana had been jammed into his mouth and his head hung low. Something dripped off his nose.

Then Em saw the most alarming detail of the scene. Winterholler, of all people, had his hand pressed hard on Isabel's wrist. His other hand held a knife, the blade tip barely two inches away from her aunt's frail and freckled skin. Isabel was twisting her hand wretchedly.

Emily took this all in in a few seconds, making a mental imprint. Then, quickly, before she was noticed, she scanned the walls, finding what she was looking for in an instant. They hadn't noticed her yet. It was time to make her entrance.

The only thing she could think to do was wake the farm.

"*Cock-a-doodle-doo!*" she screamed as loud as she could, and every pair of eyes whipped in her direction.

"Em!" Isabel yelled in horror, meeting her gaze for a split second before Emily hit the light switch and plummeted the room into darkness.

Chapter 23

After a few moments of utter sightlessness, a man's yell cracked the silence, and the chaotic clatter of the table overturning and crashing to the ground filled the room. More yelling. A meaty thump and then a long groan, likely from Pat.

Then, two gunshots—*bang bang*—with the lightning flashes showing Winterholler in a face-off with the man with the puffy ears, guns pointed at one another while the reports deafened them all.

Emily choked on the sharp acrid smell of gunpowder as she listened to someone coming toward her, fast, frighteningly fast. She couldn't see a thing after the sudden lightning of the guns. The *thud thud thud* of footsteps swelled as she desperately fanned smoke from her face, straining her eyes after the bright flashes. She sensed a rushing movement, and then a body smashed into her, shoving her hard against the wall. The heavy form lurched by and out through the open door as she crumpled against the boxes.

More incoherent yelling and someone tripped as Emily pulled herself up along the doorframe in the blackness, hands blindly searching. Finally, she found the switch and pressed the on button.

The room shot into light and her eyes were greeted with another scene, but this time the brightest thing was the red slash of blood where the table used to be.

Face down at their feet, the shoulder of the boxer's white jacket bloomed blood.

Nearby, Isabel crouched next to Pat, whose chair had overturned with him still tied to it, his back to Emily and legs sprawled. Aringa stood surveying all of this with a stunned look, his face ashen beneath his dark widow's peak.

Garrett Winterholler was gone.

"Isabel!" Emily yelled as she shot down the narrow path amongst the boxes to where Isabel leaned over Pat.

"Emily!" gasped Isabel. "What on earth are you doing here? You could've been killed!" Beside them, Aringa knelt next to his comrade.

"Come on, we have to go," Em said, tugging at her aunt's sleeve. "Now. Let's get him up."

Pat groaned and mumbled incoherently as Isabel and Emily righted his chair and Em cut through his bindings with Butler's knife, flicking it closed and tucking it into her jacket pocket. A pool of blood and saliva leaked from between his swollen lips when Em yanked the bandana out of his mouth and he coughed spasmodically, leaning over and breathing hard. Softly, he said, "That rat bastard," and spat on the wooden floor.

The air in the room reeked of spent gunshots, the iron tang of spilled blood, and spilled booze from broken bottles.

"This, this is not good," Aringa said, raking his hands through his hair, leaving divots.

"Yes, obviously," Isabel said.

"You, you here, is no good," Aringa said, looking at the three of them—Pat, Isabel, Emily—clenched together as if he'd never seen them before. "You can't be here!"

"What . . . what happened?" Em asked, looking at the back of Isabel's shaking hand.

"You, girl, how did you get out here? Can you get back?" Aringa took a spotted kerchief from the pocket of his jacket and swiped at his gleaming brow.

"I may have made a simple miscalculation," Isabel said, straightening her hat and gaining some of her composure back. "Instead of Signor Aringa, here, it was, in fact, Garrett Winterholler who was the culprit all along."

"You being here is no good for any of us! You must leave, now, immediately. *Velocemente!*" Aringa looked down at the body of his friend. "I will deal with this. There can be no police involved. Not for him."

At that moment, the guard in the dinner jacket appeared in the doorway, gun half drawn.

"No, Luca. It's not them. It's the other. That Winterholler." Aringa spat the name. "Find him."

Luca nodded and disappeared, gun fully exposed now.

Emily and Isabel exchanged glances and nodded to one another. Pat, who didn't say a word, stood, delicately, holding one palm over his side as Aringa herded them with wide arms away from the corpse down the narrow path.

When they reached the doorway, Aringa stayed behind, silhouetted in the frame. "And if any one of you ever says anything about this . . ." He didn't have to finish; his expression was enough. He soon disappeared back into the storeroom. Em would be glad to never see that man's face again.

With Emily in front, Pat limping just behind her, groaning and swearing with every step, and Isabel taking up the rear, they filed past the seashell bandstand, across the dance floor, and through the same door with the porthole Em had used.

The ground beneath them pitched back and forth, and Isabel took the lead as Em held out an arm for Pat.

"Have you been shot, Pat?" she asked, cautiously threading his good arm around her shoulders.

"Not so much. Just beaten up. May have even broken me ribs," he said shortly, painfully. They hop-limped along the wet wooden planks as Em watched their feet. "Thanks, Em," he said and coughed. "Not just for this, but for the light-switch routine. Quick thinking."

"Agreed," Isabel said from in front, where she scanned the horizon. "We shall discuss the impetuosity of your decision later, Em, but it was quite fortuitous in the end and undoubtedly saved our lives." Isabel reached back to squeeze Em's hand. "Now, how are we getting back? I'd like to get off this dressed-up barrel of bolts as soon as humanly possible."

"Captain Butler's close. Hold on." Pat held onto Em for strength with his good hand. He poked the two fingers of his weakened hand into his mouth and let out a shriek of a whistle, collapsing onto Em as soon as he was done, all his strength gone.

Isabel nodded, more at Emily than at Pat. "Our hero."

—

THE TWELVE MILES plus between the *Atlantis* and the safety of Hy House were dark, watery, treacherous, and mostly spent huddled in the front cabin of Butler's wheelhouse. The four shared bitter coffee, still fairly hot out of the tin thermos, and the sordid details of the last few hours' events.

"Yes, it was Garrett Winterholler all along. That's what Ann's letters told me. I admit," Isabel said, "coming out here was impulsive and rash, and I apologize." Isabel leaned into Em beneath the scratchy blanket.

"And coming out here *armed* was especially foolhardy," Pat said from next to Butler at the wheel.

"What do you mean," Isabel said, "armed?"

"I saw the bullets," Em informed her. "On your dresser. Four of them."

"Those were not for any gun of mine, my dear," her aunt returned. "Those I found in the box with the black rose."

"Oh!" Em's arms erupted into goose pimples at the thought of the rose softly encased in straw alongside a handful of bullets. "You"—she held up a finger—"Bridget"—she put up another—"Pat"—she held up three—"and me." She finished, holding up her pinkie. "All of us."

"Indeed," Isabel said.

After a while the shock wore off, and Isabel could relay to them what she'd learned from the letters and journals delivered to Hy House the day before. The plot of Ann's mystery suitor thickened, all veiled in Ann's pithy language. In the letters, Isabel discovered that Garrett Winterholler was indeed an expert sailor, certainly skilled enough to hold his own, at least for a few moments, on a stormy sea while tying ropes around his unconscious fiancée's wrists. And as the letters grew less rapturously in love and more somber, new and increasingly alarming discoveries coming to light, it became altogether too clear that Winterholler was not only involved in organized crime and illegal booze trading, he was also double-crossing the Mob itself. It had always been Garrett Winterholler; it made so much sense now, like a painter dabbing a final shadow onto the canvas so that the picture snaps together.

Isabel told Ann and Garrett's love story as they slid up one wave and down another at a much less frenetic pace than their initial approach to the *Atlantis*. Ann met, or remet, her intended on the battlefields of France, and fell in love there, amidst the broken bodies and mud. Then it got complicated.

As the *Nola* plowed her way home through the slashing rain, Isabel told them that Winterholler wooing Ann had seemed so innocent to all of them, and maybe it had been at first. Their chance meeting on the front lines. Winterholler couldn't have planned how marvelously situated Ann's Vineyard house was for rumrunning, nor could he have foreseen Prohibition, Rum Row, and all the rest of it. He'd have to be psychic, and neither Isabel (nor Em) believed in that sort of woo-woo nonsense.

No, it must've been a striking coincidence, and indeed an amazing revelation for Winterholler to discover that his new love interest happened to be an heiress with a very convenient cove of her own. It must've been whipped cream, chocolate sauce, and a cherry, all in one.

The rain intensified when they were halfway home, which bogged them down even more, doubling their trip time. Despite the injuries to his ribs, Pat gained mobility once he tied his scarf tightly around his chest and could even help Butler motor through the outer harbor through the clouds of rain and wind as Emily and Isabel shivered in the wheelhouse.

Finally, once they'd navigated through the maze of pilings and rain-battered boats to the dock, Captain Butler handed Isabel his umbrella to protect her from the rain. They held it clasped between them for a few seconds in the dark wheelhouse, Em doing her best to remain inconspicuous on the bunk, but not so inconspicuous so as not to notice Butler's hand gently resting atop Isabel's.

"Thank you, Frank, for all that you have done here."

"Anything, Isabel," he said simply, "for you."

The umbrella turned out to be indispensable. The rain pummeled them the twenty or so feet they trotted to Hy House's truck, which stood sentinel in the vacant parking lot. Although Isabel had probably never ridden in this truck as she always preferred the Pierce-Arrow, she blithely threw herself across the bench, making room for Em as quick as she could, who shook and closed the umbrella, pulling it in after. For the first time, Em noticed that Isabel was definitely outfitted to go after the bad guys in a double-tweed jodhpurs and jacket, all soaked through and filthy, but still retaining their sharp crease.

Pat slipped into the driver's seat but, after a few groans as he tried to manipulate the gearshift and wheel, locked eyes with Em across Isabel. He didn't have to say a word. Em nodded and popped out into the rain, jogging around the front of the truck and holding open the door. Pat wretchedly slid out, taking a spot in the back of the truck just like on their return from Dreamland, except this time under his own steam. He was so worn out he had to lift his legs, one by one, with his good hand to get them into the truck, but soon he knocked on the back window before lying down out of view with a low groan.

"You can't be serious," Isabel admonished, staring at her in the driver's seat and placing a smudgy but still elegant hand to her brow.

"Don't worry, Isabel. Pat has taught me well."

"What, in a week?"

"Do you see a viable alternative?"

Isabel stared at her incredulously for a few more seconds, then she sat straight.

The *Nola* didn't stay any longer than she had to either, making the tight turn in the rain-dark landscape in front of the pier. Butler's hand flashed from the wheelhouse, and then he and the boat disappeared from view, the hull blending with the shadows.

Emily carefully put her feet on the pedals and let her mechanical mind take over, checking valves and levers before twisting the key. She didn't try to think too hard about what her hands and feet were doing and, luckily, she didn't have to—instinct took over. The truck chugged to life and Emily eased into first like she'd been driving for years. Isabel made one breathy gasp as they hit a pothole at the top of the hill, braced herself between the dashboard and the seat as Em put her into second and coasted onto North Water Street, and didn't say another word until they pulled into the driveway.

Back at Hy House, once again, Bridget was waiting for them.

The minute the old truck rumbled over the white shells of the driveway, the kitchen door flung open and Bridget scurried out with another umbrella. Picking their wet way around puddles from the truck to the sanctity of Hy House's kitchen was so reminiscent of Em's arrival on the island that she found herself caught in a swirl of déjà vu. The presence of Isabel, however, shivering next to her as Bridget deposited them by the potbellied stove jolted her back to the present.

They stood together in complete shock like scolded schoolgirls waiting for the headmistress to mete out her punishment.

Bridget bustled around, at a loss for words but otherwise keeping it all well in hand, pushing a mug of tea into her mistress's palms and throwing an old blanket she retrieved from somewhere over Emily's shoulders. At last, the dam broke and Bridget's anxious concern and relief spilled forth: "Oh my, Mrs. Hewett! Oh my! What in the world! Let's get you into the parlor for a moment to see what's to be done. Come along."

As Bridget herded Em and Isabel like docile sheep headed for a shearing down the hallway, the cuckoo clock went into its paroxysms with a whirl and a wooden jangle as they passed. Nine o'clock. They'd been gone all day.

They entered the blessedly warm room, still in all their traveling garb, although Em had remembered to take off her life jacket on board Butler's boat. Em's wool coat was soaked through, and Isabel's hat had flopped over like a dispirited houseplant. She gripped the handle of Butler's umbrella. Out in the hall, the glass chandelier jingled, still waiting to be cleaned; Bridget hadn't had the time or inclination to finish the job.

"You stay here," she said, turning to dash out of the room. "I'll fix up some tea."

"No, Bridget." Mrs. Hewett's voice rang out as she held her hands to the fireplace, which housed a small crackling blaze. "Call the police. Somebody may have already, I hope." Isabel lowered herself into an armchair with as much grace as possible and gazed into the flames. "And then, if you please, get the tea. And some Scotch for me."

Bridget disappeared from the doorway as Isabel gestured to the other armchair for Em, drawn up snug by the fire. Perched by the grate, the warmth washed over her, and the wool of her drenched coat sizzled after a few contented moments of silence.

"It's all over, then," Emily said, looking over at Isabel, who, although disheveled and distraught, still looked beautiful and regal somehow, like Queen Victoria if she had been asked to fix a flat tire.

Isabel's eyes remained closed as she answered. "We'll call it over once the police have taken our statements, dear."

"That's an idea," came a man's low growl from the doorway. "Too bad nobody's going to call them."

Em whipped her head around to see Bridget standing stiffly at the door, her eyes wide, her face a rictus of fear and surprise. In one shaking hand she held a screwdriver, the same one she'd been using to dismantle the chandelier, and her other was trapped behind her back, wrenched at a grotesque angle by her captor.

Garrett Winterholler stepped across the threshold, pushing Bridget into the room, his left fist clamped on her arm. Blood had splashed his white button-up shirt in a bright slash, and he'd lost his dinner jacket somewhere between the *Atlantis* and Hydrangea House. His helpful-neighbor visage twisted into a sneer of hatred, a tremor twitching one eye. A mean-looking scratch ran from his left temple to just below his lip, and blood covered that side of his face, staining the white collar. In his right hand, a gun.

Winterholler shoved Bridget and she stumbled, whining in pain as her arm wrenched further out of its socket.

"Bridge," Em said in a trembling voice. She felt like throwing up; her heart slammed painfully in her chest.

"Don't you move!" Winterholler snarled, jabbing the gun toward Isabel, who was halfway out of her seat.

"You're in my house, Mr. Winterholler," she growled, her violet eyes burning and wide.

"You already gave me this!" Garrett gestured with the gun to the jagged welt on his face. "I won't trust you near me for the short time we're together." Winterholler stabbed the gun at Emily. "You! Up!"

She cringed and then stood, even though every muscle in her body screamed not to.

"Come here!"

She glanced at Isabel, who had a hand over her heart, shaking her head so hard her hair came loose.

"*Now!*" Winterholler brayed, spittle and blood spraying the space between them, and all three women startled at the harsh yell. He pointed the gun straight at Emily's forehead. "I won't ask again."

What could she do? With heavy, dread-filled boots, Emily walked toward Winterholler, who torqued his mean grip on Bridget's arm until the pain showed through the creases of her face.

Emily was but four steps from Winterholler, his brown eyes

roving greedily all over her expression. Who knew what he planned to do with her? To her. The muscles stood out in the forearm that held the gun, its iron like dead space or a black hole, sucking all the life and light from the room. The only other sounds were Bridget's panicked panting, the soft crackle of the fire, and branches scraping the windowpanes.

Emily's hands were shaking so badly she had to shove them in her pockets. And that's when her left hand closed around the smooth hilt of Captain Butler's rigging knife. Courage surged through her, and she looked away from Winterholler and straight into Bridget's wide eyes.

As Emily took her next clumsy step forward, almost as if she and Bridge were in an overture of some odd dance, a change came across the other woman's countenance. Her gray eyes lit up as if a flame flared behind each, and her eyebrows smoothed out, undoing all the creases of pain. Then, astonishingly, she winked.

In an instant, Bridget's arm flew up and, with the force of thirty-five years of pounding dough and slinging wet blankets onto lines (among the thousand other things she did with those arms on a daily basis), she jammed the screwdriver two inches into Winterholler's thigh, with the wooden handle sticking out absurdly.

Winterholler yowled a high-pitched shriek of disbelief, shoving Bridget away and pawing at his thigh. But he didn't drop the gun.

Em saw her chance. With all the strength she'd gained wrestling calves and hurling bales of hay, she locked her shoulder and rammed it into Winterholler's midsection, where his stomach and torso met. He was still surprised by Bridget's attack and she caught him off-balance; Winterholler went sailing into the hall, the air knocked clean out of him. He sprawled ingloriously in the hallway, feet in the air like an upturned bug, and tried without much success to suck in a breath.

"Go!" Bridget screamed as she went for the gun in Winterholler's hand. He saw her coming and rolled out of the way, shrieking when the hilt of the screwdriver glanced off the floor.

Isabel's hand clamped on Emily's shoulder, spinning her toward the stairs and away from Winterholler. He was trying to get at the screwdriver, gasping and clawing at it, but he was still able to keep the gun from Bridget. Just as Bridget lunged for the gun again, they ran, Isabel dragging Emily by force across the foyer, where the half-hung chandelier tinkled over the ladder. They dashed around the corner, away from the main staircase, past the dining room, and down the hall.

A yell from behind them—Bridget's—and then, horribly, a gunshot. So loud and final that Emily thought it was the sound of her heart breaking into a million pieces.

"Bridget!" she screamed, but Isabel gripped her collar and yanked hard, tugging her along behind.

The glimpse of the telephone cubby as they rushed by showed the pad, usually primly stacked on the wooden desk and awaiting messages, sprawled on the ground.

The two charged up the narrow servants' stairs, Isabel in front clumping up frantically with the umbrella, and Em with her hand on Isabel's back, glancing behind her every few seconds.

As soon as Isabel reached the top, Winterholler jumped into view at the bottom, looking absolutely unrecognizable. His cheek was bleeding again, and the whites of his eyes were brilliant in the mottled mess of his face. Emily had never been so scared in her life. A shriek escaped her chest as she and Isabel hustled up the last stairs, spilling them onto the upper landing.

They scrambled to their feet and ran as fast as they could along the darkened hallway, Garrett's footsteps pounding hollowly on the stairs, too close behind them.

As they flashed past Isabel's rooms, Isabel blurted, "Wait!" and came to a skidding stop.

"Isabel!" Emily screeched to a halt a few steps ahead. "What are you doing?"

Isabel wrenched the door open just as Winterholler appeared at the end of the hall.

A booming bark exploded from Isabel's boudoir and Connor,

in a flash of brown and white, flew past his mistress and made two beautiful leaps toward their attacker.

Winterholler was not expecting this and his mouth dropped open in a strange, garbled yell. "Yarglll?" he screamed and raised the gun as Connor's sizable paws hit his chest. *Bang!* The sharp report blasted through the hallway, knocking out all other sounds, and Connor smashed into him, slamming them both against the far wall.

The women screamed and ran for the other end of the hallway—their only escape route.

Taking the steps on the ladder as fast as she could, Emily burst through the trapdoor to the widow's walk. Raindrops pummeled her face, momentarily blinding her as she pulled herself into the sheets of rain. Turning to grasp Isabel's raised arm, she heaved her aunt out onto the roof, guiding her to a railing.

"I swear to God, if he killed my dog I will murder that man," Isabel shouted as Em grabbed the splintery trapdoor, a legion of tiny wooden spikes digging into her hands. Groaning with effort and fresh pain, Emily hauled the heavy trapdoor on its hinges to slam shut on the roof.

Safe, we are safe, she thought. But just as the hatch swung down, a broad hand—his hand—stopped it with a sturdy *thunk*. Emily screamed again, her throat on fire.

She threw herself against the door, wild with fear, shoving her entire body weight against it, but to no avail. The trapdoor was slowly pushed open from below, creaking as if it would splinter from the pressure, until Garrett Winterholler's ghoulish face appeared. He kept pushing until Em had no choice but to jump off. Like Hades emerging from the underworld, Winterholler stepped onto the roof into the wind and the rain, gun pointing directly at Isabel.

"You should've just stopped!" he screamed, punctuating each word with a stab of the gun in Isabel's direction.

Emily found Butler's knife again in her pocket, sneaking it out and flicking it open behind her back. She was just in Garrett's periphery.

"You couldn't stay out of it!" Sheets of rain cleaned his face of blood, making him seem more human, despite his snarl. He cocked the pistol.

"She was my friend! I wasn't going to stand by and let you get away with it!" Isabel shouted back. "You coward!"

Garrett slapped Isabel Hewett so hard she was half thrown over the railing, which seesawed outward with a creaky yawn.

It was at that moment, when Winterholler was duly distracted, that Emily brought the rigging knife down into his shoulder as hard as she could, where it struck and stuck, just like the screwdriver had done. The blade sank in with a fleshy impact that shook her to the bone, a feeling she would never, as long as she lived, ever forget. Stabbing someone, it turned out, was harder than she expected.

Garrett screamed and spasmed, throwing his hands in the air, almost giving up the gun, but he held onto it as he twisted this way and that, desperately grabbing at the knife sticking from his hunched shoulder, incoherent shrieks and groans spilling from his grotesque lips as he swiveled and pitched wildly around the small square of the widow's walk.

Isabel pushed off the precarious railing and took two steps forward, toward the thrashing man. Garrett stumbled back in shocked response before he remembered *he* was the one with the weapon. He partially raised it, rain bouncing off black metal, but Isabel was too fast for him.

She opened the big umbrella right under his hand, catching him off-guard and shoving the nose of the gun to the sky. "Get out of here!" she screamed. "You miserable bastard!"

Winterholler's arms pinwheeled as he wobbled backward, pitching like the mast of a capsizing sailboat, until his body slammed against the railing. With a splintery squeal, it let go and spilled Garrett Winterholler off the roof, his arms flailing back, gun in hand, Butler's knife jutting from his bloody shoulder, and an eternally surprised expression slathered across his face.

And then he was gone. The only things left were Em and Isabel and empty space and the cacophony of the storm whipping around them.

Isabel rushed to Emily, enveloping her in a hug that smelled like fear and sweat and a hint of Chanel No. 5. They held each other as the rain suddenly tapered off, as if someone upstairs had turned off a faucet.

Without a word to one another, the two shuffled cautiously to the edge of the roof, where the broken railing left a jagged opening to emptiness. They peeked over, but the roof was too high and its angle such that all they could really see was one of Garrett Winterholler's legs. It wasn't moving.

"Now," Isabel whispered, "now it's done, my girl."

The fall had knocked his shoe off and his sock was dirty.

Isabel squeezed Emily's arm. "Bridget," she said, "and Connor." Her voice was husky with tears.

Emily opened the trap again, her muscles screaming, and was delighted to see the happy smile and wagging tail of Connor, sitting and waiting for his next command. When Isabel got down to the floor, kneeling beside him, she cried as he lapped up the tears and rain from her face.

"Good boy," Isabel kept saying. "Such a good boy."

When Emily and Isabel made it downstairs, they were greeted by Bridget, who was very much alive, thank heaven, and had just alerted the police. Isabel hugged her, eliciting an astonished squeak from Bridget. Then she urged them down the hall to the kitchen and to the back door, swinging it open into the damp night and the driveway beyond.

There was nothing there; the shell-strewn driveway was completely deserted. No Garrett Winterholler, not his shoe or the dirty sock, and not the gun. The only thing to show for him was a glistening pool of blood staining the clamshells.

Blue and red lights flashed behind the stately line of sycamore trees, turning Winterholler's blood red, then black, then red again.

Chapter 24

Although Isabel stated that the reason for the party was to celebrate Seamus the Statue's reincorporation into the family fabric with a June soiree in the garden, everyone in the household knew it was really a way to say "I told you so" to seventy-five people at once.

Isabel couldn't have planned a more gloriously perfect day weather-wise, as a gentle southwesterly breeze coaxed puffs of clouds across the sky, high above the blooming apple and dogwood trees.

Bridget had pushed the parlor's radio up against a screen window on the ground floor of Hy House, and a tinny, jaunty number from the Imperial Dance Orchestra trailed down through the garden to mingle with the tinkle of water spouting, once again, from Seamus's crown.

Hydrangea House was scrubbed and festooned for the gala, in the subtlest way possible of course, with bursting window boxes and long runners of simple white linen hung from the trellis. The only real clues to the violence that had occurred two weeks before were a layer of new shells in the driveway and a rope across the broken railing on the widow's walk. Emily couldn't stop looking up there. It was like having a missing tooth: She couldn't stop worrying over the spot, even though she wanted more than anything to forget it.

Guests moved around in blues, greens, and pinks, tasteful prints of small florals and large straw hats wafting about as Fiona, in black and white and with the help of Miranda and Felicity, passed through with trays of nibbles.

Isabel had had an especially fine time planning the menu, and she'd even gotten Bridget to shape biscuits into bird shapes and dye them a deep purple so that she could watch her guests "eat crow." She'd had her florist dye two dozen white roses a pure black, using the method Emily had first suggested (ink in water, basic science). It had been successful, and now Isabel had cheerful bouquets of black roses in tasteful bunches all along her brunch table. Guests ogled the dusky flowers, often testing a petal to see if they were real. Isabel even had one pinned to her lapel as a corsage, and she'd insisted that Emily put one in her hair.

"Break down the master's house with the master's tools, is what I always say," Isabel had intoned, handing her the small black velvet bud.

To say Isabel was having a ball planning her "I Told You So" party would be an understatement. She'd even made herself a throne.

Cushions had been set up on the bench next to the weeping willow where Isabel held court, and an armchair had been brought out for Emily, a side table between them. As unusual for her temperament as it was, Isabel had insisted that both Pat and Bridget enjoy the day with them (although Fi didn't get the same treatment as she wasn't at "the shoot-out," as Isabel was now referring to it). They both sat awkwardly on chairs that Pat had found in the garage, and soon after the first hour, both found excuses to get busy.

Pat gave Emily's arm a squeeze with his one good hand as he took his leave, the other trussed up in a sling. It seems he'd been so impressed with her rescue attempt (and success, he assured her) that she now had a lifelong devotee. As he put it, he owed a blood debt to her, and the Irish took those seriously.

It was pleasant sitting in the shade of the willow, having people come and go to ogle and congratulate the old lady and young girl who had single-handedly (somewhat, Ned said at one point in the retelling of events) brought down Winterholler, that double-crossing rat, who deigned to try and fool the Mob and silence an island girl in the bargain.

"It just goes to show," Isabel's imperious voice echoed across her guests' heads time and time again, "that in the end, it's grit that matters."

Ned leaned over in his uncomfortably tight plaid waistcoat and whispered, "That's the most New-England-Yank thing I've ever heard her say."

Em chuckled. "No, she's said plenty more."

"A bite anytime she talks about resilience or grit," Ned said, holding out his hand.

"Deal," Em said, shaking on it.

They both ended up eating a lot of crow cake.

—

TOWARD SUNSET, Isabel discovered Emily where she'd found a quiet spot in between a buffet table and a trellis.

"There you are," Isabel said, rustling over in gray silk.

"Here I am."

"Getting to be a little much?" Isabel asked.

Em flushed. "It's a lovely party, Isabel, but yes."

"I thought as much. Let's slip away. I have something to show you." Isabel threaded an arm through Emily's and pulled her away from the table. "Connor!" Isabel called, and soon he was trotting up the gravel pathway to the house, leading the way, his big black bow bobbing cheerfully.

Connor also had a place of honor on his new bed, and in addition, a black rose tucked into his neckwear along with the bow, signifying he was one of the Warriors of the Black Rose. Isabel, it seemed, had an inventive side.

"Isabel," Emily said as they strolled up a trio of stone steps to the veranda.

"Hmm?"

"What did he mean, Winterholler, what he said about the cut on his face?"

Isabel's step faltered and then resumed at its normal gliding gait. They hadn't spoken about the possible murder-death-escape of Garrett Winterholler since that fateful evening. Well, that wasn't completely true. They'd talked about it so much to all sorts of people—police, officials, reporters—that they'd had quite enough when it came to talking about it to one another. That was how Emily felt at least. And yet this detail had been nagging at her. She just had to know.

"You know," Emily nudged. "When he said you gave it to him?"

Isabel caught Em's eye, smirked, and then held out her left hand, on which she wore a slim ring with a single pearl on it, Em thought to counterbalance the stunning opal she always wore on her other hand.

Deftly, Isabel unscrewed the pearl from the ring, lifting it away to reveal a tiny sticker, no bigger than a rose thorn, but very sharp. She sliced the air with it, and its point flashed. "My ring sticker," she said, screwing the pearl back on. "I never leave home without it, especially on grand adventures involving potentially dangerous criminals. We shall have to get you one." She smiled into Em's look of amazement. "Yes, we all showed quite a bit of fight, did we not?"

When they got inside, Isabel led her up the front stairs under the gleaming chandelier and down the hall, to the last room on the right, the one she and Fi had almost visited the first day. Emily the First's room.

Isabel's hand paused on the doorknob. "I thought it was time for a change," she said, and twisted the knob. "It's all yours." She pushed the door open, stepping back to let Em see.

In Nebraska, in her old life, Emily hadn't had a room of her own, not really. She and her mama, after her dad's death, had hung a curtain between them, but she'd never had a bedroom all to herself like this.

Instead of the blue-and-bronze underwater royal court that was Isabel's room, this room was austere and bare and perfect. It shared the same layout as her aunt's, with a bathroom peeking through a partially closed door, and double windows looking out over the Hy

House gardens. The windows were open to the tinkle and hum of the party floating up to them. Emily took a step into the room in disbelief as Isabel watched her from the doorway.

The walls were off-white and bare, almost no paintings hung anywhere, although their ghosts lingered in the lighter rectangles they'd left behind. There was only one, another portrait, this time of a young girl with a wide, kind smile and sky-blue eyes surrounded by icy blond locks. Her mother. Mama.

"I thought you'd feel more at home without having to share your space," Isabel said from the doorway, "except I thought you wouldn't mind sharing it with *her*." She looked with affection at her sister's portrait on the wall.

There was another matched bedroom set of furniture, like Isabel's, but these were a cheerful minty green. A cozy brown chair that looked more like an old shoe than anything else sat near the far wall, next to a bookcase. Em walked over and sat down, snuggling into it immediately. Out the window—her window—she could see the back of the Methodist church's spires and the colorful, jumbled rooftop view down to the harbor, and, as always, the indigo sea beyond.

"I'll leave you to get settled in, then. Go on, Connor," Isabel said, and pointed.

Connor walked over to the armchair and curled up comfortably in a patch of sunlight, a little round ball of dog. He looked like he belonged there.

"You found her favorite spot straight off." A wistful expression washed over Isabel's features. "The spot with a view and a bookcase." After a moment she continued. "If there are any other paintings you want, John Patrick will hang them. You have your pick of the ones in the parlor, or any in storage. Or paint your own." Isabel gave a little shrug from the doorway and started to leave. She looked fifteen years younger than when Em had arrived—fifteen years lighter.

"Em?" Isabel said from the doorway.

Emily looked over.

"I'm glad you're home." And with a rustle of starched French silk, Isabel left her alone.

Emily snuggled back into the leather chair, a perfect perch, and glanced at the pastel portrait of her mother as a child. *Home*—Em held the word in her mind. It didn't feel so strange anymore.

ACKNOWLEDGEMENTS

We would like to acknowledge the team at Ashley Hall—Chris Hughes, Cintra Horne, and Vanessa Graham—who read the manuscript and delivered awesome feedback. We are so lucky to have you and can't wait to visit the school again.

Jen Schwartz is the cat's meow for always being in our corner and for her wonderful bookstore, Briar & Brambles, in Windham, New York.

Three loud huzzahs for our most-excellent editor, Jill Hindle Kediasch, who slashed and burned and cherished all our murdered darlings along the way.

Thank you to Koehler's editor, Hannah Tonsor Burke, whose eye and ear are impeccable. Koehler's designer, Suzanne Bradshaw, has vision and also knows how to listen, an impressive combination.

Bow van Riper, the research librarian at the Martha's Vineyard Museum, is the bee's knees for offering historical leads and cross-checking our accuracy. Robert Crimmins lent his eagle eye to our editing process, resulting in a fascinating blurb.

To our amazing friends and beta readers: Lisa Davis Mitchell, Mitch, Linley Dolby, Simon Athearn and Jim Athearn, and Lorraine Besser. Great friends are hard to come by, and great friends who read your work are more precious still.

A hearty thank you and head bow to Bruce Bennett, professor emerita at Wells College, for his wise and relentless attention to craft. It only makes us better writers and researchers. And to Richard

Mihans, who's always game for collaboration and sharing insights.

Heartfelt gratitude for our fellow scribes, Traci O'Dea and Margaret Meacham, who know this path and light the way for others.

Thank you to Dyer and Jonas for putting up with us.

Last, but definitely not least, raise a Bronx cheer for Marcia Adams, without whom none of this would have come together.

www.ingramcontent.com/pod-product-compliance
Lightning Source LLC
LaVergne TN
LVHW041755060526
838201LV00046B/1014